STEALING CAPTIVITY

HUMAN PETS OF TALIN
BOOK 6

DISCLAIMER

Copyright: RK Munin, 2024
Cover Illustration: RK Munin
Profession Editing: Chrisandra's Corrections
ISBN-13: 978-1-962699-13-6

Warning: Author is dyslexic as hell.

The editing and beta reading team: Martha Collins, S.F. and Lauren Meghoo

Feel free to contact me with questions, requests, or comments:

Author@RK-Munin.com

Want to get some free novellas or find links to my social media? Everything's on my website:

www.RK-Munin.com

And, as with many writers, your reviews on Amazon, Goodreads, and/or Kindle help immeasurably, even if it's just clicking on the stars.

Thank you to all my readers!

CONTENT WARNING

- There is a description of a child dying, nothing on page.
- There are several scenes of graphic sex – all consensual
- There are several scenes involving graphic violence.
- Kasi has anxiety that wakes her up in the night sometimes.
- Ignatias suffers from "memory episodes" which is Talin for flashbacks. He has some PTSD from childhood.
- Kasi is a curvy girl and was teased and tormented when she was a kid. It comes up a few times because she suffers from low-self-esteem regarding her appearance.

To my alpha and beta readers. You guys make my writing better and keep me from having too many anxiety meltdowns. Thank you all!

CHAPTER 1

Kasi

"You're going to be in so much trouble!" Isla sang out as she walked into the small clearing where Kasi was working.

Kasi turned to her friend with a wry smile. "Only if you tell someone."

"Why wouldn't she tell someone? This is not where you're supposed to be." Tisuran admonished as he appeared at the far end of Kasi's experimental crops' field.

"You're overreacting," Isla replied.

"I'm being cautious," Tisuran countered. "The inspector from the Committee of Pet Welfare will be here any day now; you need to remain in the village."

"I would've been back before you even knew I was gone," Isla said, and Kasi had to slap a hand over her mouth to keep from laughing. Her friend was many things but good with time management wasn't one of them.

Tisuran briefly sounded his annoyed rattle, filling the air with the buzzing of a nearby swarm of angry wasps. "You shouldn't have 'been gone' in the first place."

Isla answered his question with a question. "I thought you were going to wait for me at our domicile?"

"Someone pointed out that Kasi is never in her room, so when you said you were going to talk to her, I thought you might have to walk all the way out here," he stated. "You should know better than to come out here without me. Your intentions were good, but your method wasn't sound. Besides the arrival of the inspector, there are dangers out here, as you well know!"

"Now look who's in trouble!" Kasi teased Isla. The woman's tendency to *act first and think about consequences never* was well known. Last time she'd done that she was attacked by a gorg, Sorana's only predator. Tisuran had saved her, but it left he warrior even more protective of Isla.

"It's midday!" Isla protested with a little laugh, ignoring Kasi. "No gorg will be awake and hunting in broad daylight, and we aren't even that far away from the village. It's perfectly safe for me to be out here without you."

"What Kasi said still stands," Tisuran argued with a comforting rumble that sounded very much like the purr of an Old Earth animal called a cat. "You're in trouble."

Talin's faces weren't mobile, so they couldn't display emotions the way humans could. Instead, their species had developed many different sounds to denote their emotions. They moved the backplates running down their spine to make rattles or sounded rumbles from their chestboxes. The purring rumble was a favorite for Talins to make whenever they were around humans. Especially when it was their human, like Isla was for Tisuran.

Isla faced her Talin unrepentantly. "I'm in trouble? How ever will you punish me?"

"I will find something horrible!" he growled. "I'll hide your information square or make it so it only plays that child's vid you detest so much!"

"You wouldn't dare!" Isla said with a dramatic gasp.

"Test me and find out," he said.

The big warrior rushed at her with a demanding rattle that sounded a lot like a large metal weapon being banged against a metal shield. Isla laughed as he scooped her up and cradled her against this chest.

"I'll dye your quills that green color you hate!" she fired back, not at all intimidated by the fierce Talin covered in hard keratin plating.

Tisuran sounded a rumble of amusement before he went back to purring. "You know I'm not worried about you being attacked during the day."

His sincere tone made Isla's smile fade a little. "Then what is there to worry about?"

Tisuran's purr was interrupted briefly by an impatient rattle. "As I said before, the inspector from the Committee for Pet Welfare could arrive at any time."

"I know the inspector is coming," Isla reminded him with a huff. "That's why I came out to get Kasi! I knew she'd forget. Look, she isn't even wearing her collar."

Kasi touched her neck self-consciously. Under Talin law, all adult humans were required to wear collars, but of course those weren't enforced here on Sorana. She'd completely forgotten about the plain, serviceable collar she'd been issued when her group traveled here with Palforma and Zia. She'd taken it off once they'd arrived and never bothered putting it on again.

She grimaced and opened her mouth to apologize, but Tisuran didn't spare her a glance. He was still focused on Isla.

"I'm sure she'll fix that once she's back in her domicile," he countered. "You should've sent one of us to fetch her and not gone yourself. If the inspector had arrived before me, he would've seen two humans without Talin supervision outside the safety of the village."

Isla rolled her eyes. "If you hadn't shown up to admonish me like a child, we'd already be back in the village."

"Maybe not," Kasi said, then winced when both of them turned their gazes to her. "I only need another hour and

I'll be done here. I promise. If I don't set up the machines to auto-maintain the field, I'll lose the whole crop."

Isla focused her gaze over Kasi's shoulder. "What are you trying to grow this time?"

"Old Earth strawberries!" Kasi said, excited to share. "Same as last time, but I think I've got everything perfect now."

Isla gave her a look of admiration. "I can't believe you're able to do something like this with that old dusty sample box Zia found."

Kasi beamed, pride making her stand up a little straighter. "It wasn't that hard, not with all the fancy tech Commandant Holian sent."

"I was curious why the last shipment of goods included so many agricultural machines," Tisuran commented. "I'd thought it was a mistake. I should've known better."

"Yeah, Commandant Holian doesn't make mistakes," Isla agreed. "At least, that's what I've heard from you and all the other retired soldiers who've settled here."

"I promise to be quick," Kasi wheedled. "I only need to double check the programming and run a few soil tests."

"If I let you finish, will you be able to stay away from the field for the next ten rotations?" Tisuran asked. "The inspection should be done by then and the inspector on his way back to Talarian to file a report about how we're following all the rules."

"Absolutely," Kasi lied. "You guys head back, and once I'm done I'll follow. I'll be back in plenty of time for the evening meal."

Tisuran rattled out a negative sound. It was one of the only rattles that wasn't loud; it sounded like a hand slapping down on a thigh. Kasi wasn't surprised to hear it and the words that followed.

"We're not leaving you here alone," Tisuran said. "I'll help you do your work, and then we can all walk back to the village together."

"Yeah, that sounds fun!" Isla agreed and wiggled in Tisuran's arms, her eyes locked on one of the agricultural-bots.

Kasi was quick to step in front of the bot, blocking it from Isla's sight. Because she spent so much time in her fields and with these bots, they all had names and personalities. Isla might not mean to, but she was a little clumsy around tech. Dotti already had enough issues with her moisture testing unit; she didn't need Isla accidentally making it worse!

"There isn't much you can help with," Kasi assured Isla. "It's mostly me working with the equipment programming and making sure it has the dimensions and orders correct."

Isla pouted. "You just don't want me touching your stuff!"

"You can touch anything that's in my room," Kasi countered with a laugh. "But not this equipment. You have the worst luck when it comes to machinery!"

Isla tried to look upset and ended up laughing also. "I know! It gets me out of so many chores!"

"You don't have chores anymore," Tisuran objected. "Not if you don't want them."

"I'd get out of chores back on Wimol," Isla amended. "I didn't mean to suggest you guys force us humans to work. Some of us just can't help it." She gave Kasi a pointed look, but it was Tisuran who interrupted his purr to make the glass-marbles-clinking-in-a-bag sound of an amused rumble. It was the Talin version of a laugh.

"Says the human who took it on herself to organize the entire Twelve Nights of Halloheen celebration not long ago!" he said to Isla, his amused rumble getting louder before it subsided back into a purr.

"That wasn't work; that was fun," Isla argued.

"And this is fun for me," Kasi added.

"We will let you have your fun," Tisuran said and nodded his head in the direction of a shady spot with soft spongy ground cover. "We'll be there. If we can help, then simply call out."

"Sure thing," Kasi agreed with a chuckle as he carried Isla away. He purred as Isla explained the difference between fun-work and work-work.

His attention might be on her friend, but Kasi knew Tisuran was well aware of the woods around them and how far away Kasi was. As one of the many retired soldiers on Sorana, he felt it was his duty to take care of all the humans around him.

It was as endearing as it was annoying!

She'd been working hard before the two of them showed up, so she gave herself a break and leaned against Dotti. She watched the two of them get comfortable in the shade, with Tisuran making sure Isla was shielded from both the sun and the slightly damp ground.

Tisuran was a typical Talin: tall, broad, and heavily muscled, with hard, keratin plating covering his entire body. As with all Talins, he had just the hint of a nose on his face and no ears, only earholes. The fashion for both men and women was to only wear pants and a belt that had a pouch on one hip and an Identification Cube hanging off the other. No shirt or shoes for them. Did they even own other garments, like a coat?

Watching Tisuran gently run his fingers through Isla's wild hair reminded Kasi that for all their strength, every Talin on Sorana was exceptionally gentle with the humans. Even if they weren't in a relationship with one.

Turning away from the couple, Kasi caught her reflection in the metal dome on top of Dotti. She grimaced at what she saw. She was much bigger than most of the other humans. Her whole family had always been big, and she was no exception. She probably weighed twice what Isla weighed. Strong muscles covered with a cush layer of round fat. A body shape her mother referred to as durable.

Maybe that was the reason none of the Talins were interested in her. Who cared? She had friends, her field, and the ability to pursue her passion.

"And who needs a partner anyway? I have you," she whispered to Dotti with a crooked grin.

Giving a last pat to Dotti's dusty side, she pushed away any negative thoughts and focused on what needed to be done. Tisuran would make her leave when it got too close to the evening meal. That wouldn't be enough time, so she'd simply have to sneak out later.

Ignatias

Ignatias piloted the shuttle through Sorana's atmosphere with less care more speed than he'd normally use. He didn't want to cause any energy wakes that would alert the orbiting exosphere monitors to his presence. It wasn't a wise maneuver, but this was his first assignment with the Committee of Pet Welfare. He was going to perform optimally and give them no reason to question his placement.

His plan was to land unnoticed and early so he could observe Sorana colony without their knowledge. It would allow him to write a true and accurate report about the treatment of humans here.

Beyond being allowed to interact with humans on Sorana, he hoped to find favor with the Committee and perhaps be pushed forward in the adoption queue. It didn't happen often, but if a human was being abused or neglected, the Committee had the power to reassign the human to another Talin owner.

He wanted a human of his own so badly it was all he could think about some days. Being picked for one of the coveted jobs with the Committee was a gift from the

Ancestors. Even if he wasn't moved up in the queue, this job would put him in close proximity with humans on a regular basis.

WARNING

His screen flashed the word a few times, accompanied by a familiar angry sound. Then the display filled with telemetry data. The shuttle didn't like the angle or speed of his descent, and the outside shell was heating to a dangerous point for hull integrity.

He'd served on and then commanded many ships over his distinguished career. He knew what the official tolerances were, but more importantly, he knew what the ships could actually achieve.

It was his vast knowledge and skillset that led to the Apogee Assembly offering him the position of Chief Administrator of the War Committee. It was a position of immense power and prestige. Everyone was shocked when he turned it down. Many tried to change his mind; even his parents voiced their extreme disappointment. Despite all of them, he was unmoved.

Prestige meant nothing to him anymore. He'd done his duty for the Talin Empire and the glory of his clan and family. It was time for him to focus on selfish goals–like acquiring a human.

WARNING

Looking over the display, he noted readings at the very edge of what he knew the shuttle was capable of. Checking his position relative to the exosphere monitors, he found the ship was safe from detection. Engaging the reverse thrusters, he slowed the shuttle and watched the numbers on the display change. The warning disappeared and the angry sounds stopped.

He studied the planet carefully as he piloted to the spot he'd selected when he'd first planned this mission. He'd picked a clearing that would force him to spend many marks hiking to the village, but it would allow him to land without being seen by any of the residents.

That was one thing he was going to insist on in his report regardless of what he saw once he was on the ground– the colony needed more observation satellites and ground monitors.

Sorana was vulnerable to thieves doing exactly this, slipping in with a small shuttle undetected. He was astonished that a colony planet owned by Prime Son Searin, potential heir to the Talin monarchy, wasn't better guarded. He had the resources to set up much better monitors and defense systems.

Although the colony might not produce anything of note, it was still highly valuable. Humans were a precious and rare commodity among Talins, and his data reported many human pets living on Sorana!

Perhaps they believed the high number of retired Talin soldiers also living on Sorana was deterrent enough. Ignatias was determined they'd realize the idiocy of that thought process. His report would have some strongly worded reprimands, unless the leadership in residence implemented everything he suggested immediately.

Despite the pressure he'd put on the shuttle, it landed perfectly, barely fitting into the small clearing he'd chosen. It wasn't a coincidence that the shuttle was now surrounded by high trees. When he deployed the masking shell, the shuttle was virtually impossible to find from both the ground and the air. Even in the early years of his career he'd been lauded for meticulously preparing for missions, including any contingency he could dream up. He saw no reason to break the habit now.

He gathered his pack and set out at a fast pace for the village. He should be there within four marks and be able to observe the inhabitants without their knowledge.

As usual, everything was going according to plan.

CHAPTER 2

Kasi

Kasi suffered only a moment of guilt as she snuck out of the village using one of the narrow, lesser-used paths. Unlike Kasi, everyone was following the rules so there were no roving Talins monitoring the village. It was easy to disappear into the red, brown and yellow jungle that covered the planet.

The dangers on Sorana were few and it would be hours before the sun set, giving her plenty of time to check on her experimental field and be back before nightfall. Because she was a cautious soul, she carried two walking torches with her. The little bots with their three legs attached to a bulbous body could illuminate the entire field easily. Their light would keep her safe from any gorg that might come looking for a tasty snack.

She didn't plan to be out past dark, but it was better to be prepared than to be dinner.

Isla liked to tease Kasi by claiming she got all the prudence while Isla got all the recklessness. Kasi would argue that Isla had all the serenity and Kasi all the anxiety. Kasi had always struggled to calm her mind, especially at night. When she should be sleeping, her brain would insist on analyzing all kinds of things that made her uncomfortable or restless. Having shared a cabin with Isla for a couple of years, she knew her friend fell asleep easily and slept soundly through the night.

Kasi envied her! Her mind was always buzzing and sometimes the thoughts weren't pleasant or fun.

It wasn't so bad during the day when she had work and projects to distract her, which was why this field was so important. She'd always been entranced by plants and filled with regret that she couldn't experiment with growing before. Now that she lived on Sorana with Talins willing to indulge the humans, there was every reason to spend her time and some resources playing with the plants!

Honestly, it was a dream come true.

It didn't take long for her to be out of sight of the village. Even carrying the walking torches balanced on her shoulder, it didn't take her long to reach the field. She was horrified. Dotti was stopped in the middle of a row, sampling and resampling the same spot. She must've been there for a while because the area under her was bare and deeply furrowed.

Pushing out a loud breath of frustration, Kasi set the walking torches down on their spindly legs and turned them to automatic. They'd remain in a dormant state until it got dark and then they would automatically light up and move to stay close to her.

With her hands free, she opened up the storage box where she kept the agricultural-bots' controllers. Pulling out Dotti's controller, she tapped out the instructions for the bot to stop its program, move to the end of the row, and shut down.

Dotti didn't obey any of the commands. Kasi double checked to make sure she had the correct controller then tried again. Dotti didn't stop. If any of the bots were going to malfunction, it was going to be Dotti. She was the only bot they'd brought with them from Wimol. She was an old model and probably should've been left behind.

"You would've ended up in an Ugarian scrap yard back on Wimol," she told Dotti, dropping the controller back into the box. "But I insisted you had to come with us. Then you wouldn't work when we got here. Do you know how much I had to beg Zia to fix you? I had to clean her domicile for weeks!"

Predictably, Dotti didn't respond and kept sampling the crater she was digging.

"Is this how you thank me?" Kasi asked with a shake of her head. "I'm going to take you apart myself if you keep this up!"

The bot didn't pause, making Kasi laugh. What was she expecting Dotti to do, suddenly start behaving?

"Fine, I'm not going to take you apart, but I need you to stop before you hit the water table," she said, walking between the rows to get closer to Dotti.

The bot was about ten feet tall, with a smooth square body and eight stubby legs that moved with surprising delicacy for such a massive bot. Unlike the newer bots, Dotti's control circuits were all inside the shiny dome on her top. Kasi was going to have to climb up to get access.

Thankfully she hadn't started wearing the wrap garments they'd all been issued to fit in with the Talin Empire's idea of human pets. She was still dressed in her sturdy work pants, durable shirt, and practical boots. All of that should make it easier to scale the bot.

Standing on the tallest spot of piled up earth, she timed Dotti's movements and jumped. Her first attempt failed completely.

"Putre!" she exclaimed, using the curse word that had become popular on Wimol a few years ago. Then she winced and looked around. She'd been pretty loud, but she didn't hear the sound of running feet, which hopefully meant no one heard her.

Getting to her feet, she ignored the soreness in her hip and focused on Dotti. "I don't suppose you could edge a little to the left? That would make it easier to jump on top of you."

Dotti must have been feeling contrary because she moved slightly to the right.

"Not helpful," Kasi muttered. It never crossed her mind to leave Dotti to her destruction. She was shifting a half an inch every turn, and if Kasi didn't stop her now, most of the field would be destroyed by morning. She couldn't let that happen.

"Listen, you dumb, overgrown watering can," she said, shaking out her limbs and getting ready to leap again. "If I break a limb out here, I'm going to turn you into an elimination unit for one of the new domiciles. If you let me get on top of you, I'll find another job for you that doesn't involve destroying my hard work."

It took three more tries before she got hold of a grab bar well enough to stay with the machine. Her feet scrabbled for purchase and one boot landed on a small lip where two panels met. It was just enough for her to grab a higher bar with her free hand and pull herself up.

"I need to work out more," she huffed, wiggling her body onto the slightly convex top of the machine. When she was feeling charitable she called herself curvy, but in truth, she was chubby. She'd always been big, and for the most part she'd come to terms with it long ago. Her thin, elegant friends, like Isla and Zia, never made her feel bad for her body shape, but sometimes it was hard to be the only one her size.

She sat on the top of the moving machine and blew out a sigh. Shaking out her arms, she gave herself a moment to recover before she tried getting the panel to the internal controls open. Dotti was used to carrying a belly full of soil supplements, so Kasi's weight didn't affect her at all.

"You know, this is kind of fun," Kasi commented as Dotti moved under her. "I should see if I can program you to be ridden. None of the Talins would like it because it isn't what you're designed for, but they don't know how to have fun."

Dotti finished another circle and shifted an inch to start more destruction.

Turning around, Kasi faced the dome covering Dotti's brain. "I need to get you shut down. We'll see about going for rides some other time. Maybe we could repurpose you as a kids' ride. I know Ren and Lamarin would have a blast riding around on top of you."

The dome opened up easily and it didn't take long to instruct Dotti to walk to the end of the row and power down. Now that she had a new role for the old bot, Kasi felt better. Even though Dotti had destroyed a portion of her field, she didn't want her turned into spare parts.

"Holian said more bots were coming," she muttered, sliding off the bot and landing in the soft dirt, "but I wish they were here already."

The biggest issue was now she was down a bot. There had barely been enough, and with only two left working, the field was going to suffer. How often would she be able to come out here? Maybe she could talk some of the Talins into standing guard while she worked. That way her field survived and the inspector would never need to know.

She was so absorbed in plotting and planning that she didn't even notice the shadowy figure until it was on her. Something made her turn to find an unfamiliar Talin standing right behind her. His keratin plating was a light brown that darkened down his arms and legs. Vermilion eyes stared at her intensely, and the faint scent of caramel hit her nose.

She was so stunned that she only managed a surprised squeak when he scooped her up.

"Please don't be afraid," he said, rumbling out a purr. "I'm going to take good care of you."

CHAPTER 3

Ignatias

The human in his arms remained stunned and silent for several submarks, allowing him to run at full speed through the forest. Unfortunately, she didn't stay that way. Her entire body jerked in his arms and then she spoke.

"I'm being human-napped." Her voice was barely a whisper and he believed she was talking to herself, but he answered anyway.

"You're being rescued."

"I will not make this easy!" she said far more loudly. "I won't be taken to a secondary location!"

Then she started screaming and flailing. Her movements didn't hamper his ability to carry her, but they did force him to reduce his speed. He didn't want her to accidentally hit her hand on a tree and hurt herself.

Her screaming concerned him. Not because it was loud, but he worried that she could damage her vocal cords or throat. It was frightening how easily humans could be damaged, even through their own actions.

He didn't want to stop, but the human was panicking and he needed to calm her. He was already concerned by her dirty appearance; she looked like she'd been knocked to the ground several times. There was dirt all over her clothing and her mane was a short messy halo around her head.

Finding a sheltered spot within a thick grove of trees, he set the human on her feet and ducked his face away from her flailing fists. He didn't worry she could hurt him—humans were too soft to do any damage—but he didn't want her to injure herself on his tough hide.

"Easy, Pretty," he murmured gently, quickly capturing both her wrists and holding them in one of his hands. She stopped screaming then, her breathing ragged and rough. The poor thing was out of breath from fear!

"I'm not going to hurt you," he rushed to assure her. "You're safe with me. I can see you've been abused by your owners and I'm here to stop that."

She stared at him with wide eyes. "A-a-abused? No one was in the field but me."

"They're making you work," he explained. She must have been purchased at a slave auction. Only a former slave could be treated like this and not realize it was inhumane. "Humans are too fragile to work as I saw you doing. It will shorten your lifespan and could cause you irreparable harm. Look at the state of you."

Following his eyes, she looked down to take in her clothes while he continued to talk. "These fabrics are too coarse for your delicate skin and those shoes are unnecessarily heavy. Your mane is cut short, so you've either been sick or forced to cut it because no one is willing to help you maintain it."

Still holding her wrists locked in one of his hands, he used his free hand to look at one of her palms. "You've built up callused skin here, something that only occurs from repetitive labor. All of this tells me that your owners are abusing you horribly."

"Owners?" she repeated slowly, then shook her head and started talking quickly. "You misunderstand, no one was making me do anything. I wanted to be in the field. I wasn't supposed to, so I snuck out to check on the agricultural-bots. I'm not being abused!"

"Lying to protect your owner," he murmured. "I'd heard your species tends to favor loyalty over logic, and now I see it in action."

He saw amusement then worry flash across the human's face. Unlike Talins, humans were as easy to read as a brightly lit Identification Cube.

"This is bad. I can't…we need to…I…" Her voice trailed off and she bit her lip and looked down, obviously deep in thought.

She must be trying to understand that she was safe now. Switching masters was probably startling for her; it might take some time to process. While he let her consider her new circumstances, he looked her over.

Her hair was a dark, gleaming brown that reminded him of some of the older woods used in decorative architecture on the Talin home planet, Talarian. The color of her hair complimented the bright copper color of her eyes.

Her skin was darkly tanned, and he was unsure if it was her natural coloring or caused by too much exposure to the sun. Every Talin knew that humans with naturally dark skin were wonderfully healthy, but humans whose skin grew dark due to UV exposure were prone to illness and certain types of diseases.

Could he already be too late? Had the Talins of Sorana worked this little human to an early grave?

Worry made him lift her arms up a little so he could push her loose sleeves up past her elbows. To his immense relief, the color of her skin didn't change to a lighter shade as he revealed her arm.

"Hey, stop that," she protested, tugging ineffectively. Her lush lips were turned down in a frown and her luminescent, light brown eyes were narrowed with irritation.

"Easy," he said, sounding a soothing rumble. "I needed to check your health."

Her eyebrows shot up. "By looking at my elbow?"

Her willingness to question gave him hope that her spirit hadn't been broken by her owners. "I was worried for the health of your skin. Don't fear. I'll make sure you're seen by healers once we're away from here."

She still looked confused but also determined. "I'm not abused. They don't make me work. I wanted to be out checking on the field. It's my personal project. See, I'm trying to grow an Old Earth fruit called a strawberry and–"

Her explanation was interrupted when two walking torches came trotting through the trees and stopped near them. Their lights weren't on yet, but it was obvious she'd programmed them to stay close to her. Did that mean she'd expected to continue working late into the night? How disgraceful!

"Do you labor to feed yourself and the other humans?" he asked. "Do your owners require you to grow your own food? This is deplorable! I swear to you that I'll see them all brought to justice."

"This is not going well," the little human mumbled under her breath. Looking up she met his eyes, her gaze bold and undaunted. "Could we go back to the village? Talk to Palforma about—actually no, don't talk to Palforma. Um, talk to Tisuran or Idrisan. They can explain everything. And everyone else will be there. You'll see all the other humans are clean, dressed in the wrap outfits, and wearing comfy slippers. Just like they should be. I'll get cleaned up and change into mine."

It was difficult, but he kept himself from sounding a harsh rattle of anger. "I won't set foot in that village built of lies. I can see my decision to arrive early and unannounced was wise. Given warning, your owners might have successfully hidden their nefarious activities from me. Now their ploy has been revealed. We'll leave this place, and I'll send my report out as soon as I'm within range of a comm's array powerful enough to reach Talarian."

For the first time, the little human looked scared. "Please don't do that."

"Don't be afraid, Pretty," he said, letting go of her wrists to wrap his arms around her and draw her against his body in a gentle clutch. Her body felt soft and perfect in his arms, as if she was always meant to be nestled against him. "There won't be any reprisals because you weren't able to convince me to follow along with the lies. I'll keep you safe."

He'd use every political favor he possessed to make sure she ended up with him. Even if he was forced to issue threats, he'd find a way to keep this human. This sweet female would live in safety and luxury with him for the rest of her life!

"I like you calling me pretty, so, uh, thanks for that," she said, her voice muffled against his chest. "And it's sweet to keep promising me you'll keep me safe, but I swear I'm not in danger. Or being abused, or anything like that."

It was clear she believed what she was saying was true, making him even more sure that she was a wild-caught human used to being badly treated. It might take some time to earn her trust, but he'd show her how humans were meant to be pampered and cared for.

Some noise caught his attention, and turning his head, he focused on listening. It was faint, but there was the sound of footfalls in the woods. It was the light, surefooted tread of someone trained for battle.

He looked back down at her. "They're searching for you."

He was watching her carefully, so he knew to cover her mouth with his hand when she parted her lips to scream. He muffled most of the sound, but she was making enough noise that they would be found if he didn't start moving again.

"I'm sorry," he murmured as he gathered her up in a much less comfortable hold than earlier. Once he'd put some distance between them and their pursuers, he'd be able to restrain her in a better way, but for now, she was going to have to put up with the discomfort.

She struggled against him as he held her tightly to his chest and ran. She stopped struggling within several strides, probably having already worn herself out. Poor thing must be exhausted after laboring all day. It was nearly nightfall and he feared she might not have even been given a meal that day!

"My shuttle is well hidden, but it will take us four marks to get there," he explained as he ran. He wanted to sprint but knew it would be better to maintain a steady pace than risk wearing himself out too early. He'd need plenty of energy in reserve if his pursuers got close.

"Once we're onboard my shuttle, it won't take much time to get to my ship. The ship isn't much, but there is plenty of food fit for a human and I packed a sachie squeeze. I've heard humans are fond of those. You can have all the blankets and pillows and the sachie squeeze to build yourself a nest to your liking. If there aren't enough, we can stop on the way back to Talarian and purchase more items."

He hesitated before he said the next part, but decided it was important to establish their relationship early. "I'll be a good owner."

It felt immensely satisfying to say those words out loud.

She'd stopped struggling or trying to shout, but he knew the moment he removed his hand she'd start again. For all she knew, he was taking her to a much worse situation. Past experience probably kept her from trusting anything she was told.

Time would show her the truth. He wished he didn't have to cause her distress to save her. Determined to get her to a safe place, he increased the pace a little to try and reach the shuttle sooner. Once there, she wouldn't need to be restrained any longer and would probably feel somewhat better.

When she started whimpering, he grew worried and found a place to stop.

"What's wrong, Pretty?" he asked, setting her down on her feet and removing his hold over her mouth.

"Hard to breathe," she gasped, sucking air into her lungs.

Mortification almost made him rattle out a sound of distress. "Was I holding you too tightly?"

She nodded her head, bending over at the waist and bracing her hands on her thighs. "Waaaay too tight."

"I'm sorry," he apologized with a quiet comforting rumble. He resisted the urge to draw her back into his arms. It was a far different thing to have one in his arms than to watch educational vids or pamphlets about humans. Nothing he'd watched or read prepared him for how easy it would be to accidentally deprive a human of oxygen. "I'll be more careful from now on."

Straightening up, she shook her head. "I can walk, and I promise I won't run away or scream. I'm a good hiker. When I first got to Sorana, there was a group of us that explored for days at a time."

He made a very quiet negative sound, still aware that there were others searching for her. They probably didn't realize he was here yet and that was an advantage. No human would be able to cover this much distance so quickly. Her old owners wouldn't realize they needed to expand their search far into the forest of Sorana.

"We won't cover enough ground if I don't carry you, but because you've promised to be good, I can carry you in a more gentle way."

She let out a deep sigh and opened her mouth to say something when several Talins appeared from the dense woods. He couldn't understand how they'd found him so quickly, and even worse, there were three of them and they all looked capable and strong.

"Stay back, Pretty," he ordered, pushing her behind him. "I'll protect you."

Or die trying.

CHAPTER 4

Kasi

"Hi, guys!" Kasi called, peeking around her kidnapper's bulk. "This is all just a big misunderstanding. Let's sit down and talk it out. I mean, I'm sure everyone is going to laugh, or uh, rumble? Rattle? Whatever. You'll make sounds because it's funny."

The guy protecting her pulled off his pack and dropped it next to her. She could see his backplates move as he sounded a loud, aggressive rattle that sounded like rapidly fired projectiles.

"I won't let you take this human from me," he warned Palforma, Sandorian and Idrisan. "It's best you leave here and let me continue to my shuttle. If you try to stop me, I won't be merciful."

Wow, that sounded like he was ready to fight all three of them by himself. Bad idea! The guy might be almost as big as Palforma and was probably a skilled fighter, but he was facing three accomplished warriors. She knew from the stories circulating around the village that every Talin on Sorana was deadly.

This stranger was only trying to save her and now he might get really hurt!

"There's no need for conflict," she said, jumping out to stand between him and her friends.

'Don't be afraid,' Palforma tapped quickly. After a head injury that ended his military career, Palforma struggled to speak verbally, especially during times of stress. He'd met the deaf human, Zia, when his non-functioning shuttle was pulled onto the junk trawler where she worked. She took charge of him and got his INT programmed with the silent tapping language of the Norka so they could talk. It was life changing for him and he'd been devoted to Zia ever since.

He was probably the most reasonable Talin on Sorana, so Kasi focused on him. She needed Palforma to understand that violence wasn't called for and to help convince the stranger of the same thing.

"I'm not scared," she assured him, tapping her answer as well as speaking it verbally out of habit. "I'm not hurt either. This isn't what it seems."

She felt a hand on her arm and a tug. The stranger was gently grasping her and trying to place her behind him again.

"I know you're conflicted," he said while purring. "But it's harder for me to protect you if you won't stay back."

"Let go of her!" Idrisan growled, sounding an aggressive rattle so loud it caused several small creatures in a nearby tree to flutter away.

Sandorian spoke up. "You'll be punished severely for stealing a human!"

"Stealing?" the stranger scoffed. "I was sent here to make sure none of you were breaking the law, and what do I find? A human with no collar, by herself, toiling in a field! It's all of you who will be punished!"

"Not helping," she muttered, trying to pull her arm out of the stranger's grip.

"Committee Citizen Ignatias?" Idrisan said.

At the same time, Palforma tapped rapidly. 'I didn't think he'd get here for another rotation.'

"Ignatias," Kasi murmured, liking the name. It sounded dignified and steadfast, like the male himself. "That's a good name."

"I'm glad you like my name, Pretty," Ignatias said, his voice strained as he tugged on her arm again. "But please step back now."

Sandorian sounded an angry rattle. "He's early and unannounced. He must have planned to steal a human from the beginning!"

"He's not stealing me!" Kasi told them. "I mean, he was, but only for the nicest reasons."

She really wished Zia, Isla, Henni, or any of the other humans were here to help her calm the situation down. Talins were quick to turn unreasonable when humans were involved.

"Come, Pretty. Take shelter behind me," Ignatias urged, pulling on her arm with more force this time.

She dug in her heels. "Give me a moment to talk to them."

"Not while you're in a position of danger," he argued. "You may continue to speak to them while standing behind me."

She was surprised none of the guys were reacting badly to him touching her. One of the number one rules on Sorana was that there was no touching the humans without their permission, except in times of emergency.

She turned to face Ignatias. "If I stay in the middle, you're a lot less likely to fight. We need words right now, not blows. You think I'm being abused, and these guys think you're an evil thief. Everyone's wrong, so let me fix this."

He was keeping a wary eye on the three men even as he spoke to her. "If rescuing you from a life of manual labor and abuse is thievery, then I'll wear the label proudly. I'm here to fight your battle, Pretty, not sacrifice you to them to keep myself safe."

She almost yelled in frustration. No one was listening to her! "That's just it, I'm not–"

Tisuran suddenly appeared behind Ignatias, shocking her into silence mid-sentence. Ignatias started to turn, realizing danger was close. He wasn't quick enough and Tisuran was able to shove a small black object hard against the slip of exposed skin all Talins had on their necks. Ignatias didn't have time to even complete his turn. The moment the object touched him, he jerked, went stiff, and pitched forward.

Scared that he was going to hit the ground face first and hurt himself, Kasi pushed her shoulder into his chest and locked her legs. She might be strong, but she wasn't lift-a-Talin-by-herself strong. She managed to slow his descent but they both started falling.

It all happened so quickly she didn't have time to brace herself before she was flat on her back with the wind knocked out of her. At least he'd fallen a little short and his head ended up on her chest instead of hitting the ground and maybe doing damage to his face!

Trapped under his bulk, she tried to ignore how good Ignatias smelled.

Just like caramel. Sweet, rich, buttery caramel.

Focus, she admonished herself. Now was not the time to be thinking about Ignatias smelling good enough to lick!

"Help!" she squeaked, unable to pull in a full breath.

"Kasi, why did you jump toward him?" Tisuran cried as he grabbed Ignatias by the shoulder and rolled him off her.

Ignoring the warrior looming over her, she scrambled to her knees to check on Ignatias. His eyes were closed, his body relaxed, and his breathing even.

"He's not hurt," Tisuran said, dropping to his knees next to her. "I only rendered him unconscious. Are you injured?"

The other men joined Tisuran, all asking her if she was hurt and what happened.

"I'm fine." She was forced to repeat herself several times before the Talins heard her. When they quieted down, she asked the important question. "What are we going to do about Ignatias? I don't suppose you guys have some kind of serum to make him forget the last few hours, uh, I mean marks, do you?"

Idrisan made the thigh-slapping sound of a negative rattle. "There's no medication that works like that."

'Not without running the risk of killing him,' Palforma tapped out.

Suddenly she felt like crying. "Then we have to figure something else out. We can't accidentally kill him. He was only trying to help."

"Help?" Sandorian said incredulously. The accompanying rattle of frustration sounded like a swarm of angry hornets. "He arrived early, didn't announce his presence, then stole you. I don't see how that is helpful at all."

Put like that, it sounded bad. "He was only trying to do a good job. He got here early, saw me, and thought I was being abused. This was a rescue attempt."

Tisuran sounded a demanding rattle that made Kasi think of two large metal items being banged together with force. It was a challenging rattle, and she knew he was about to ask some uncomfortable questions.

"Where were you, Kasi, that he was able to steal you away?" he asked. "We would've known if he was in the village, so where did he find you?"

Her words came out hesitant and odd sounding as she tried to think of a plausible excuse. "Um, well, I was really full after dinner, and I decided to go for a walk."

Tisuran's demanding rattle sounded again. "Kasi?"

"No really, I just wanted to go for a walk," she insisted. Ignatias was unconscious. He couldn't counter the lie.

"And where did this walk lead you?" Sandorian asked, sounding a rumble of amusement.

She shoved her hands in her pockets and looked down at Ignatias. He was lying on his back and looked peacefully asleep. She kinda wished she could join him.

"Since I was walking anyway…I…uh, I thought I'd stroll over to my field. You know, because it's a pretty walk anyway." Yes, that was it! "And it was good I did, 'cuz Dotti was making a mess and I needed to—"

Her efforts to come up with a convincing story were interrupted when the two walking torches trotted up to her and turned on, illuminating the area around them. She hadn't realized the sun was setting and it was rapidly getting dark until that moment. The bright lights of the walking torches made it clear how dim the forest had gotten.

Almost as one, the warriors took in the walking torches then turned their eyes to her.

'They followed you,' Palforma tapped. She'd never seen taps look so accusing.

"They'd only be following you if you programmed them too," Tisuran stated with an angry rattle. "You promised you wouldn't go back out if I let you finish your work earlier. You either lied to me or decided to ignore my wishes."

The hurt and disappointment in his voice made her wince. Pulling her hands out of her pockets she threw them up in the air and went on the defensive.

"If you let me check on the field while he was here, none of this would've happened!"

Sandorian sounded another amused rumble. "This is our fault because we wanted to keep everyone on Sorana safe?"

She glared at him, not pleased by his not-helpful comment. "I only meant that you guys were being way over the top about the inspection."

"Were we though?" Tisuran asked, pointing to Ignatias. "Or were we acting with an absolutely appropriate level of caution that you decided to ignore and now we might have to do something drastic?"

That got her attention. Stepping closer to Ignatias as if she could protect him, she crossed her arms over her chest and tried to look intimidating. "What do you mean drastic?"

Palforma let out a loud demanding rattle to get everyone's attention.

'Enough talk,' he tapped. 'Sandorian and Tisuran, carry Ignatias back to the village and secure him in the old storage building at the east side. Idrisan and I will guard Kasi on the walk back. We need to contact Prime Son Searin and Commandant Holian before we do anything with Ignatias.'

Kasi let out a relieved sigh. Nothing was going to happen to Ignatias right away. She had time to convince everyone he wasn't going to hurt her and maybe even talk him into doctoring his report about Sorana.

The only problem was that she'd never been that great at persuasive arguments. Looked like she was going to need to learn and fast!

CHAPTER 5

Ignatias

He woke in a rush, blinding pain making him hiss out a breath and forcing him to keep his eyes closed tight. He wanted to press his hands to his face, but he found them bound over his head. He was laying on a smooth, hard surface and an experimental tug at his legs informed him they were bound also.

He wasn't surprised. He remembered everything that happened. The pain was a common reaction to being hit with a knock-out block. At least he'd woken up. It was rare, but sometimes Talins didn't wake up when a knock-out block was used on them.

"You're awake!" A gentle hand cradled the back of his head and lifted. He recognized Pretty's voice at the same time the smooth rim of a medicine vial was held to his lips. "They said your head would hurt when you woke up, but this'll help."

He opened his mouth and let her pour the liquid in. The familiar taste of a mild analgesic hit his tongue. It didn't take long for the fast-acting medication to take effect. With the pain diminished, he risked opening his eyes.

Pretty was kneeling next to him, still cradling his head with a concerned expression on her sweet face. Lifting his head out of her hands, he took in his surroundings.

He was in a small, bare room, with restraints on his arms and legs secured to the exposed support beams in the walls. The space looked to have been used for something industrial, or maybe it was a place of punishment for misbehaving humans. That was the only explanation for both of them being in here.

"I've failed you," he whispered, pulling his head away from her soft hands and thumping himself hard against the unforgiving floor. He wished she hadn't given him the pain medication; he didn't deserve it. "The three distracted me like some untrained new recruit, allowing a fourth warrior to sneak up from behind. How could I have been so stupid?"

Pretty frowned and laid a hand on his forehead. "First thing, no more knocking your head on anything. That's not going to make you less stupid, right?"

He blinked, taking a moment to let her words sink in. "Was that an attempt at humor?"

Her adorable nose wrinkled as if she was smelling something bad. "Yeah, sorry. All my jokes are bad. I didn't mean to imply you're dumb, okay? I'm sure you're really smart. You'd have to be to get a position on the Committee for Pet Welfare, right? Idrisan said that tons of Talins apply but only a few get jobs. Is it true that only half of you get paid? That the rest of you willingly work for free? That doesn't seem fair at all."

He could listen to Pretty's melodic voice all day, even if she was talking in circles. How could she be making jokes and trying to have a normal conversation with him? Especially when he was the reason she was in the cold barren room.

At least she was dressed appropriately. She was wearing a dark purple omnie with black embroidery around the edges. The omnie coats were lined in nano-infused faux fur that automatically adjusted the garment's temperature to keep the human warm. Although it was an expensive item, the expectation was that every owner would acquire at least one for their human. The one she was wearing looked brand new, and he suspected it was only recently purchased for her, probably in anticipation of his visit.

As she moved a little closer, he saw the hint of a matching wrap under the omnie, and glinting among the clothing was a standard issue collar. He couldn't see her feet, but he was sure she was wearing the standard slippers most humans wore that were also imbued with warming nano technology.

Not only had she changed clothes, but she'd also cleaned up. Her face wasn't smudged with dirt and her short mane gleamed from being well groomed. They must have let her use the cleansing facilities while he was unconscious.

As much as he was happy to see her dressed more appropriately and free of dirt, he hated that it was all an illusion. How long had they been locked in this room? Were they going to care for her appropriately or punish her further by denying her food and water?

"How long will they punish you?" he asked.

Her brows furrowed in confusion. "I'm not being punished. Actually, you're not being punished either. You're, um, being detained."

What kind of lies did these Talins tell their humans? Did she think this cold, bare room was luxury? Was punishment being forced to sleep outside? The more he learned, the worse Pretty's life seemed.

"If you need to, you can lay on top of me, Pretty," he offered. "I'll be slightly softer than the floor and a lot warmer."

The skin of Pretty's face got darker, and her eyes slid away from his. "Um, that's sweet of you."

Was she embarrassed by his offer? She probably felt responsible for his capture and current situation. Her care and concern clearly showed a growing fondness for him. It might even be possible to convince her to sneak out and find the release remote for his restraints. Once free, he'd be merciless. There would be no second chances for any of these warriors.

All of that would happen later. Right now was about continuing to gain Pretty's confidence and affection.

"I'm not angry with you, Pretty," he assured her. "I understand that you might have friends and family among the humans here. That would make you reluctant to leave, even when offered a better life. You might not believe me yet, but I can save all the humans."

Her eyes were on him again and her mouth was strangely scrunched to the side. "It's nice that you want to save me, or, uh, all of us, but we don't need it. Not really. Like I said back in the woods, it's all a big misunderstanding."

Should he pretend to believe her to gain his freedom? He hated to let her think that this treatment was acceptable, but he might not have a choice. "How have I misunderstood, Pretty?"

"My name is Kasi," she said, the skin of her face darkening again. Then he remembered it was called blushing and it could be caused by many reasons, including embarrassment or desire.

"It's nice to meet you, Kasi. My name is Ignatias of the Towiv Family within the Rolinan clan," he said, then decided to add the formal greeting. "May the Ancestors grace you with wisdom and loyalty."

"I know how this goes!" she stated with excitement. "I'm supposed to say, uh, *and have honor in*…no, that's not right." She ran her fingers through her short dark mane, fluffing the perfectly laid strands into a charming mess as she thought. "Don't help me, I'll remember…it goes: *And lead you to honorable action!*" She concluded the traditional greeting with a bright smile.

"That's it exactly," he praised her. "May I still call you Pretty even though we know each other?"

"Sure, if you want to," she agreed and ducked her face down shyly. He wasn't an expert on human expressions, but this one seemed as if she was pleased but trying not to show it.

"I'd like to sit up and face you if I could," he said, testing the bonds holding him and making the cables clatter against the floor.

"Oh, yeah, that can't be comfortable," Kasi agreed. "I can't do anything right now."

That sounded like she might be willing to find and steal the remote later. This was a good sign. "What should we do to pass the time? Do you need to clutch or cling to me? I can't hold you, but you could still take comfort in snuggling close to my body and wrapping your arms around my neck."

"A lot of your suggestions seem to involve us touching," she commented with a small smile. "I think I could argue that it's more about you than me."

As she spoke, she laid down next to him, rested her head on his chest, and draped an arm over him. He couldn't feel much of her because of the heavy omnie, but the skin of her face was soft and her warm breath ghosted across his hard keratin plating. His scent glands started to ache, and he desperately wanted to wrap his arms around her and hold her close.

"I want to tell you a story," she said, her voice soft and tentative.

"A story?" he asked. "What would be the nature of this story?"

"It's about where I came from and how I got here," she explained. "It's not that exciting or entertaining, but I think it'll help you understand this place."

"Everything about you is interesting," he rushed to assure her. Realizing he wasn't rumbling, he started up a strong, soothing rumble to help comfort her.

"Oh, I like it when you purr," she murmured, rubbing her cheek against him. "And you smell like caramel. It's really nice."

"Tell me about your past, Pretty," he urged. "I won't stop my rumbles unless you ask me to."

"It's sweet that you call me pretty," she commented. "Even though I'm only average."

"I assure you, you're not average at all," he argued. He strained against his bonds even knowing he couldn't break them. For a submark, the urge to hold her overrode his common sense.

"Easy," she said, levering herself up on an elbow. "Don't hurt yourself. The guys said this position wasn't going to bother you. Were they lying?"

"I'm not in pain," he said. "But I don't like being restrained."

"Most people don't. Unless you're into that kind of thing, then it's probably a lot of fun. There would be safe words and all that stuff, but I'm getting off topic," she said in a flurry of words. "As long as you're not uncomfortable, I guess I can tell you my life story. No, not the whole thing, maybe only the highlights. You don't need to know about the time I knocked out a tooth or got lost trying to keep up with Zia and Isla. I was a bit of a late bloomer and short so those two were always outpacing me, except when I tripped one of them!"

She chuckled from the memory, then cleared her throat. "Right, I said you didn't need to know that stuff, and there I go, blabbering on about it. Let me try again. Most of the humans here on Sorana grew up on Wimol. It was a pretty typical human town, meaning we were free, but poor."

Ignatias couldn't help it when his body jerked from surprise. "You were wild humans?"

She snorted out a laugh. "You make it sound like we were running around in the forest scrounging for seeds and fruit. I know you guys use the term wild-caught for humans that weren't raised among the Talins, so in that respect we were wild. But we had a strong community with homes and everything. We weren't feral."

"I didn't mean to imply you were lesser than," he rushed to assure her. "I'm simply shocked so many of you survived. From the official stats I read, there are a good number of humans living here on Sorana, and you're telling me they all came from a wild colony of humans? It's impressive that so many of you lived without help."

"That's true," she conceded. "The universe isn't an easy place and tends to be really cruel to any species without a homeplanet."

She adjusted herself to lay a little more on top of him. Now her face was closer to his, making his scent glands ache even more. He wanted to rub his bonding oil on her. If he had that impulse with another Talin, it would be shameful, but this was a human.

According to all the literature, humans found Talin bonding oil comforting. Besides, it wasn't as if he could accidentally scent-bond to a human. There were rumors, but they had to be fanciful because humans didn't have scent glands to create bonding oil. How could a Talin bond with a creature that didn't have oil to bond them with?

"You smell like caramel," she murmured, rubbing her cheek against his chest. "I really like it. Zia says Palforma smells like vanilla to her, and Isla tells everyone that Tisuran smells exactly like maple. They both smell a little like soap to me, not bad, but not wonderful either. I think there's something important about the Talin that smells good to us. Like it's a way for us to pick out the Talin we want to be with."

He didn't know what caramel was, but all he needed to know was that she was fond of the scent and seemed to be looking for a reason to stay close to him. It made him determined not to leave this planet without her, no matter what he had to do to achieve his goal.

CHAPTER 6

Kasi

Was it creepy that she was cuddling up to a guy who was restrained? It wasn't kinky because he wasn't enjoying it, but was it wrong?

She'd tried to talk Palforma and Sandorian out of putting him in shackles. Of course they hadn't listened to her. She also wasn't surprised when they'd taken the remote release with them. That wasn't a concern, because she knew where the uni-key was kept so it'd be easy to release Ignatias once she explained everything to him.

Snuggling against him wasn't about warmth. The omni kept her perfectly warm. Something about him gave her the impression of loneliness. Zia would call her crazy, but Kasi felt the need to comfort this Talin.

"Tell me about Wimol, Pretty," Ignatias urged, his chest rising and falling under her cheek as he spoke. "Make yourself comfortable on me and talk of your childhood."

She pulled in a deep breath and thought of the most important things he needed to understand. "Wimol was like all the human communities out there because we were poor, but we were also strong. No one went hungry or homeless, we took care of everyone. When Zia was young, she needed these super special implants that were really expensive. The entire community saved money. Someone even donated a huge amount just in time and made it anonymous. I have my suspicions about who did it, but it's not my place to ask if she wanted it to stay secret."

"You cared a great deal for each other," he murmured, his deep voice making a shiver move down her spine. She should've insisted on a trade, her story for his story. Maybe later she'd insist he talk about himself.

"We did," she agreed. "We all love each other a lot. Some left the colony to find better jobs, like Zia. They didn't forget about us and often sent money back to help."

"It seems that the Wimol humans were coping well with their poor circumstances," he commented.

"Exactly," she agreed, feeling like he might be starting to understand. "It all means we had a choice. The humans on Wimol didn't have to come here. We could've kept working for the Ugarians. It wasn't an easy life, but it wasn't a death sentence either."

"What are you trying to explain to me, Pretty?" he asked.

"That we agreed to be pets out of choice, not force," she explained. "Palforma and Holian didn't buy us. They persuaded us."

His purring stopped for a moment, and he rumbled out a sound very similar to a poorly tuned engine. It was a sound that indicated confusion. "Why is that important?"

She hesitated to say the next part, but she had to make him understand. "It means that the humans here aren't really pets, we're free. We agreed to move with the understanding that being pets was a ruse so we could live within the safe borders of Talin-controlled space and have access to your trade networks."

"They told you being a pet was only pretend?" he asked.

She didn't think he'd believe her right away, but judging by the tone of his voice, he thought she and all the other humans had been naive. She wanted to tell him about the many happy human/Talin pairings among the Sorana population. Use those couples as proof that humans and Talins could get along as equals, especially when scent-bonding was involved. But those weren't her stories to tell. It was up to the couples to decide whether they wanted to talk to Ignatias about being scent-bonded.

"It really is pretend," she insisted, stifling a chuckle. "That's why I wasn't wearing a collar when you arrived. We don't have to wear them unless someone like you is going to visit. Oh, and that's why I wasn't dressed *appropriately*. We get to dress anyway we want around here. We can also do just about anything we like as long as we're being safe about it."

"You can't convince me that you wanted to perform harsh physical labor," he argued.

"It wasn't harsh physical labor," she countered. "I was dirty because Dotti was..." her words trailed off mid-sentence with a sigh. "You know what, never mind. You wouldn't believe me anyway."

He was quick to respond, his purring getting loud for a few moments as he spoke. "I believe you think this is the truth."

"That's the nicest way anyone has ever called me foolish," she muttered. Suddenly she was tired. She'd been working hard for weeks getting her field ready. Her sleep was always being interrupted by her anxiety, and she couldn't remember the last time she slept through the night. Combine that with the excitement and worry of earlier, and she was one worn out human.

"I think I'm going to take a nap," she mumbled, letting her eyes drift shut and tucking her legs up under her omnie to keep them warm. "We can talk more when I wake up."

"Sleep, Pretty," he urged her, his purring a soft, rhythmic vibration in her ears and against her cheek. She felt him move a little under her, and when he spoke next, his voice sounded a little closer. "Your new master is here to comfort you."

"Whatever," she mumbled, then slid into sleep with an ease she hadn't experienced since childhood.

Ignatias

Ignatias strained his neck to watch Kasi quickly drop into slumber. The poor thing had to be exhausted. The way she was trying to defend her old owners was sweet and something he'd expect from a human. They formed emotional attachments quickly. There were plenty of stories of humans bonding to their owners or other humans at a first meeting.

They were really too vulnerable to be out in the universe on their own. The best thing that ever happened to humans was being discovered by Talins.

Lowering his head back down to the cold, hard floor, he thought about strategy. He didn't expect the Talins in charge of the Sorana colony would let him live. He could easily cause all kinds of problems that included potential death sentences. That was a risk these warriors wouldn't be willing to take.

It was imperative he get himself free and leave Sorana with Kasi.

The door to his cell opened to reveal two Talins he recognized from the woods. He pulled back his lips to show his teeth and flared his quills threateningly.

"Don't wake her," he whispered. It was hard to sound menacing while whispering, but he hoped these Talins weren't so cruel as to wake Pretty. It was their fault she was so tired in the first place. What kind of males worked a delicate human to the point of exhaustion?

Neither of them rattled or rumbled as they took in the slumbering human. "Why am I not surprised Kasi is in here?" one of them said in a quiet voice.

Did his words mean Kasi had snuck in to be with him and truly wasn't being punished? That made his affection for the human grow, but his concern did also. If she didn't need to be in this cold room, then she should be in her regular room with a soft nest to sleep in.

Unless of course they didn't allow her a soft nest. They probably housed the humans in rooms similar to this one so it wouldn't matter where she slept.

"I'm surprised she's asleep," the other one whispered as the two moved silently into the room. One of them unfolded a blanket and laid it gently over Kasi. She mumbled something in her sleep, snuggled her head under the blanket, and went still again.

"That blanket was for you," one of them explained, dropping gracefully into a seated position on the floor next to Ignatias. "I guess the two of you get to share it."

The other male did the same on his other side. They were close enough that he could look at both of them without needing to strain his neck.

"I'm Sandorian of Wyn family within the Anize clan," the one on his right said in a low voice.

"I'm Tisuran of Sart family within the Glanorn clan," the one that had brought in the blanket whispered. "We wanted to talk to you without any humans around."

"Sleeping humans don't count," Sandorian added with clear amusement in his voice as he pointed at Kasi.

"Are you here to threaten me?" Ignatias asked.

"Would it work?" Sandorian asked, the amusement still there.

Ignatias didn't answer him. Instead he turned his focus on Tisuran. "What do you want to tell me?"

"We're going to keep you captive here for a while," Tisuran began. "We're still not sure what to do about you, but while we wait to hear back from our superiors, we decided it would be best to show you the true Sorana."

"I've seen what you do," Ignatias spat out. His harsh words came out loud, causing Kasi to stir. They all watched her move her body further on top of him while mumbling something about lumpy mattresses. She didn't open her eyes during the process, and once she was settled and breathing evenly again, Ignatias moved his eyes back to Tisuran. "How could you treat them like common laborers?"

This time both Tisuran and Sandorian let out soft rumbles of amusement before Sandorian spoke. "You'd understand how funny that was if you only knew how hard it is to make the humans do anything they don't want to do."

"They are not the mild, compliant creatures you think they are," Tisuran added. "At least the ones here on Sorana aren't."

"Kasi told me she and the other humans here are wild-caught," Ignatias said. "It still doesn't give you the right to be cruel to them. There should be ways to gently introduce them into captivity without hard labor or threats."

The two men exchanged glances before meeting his gaze again. It was Tisuran who spoke. "Most everything you're thinking is wrong. It's true we aren't following the laws and statutes, but for good reason. They are antiquated and unnecessary. We hope you'll come to understand that."

"Otherwise we'll have to do something unpleasant," Sandorian said under his breath.

Ignatias remained silent at the threat. He didn't trust himself to speak quietly and he didn't want to risk waking Kasi.

"We would like to know where your shuttle is," Sandorian added. "We haven't found it yet. We've located your ship tethered to the further moon, but not the shuttle you used to get planetside."

"If you get close to my shuttle you'll regret it," he warned them. "I set up hidden weapons systems around it after I landed."

It was a bluff. He would never set up any kind of traps where a human might stumble on them, but they wouldn't know that. He'd learned long ago that appearing to have an advantage could often give him the advantage.

The tactic worked because Tisuran reached for his Ident and started tapping rapidly. Then spoke as he read something off the Ident.

"No one's triggered hidden traps," he announced with relief. "I'm calling everyone back." They must have had people searching the woods for his shuttle. It felt good to know his shuttle would be there when he needed it.

Sandorian looked down at Ignatias. "If any of them had gotten hurt or killed because of you, I'd cut you into pieces so small they'd only be detected by a trace tracker-bot."

"Is there anything else you want to tell us about?" Tisuran asked, his voice tight with tension.

"I wouldn't approach my ship either," he warned. Another bluff they took seriously.

"Not even Higorian was this paranoid on his worst days," Tisuran grumbled. "Do we need to worry about humans stumbling on your traps in or around the village?"

This he didn't lie about. "No, I didn't do anything close to the village. The humans are safe."

"Then I'm done talking to you for now," Sandorian announced, getting to his feet. "You can be Palforma and Oriscon's problem tomorrow."

"Tell Kasi to fetch us if you need to relieve yourself," Tisuran said, standing up and joining Sandorian at the door. "Otherwise, someone will be here in the morning."

The men left and the door shut silently behind them with a rush of cold air. He was surprised they left Kasi with him, but perhaps he shouldn't be. It was simply more evidence of their neglect.

Forcing his body to relax, he tried to let slumber take him. It would help him escape tomorrow if he was able to rest tonight. Kasi's warm, soft body lying on top of him helped. Her peaceful presence gave him something to focus on other than the growing stiffness in his limbs. He only wished he could tug the blanket covering her a little because one of her dainty hands had escaped its confines and was exposed to the cold.

"My pretty human," he whispered. "Beautiful, Kasi, you need to tuck your hand in under the covers for me."

He had to repeat himself several times before she roused enough to do as he asked. He felt a huge sense of satisfaction when her little human hand disappeared under the warm blanket. In a small way he was taking care of her. He hoped this was the beginning of a long life of him getting to care for this human.

CHAPTER 7

Kasi

Kasi woke up stiff, but well rested. It wasn't until she tried to sit up that she realized she was lying on top of someone!

"I'm so sorry!" she cried, moving herself off him in a tumble of limbs and tangling herself in a blanket she didn't remember bringing in with her. Someone must have visited and draped it over her. She'd have to find out who it was and thank them for both the blanket and not forcing her to return to her domicile for the night.

"Why are you sorry?" Ignatias asked, starting up a loud purr as he spoke. "It's only me, not one of the cruel masters you serve."

She wrinkled her nose at his words. "I'm sorry I forced you to be my bed. You had to lay on the uncomfortable floor, and I was extra weight on top of you." She looked down at her round body. She always appreciated how strong her body was, but no one would call her svelte. "I'm really heavy. That couldn't have been pleasant."

Ignatias made a scoffing sound. "You're not heavy, Pretty. It was my privilege to be your bed for the night, although I wish I could've held you so you hadn't woken and fallen to the floor."

His words made her smile. "You're nice, and it wasn't much of a fall. More like rolling over with a slight descent."

He sounded the marbles-clinking-together-in-a-bag rumble of amusement. "You have a quick mind, Pretty. How do you feel? Do you hurt anywhere? The official roll has two healers living here. Has either of them seen you to verify you're well?"

She made a dismissive gesture with her hand as she got to her feet. "I saw Joslum yesterday. She said I was fine but to stop jumping on top of rogue agricultural-bots. Let me see if anyone is up and can release you. You have to be super uncomfortable after being forced to lie in one position all night."

Once on her feet, she wrapped the blanket around herself before walking to the door.

"You don't need to go out in the early morning cold," he objected.

She could tell he was going to insist she settle back down and snuggle up to him. As much as she wouldn't mind doing just that, she was worried about him. One thing she'd learned quickly since living here was that Talins tended to be stubborn and stoic. It was often up to their humans to make them rest or eat enough.

It was hilarious that Talins thought they were taking care of the humans!

"I'll be right back," she assured him as the door slid open and the damp morning air rushed into the room.

Shivering, she drew the back of the blanket up over her head like a hood. It was winter on Sorana right now which only meant that it was a little cooler than the normal tropical temperatures and a thick fog would form overnight, cloaking everything in gray. A few of the humans living here came from places far colder and said this was nothing. After a lifetime of dealing with Wimol's heat, Sorana's winter felt downright freezing to her.

She couldn't see the sun through the thick mist but got the feeling it wasn't much past sunrise. It wouldn't be long before the fog burned off and it would be another lovely day with blue skies and gentle breezes. Sorana was a perfect planet, even if it was a little colder than she was used to.

She needed to find someone to release Ignatias. He must need to use the facilities, probably urgently!

Before she could even take a step out the door, Palforma and Oriscon appeared on the path walking toward her. Palforma was carrying a tray of food, and Oriscon had a thick roll of bedding balanced on one of his broad shoulders and a heating box on the other.

"Looks like breakfast is here!" she said, stepping back so the men could enter.

"Rise with the Ancestors," Oriscon said. Unlike most traditional Talin phrases, Kasi had no problem remembering the answer to this one because they all used it every day to say good morning to each other.

"Let their wisdom guide us," she responded, taking the tray Palforma was offering her. "This looks delicious! Thank you."

With his hands free, Palforma was able to tap while Oriscon lowered his burdens to the floor. 'We're going to take Ignatias to use the facilities and then bring him back here to eat breakfast. We'll secure him in such a way that he can sit up, but we'll need to keep his hands behind his back and secured to the wall. That means someone will need to feed him.'

After repeating Palforma's words so Ignatias knew what was being said, she tapped and spoke her reply.

"Can't we take the restraints off completely?" she asked. "There's no other city on Sorana. And only Zia can use the comms array. He can't leave or send messages out."

"That would be too dangerous," Oriscon answered. "He has a shuttle hidden somewhere in the forest, meaning he could easily escape the planet. We don't have a ship in orbit right now, and Heginium and Zia are still working on fixing our only shuttle."

As he spoke, he worked to unlock Ignatias's manacles. Palforma was quick to take up a position so once Ignatias was free, the two men sat him up and secured his hands behind his back. She was surprised that Ignatias didn't try to resist them, and once he was on his feet, he docilely let the men guide him out of the room.

"We'll be right back," Oriscon told her. "Why don't you visit your domicile?"

"Good idea," she agreed, setting down the food and following them out of the small building. She ducked left as they went right. After using her domicile's elimination room, she took a little extra time to wash her face and brush her hair. Feeling more awake, she hurried back to the storage building.

She beat them there so she set about unrolling the heavy bed and releasing the fill straps so it would fluff up. Then she dragged it into place so when they secured him again, it would be under his body. After that was done, she set up the heating box, happy to note it was fully charged. Soon the room would be pleasantly warm. She wished someone had thought to bring one last night, but they'd all been distracted by the problem that was Ignatias.

By the time Palforma and Oriscon marched Ignatias back into the room, the bed was fully fluffed up and she'd covered it in soft blankets. They marched him to the head of the bed and forced him to sit. Then put his back to the support strut and secured his hands there.

"Can he have one hand free?" she requested.

'No,' Palforma tapped. 'He could accidentally hurt you while trying to get free.'

Ignatias hissed out a breath when she repeated Palforma's words. "As if I'd do anything so despicable," he spat out with the swarm-of-buzzing-insects sound of an angry rattle. "You've grown so callous toward the humans you think everyone would act as you do."

Kasi sighed. "He's not going to hurt me. I spent the night sleeping on top of him and he didn't shake me off, even though that had to be uncomfortable."

Palforma didn't tap but his negative rattle told her he wasn't going to budge.

"Fine, I'll feed him," she agreed. "But he can't stay tied up all day and night. You'll come back and let him walk around some more, right?"

"We have plans to show him around the village and Sorana," Oriscon explained as he stepped to the door. "We want him to meet the humans and see what it's really like around here."

"Really like?" she pressed. "Do you mean we aren't going to be pretending anymore?"

'There's no point in pretending,' Palforma said with the wish-washing-then-snap of a derisive rattle. 'He's seen enough of the truth to think the very worst of us. We need to show him the rest of the truth so he understands our honesty.'

"That makes no sense," Ignatias grumbled after Kasi translated.

Palforma ignored him. 'Take your time with breakfast. We'll back in a few marks to collect both of you for the tour.'

Oriscon let Palforma exit before he leaned in close to whisper in Kasi's ear. "I wouldn't trust Ignatias with your fragile human heart, Kasi. You might end up damaged."

"We're tougher than you think," she countered, pushing Oriscon toward the door. "I'll see you later. Go rise with the Ancestors or something."

Sounding a rumble of amusement, Oriscon left Kasi alone with Ignatias. He was watching her closely, his long legs splayed out as if to give her room to sit between them.

"Come eat," he ordered, nodding his head at the tray of food. "Humans are easily weakened from lack of sustenance. All of this is safe for human consumption so please sit and fill your belly."

"We're both going to eat our fill," she said, picking up the tray and placing it next to the bed before she took the spot between his legs. She surveyed the food then grabbed an entire round of flat bread and used a large serving spoon to pile delicious vegetables covered in a tangy sauce on top. Then she folded it to hold everything together and held it to Ignatias's mouth.

"You should eat–"

She shoved the food into his mouth, cutting off his words. He sounded an angry rattle to signal his annoyance as he chewed. After several movements of his jaw, he sounded a rattle of surprise.

"That tasted good," he said after swallowing, his tone clearly conveying his shock.

"Don't sound so surprised," Kasi said with a laugh. "We might be a small colony, but we have all the same food preparation machinery as everyone else."

"I didn't mean—"

Kasi shoved food in his mouth again.

"This is fun," she said with a giggle. "This might be my new favorite activity. Filling your mouth with food every time you say something I don't like."

Realizing she wasn't going to stop, he let her feed him the rest of the flat bread. Once that was done, she grabbed a bowl of her favorite hot, thick, soupy grain dish, and sipped. There were two bowls there, one plain and one sweetened. Kisha must've put the tray together because she made the sweet bowl exactly the way Kasi liked it.

Because Talins traditionally only ate one meal a day, they'd never divided foods into breakfast, lunch, or dinner categories. She and the rest of the humans had been quick to explain that some flavors didn't agree with the human palate early in the morning. Flatbread and the sweetened, hot grain dish were almost universally liked by the humans. The vegetable dish was something they put up with because the

Talins insisted humans needed more nutrients included in the first meal of the day.

"I know Talins aren't fond of sweet food, but do you want to try a little?" she asked, holding up her bowl.

Ignatias sounded a negative rattle. "No, Pretty. You need to eat."

"I promise I always get enough food," she said with a grin. Holding the bowl in one hand, she poked her round belly with her fingers. "I've always been fat. I mean, there's plenty of muscle under there too, but it's all covered in a thick layer of blubber."

Ignatias sounded an angry rattle, making Kasi flinch and almost spill her breakfast. He cut the rattle off abruptly and went back to a loud purr.

"You shouldn't say such things," he insisted. "You're perfect, Pretty. Your shape is exquisite, and you feel wonderful in my arms. I've never rested better than when you slept on top of me."

Kasi wasn't sure how to respond to his statements. She'd never had anyone say so many nice things about her appearance at once. No one on Sorana was mean to her, and she'd left behind all the petty insults with the Ugarian's back on Wimol. Still, all her past experiences stuck with her, and she had an image of herself as an ugly human.

Ignatias made her want to believe she was pretty.

"Um, thanks," she mumbled.

"You don't sound like you believe me," he said. "I'm sure it will take time for me to undo the unkindness you've suffered. I'm patient. I'll make sure to tell you every day how beautiful you are."

"You don't need to," she said, even though she wanted to hear those words again and again.

"I want to. Will you sleep on top of me again tonight?" he asked. Then surprised her with a, "Please."

"Yes, um, maybe. I don't know." Feeling flustered, she picked up a bowl of plain breakfast grain soup and held it up to his mouth. "You need to eat too. When you finish this, I'll eat some more. We'll take turns until we're both full."

He purred as she tipped the bowl slightly so he could sip the thick concoction. She focused on keeping the bowl steady and was proud that they managed not to spill any of the food on him or the bed.

Putting the empty bowl down, she picked up another bowl full of cut up fruit. It was common to end a Talin meal with it, as if the bland fruit counted as a dessert. It wasn't bad, and the Talins were constantly pushing all the humans to eat it because of its dense nutritional value.

She popped a piece of pale pink fruit into her mouth then picked up another to offer Ignatias. She thought he'd delicately accept it with his lips, but instead, he opened his lips and took both the morsel and her fingers into his hot mouth.

She gasped as he sucked on her, his tongue exploring her fingers. He was careful to keep his sharp teeth away from her delicate flesh. A wave of lust washed over her, making her feel overheated. She'd never had someone do something so seductive, and he probably didn't even realize what he was doing!

She opened her mouth to suck in a breath and tell him to stop but choked on her food instead.

Coughing and embarrassed, she jerked her hand away from him and snatched up a canister of water, drinking between coughing fits.

"Go for help!" he demanded. "Quickly, before you aren't able to move any longer!"

Finally catching her breath she spoke, her voice hoarse. "I'm fine."

"You're struggling to breathe, Pretty. That isn't good," he argued.

"I just swallowed wrong," she explained. "We humans do that occasionally. It's nothing to worry about because the food didn't get caught in my throat or anything."

"Food can get caught in your throat and block your breathing?" Ignatias roared, clearly starting to panic. "How has your species survived so long?"

His sincere question made Kasi laugh. "That's something a lot of us ask on a daily basis! Especially Joddy when his allergies get bad between treatments."

"This isn't a laughing matter!" Ignatias sounded a rattle that was similar to the angry-buzzing-insects sound of the annoyed rattle but muted. It took Kasi a moment to remember what this sound meant; he was anxious. "You could be damaged and suffer further ill effects later."

Being all too familiar with anxiety, Kasi rushed to soothe him. Scooting closer, she set down the water canister and cupped his cheeks with her hands. He went perfectly still and silent as she petted his face. "I'm not injured or ill. I won't get worse, and I won't get sick. At least not because of swallowing wrong. I promise."

"I'm worried," he whispered. "I've only just found you, Pretty. I don't want anything bad to happen to you."

She refrained from pointing out that he was the only bad thing that had happened to her on Sorana. Hopefully by the end of today he'd see all the humans were happy and healthy and would be open to letting them explain.

The smell of caramel filled her nose, making her feel relaxed. She gave him a closed mouth smile out of habit, before speaking again.

"Nothing bad is going to happen to me. I'll be with you all day, and we're going to meet a bunch of people and see a lot of stuff. It'll be fun."

No sooner had those words left her mouth than she could hear people walking outside. Letting go of Ignatias's face, she got to her feet to move the tray out of the way.

"I guess it's time," she said with forced cheer and crossed her fingers, toes, and even her eyes that today would go well.

CHAPTER 8

Kasi

Kasi wasn't surprised when Zia showed up with Palforma, Tisuran, and Oriscon. Zia was the unofficial leader of their little colony. She might've been born deaf, but she never let that hold her back. Kasi had always admired Zia's intense courage and confidence. Unlike her friend, Kasi always second guessed everything she did.

'Good morning, Kasi,' Zia tapped before giving Kasi a fierce hug. Unlike Palforma who could hear but had trouble speaking, Zia couldn't do either. She had implants that would scroll the words spoken around her across her eyes, but she liked it better when others tapped.

"Morning!" Kasi said, tapping and speaking. Maybe she could talk Ignatias into getting Norka downloaded into his INT today.

Zia turned her attention to Ignatias. 'Rise with the Ancestors.'

"Let their wisdom guide us," Ignatias responded. "I would've tapped, but as you can see, I'm unable to use my hands. I promise you'll receive good care in the future, little human. You don't have to live this way."

Kasi felt her mouth drop; he'd understood everything they'd been saying all along? Before she could question him, Palforma sounded a rattle of affirmation. 'I thought as much. I was curious to see if you'd continue the ruse with Zia.'

"I couldn't let Zia think I couldn't understand her," Ignatias snapped at him. "She might suffer emotional damage."

There was a beat of silence before Palforma, Tisuran, and Oriscon let loose with amused rumbles loud enough to fill the room, and Zia was making her soundless huffing laugh. Only Kasi didn't find it funny.

"Stop it," she scolded them. "He was trying to be nice and all of you are laughing at him. That's cruel! He was tied up all night and didn't complain. He probably didn't get any sleep and still he's working hard to be kind to Zia. I'm ashamed of all of you."

Because she would never be labeled as having "grace under pressure," she started tearing up as she spoke, making her voice watery and taking strength away from her outrage. At least everyone stopped laughing, although now they were gaping at her as if she'd started honking like a confused dran bird.

"Don't be upset on my behalf," Ignatias said before anyone else spoke up. He was purring and shifted his body until his legs were stretched out. "Come sit on my lap and cling to me until you feel better."

Kasi really wanted to take Ignatias up on the offer, but she was determined to stand on her own two feet, metaphorically and literally. She faced her friend and pointed at Ignatias before tapping rapidly. At least she didn't have to talk at the moment; she might have started crying.

'Unlock his cuffs and let him stand up, right now!' she demanded.

Tisuran and Oriscon jumped to do as she ordered, and soon Ignatias was standing up with his hands secured in front of him. She didn't like that he was still restrained but knew this was as good as she was going to get.

Zia stepped up close and waited until Kasi met her eyes. 'I'm sorry I laughed,' she tapped. 'I didn't think about how it might be perceived.'

'I know,' Kasi answered and tried to give Zia a smile. 'I think I might be overly sensitive to being laughed at.'

'Those Ugarian kids were idiots,' Zia said, her tapping turned jerky with anger. 'I wish you'd told me that they were giving you a hard time when it was happening. I'd have taught them not to pick on a human.'

'They would've found other ways to be mean to me,' Kasi said, feeling silly for letting her emotions come to the surface so fast. 'Besides, that was a long time ago. I should've gotten over it by now.'

'Sometimes wounds leave us with scars,' Zia argued. 'Scars are never as durable as regular skin. They change us.'

As much as Kasi agreed with Zia, she didn't want to have this conversation anymore. 'Where are we taking Ignatias first?'

'The individual domiciles and the dorms,' Zia answered, letting Kasi change the subject. 'Then to the nursery, the producing fields, and finally to the communal house for a meal. I've told everyone to resume their normal duties and activities, so he'll see what we all do here on an average day.'

'Can we skip my domicile?' Kasi asked with a half grin. 'It's a mess.'

Zia shook her head and turned to face Ignatias. Kasi turned with her, startled to find everyone had been watching their conversation. Feeling a little embarrassed, she hurried to Ignatias's side. Tisuran moved out of the way so she could walk next to him with Oriscon on his other side.

Ignatias started purring and pressed his arm against her. If his hands weren't bound together, he'd probably have wrapped an arm around her.

"You can clutch or cling to me anytime you need," he offered. "I'll never reject your touch."

"Thanks, Ignatias. You can ask for a hug if you need it," she responded. "I won't turn you down."

Zia clapped her hands to get their attention. She gave them a warm, closed mouth smile before she started tapping.

'Let's begin. We have a lot of things to do today. This way.' Turning, she led everyone out of the room.

Ignatias

He wasn't sure why everyone had laughed when he'd explained that he didn't want to hurt Zia's feelings by pretending not to understand Norka, but he'd felt elated when Kasi jumped to his defense. He wasn't bothered by their amusement, but he could tell some past trauma had been triggered in Kasi.

He'd badly wanted to snatch her up and hold her tight, but everything he read about humans said they needed to be allowed to talk to each other if there were hurt emotions. Owners were only supposed to intercede if the interaction continued to get worse or turned physical.

His patience was rewarded when the smaller human, Zia, was quick to apologize and revealed that there was something from Kasi's childhood still affecting her as an adult. He suspected it had to do with her belief that she wasn't a beautiful human.

As they walked, Kasi stayed close to him. He was familiar with having to divide his attention, so it wasn't hard to be aware of her and watch his surroundings as they walked to the center of the village.

Zia stopped where several walking paths converged and turned to face him. She pointed to a large, multistory building.

'That's the dorms. Each room has its own private elimination and bathing facility but no food preparation area. Usually people are only there until we can build them a domicile of their own, but a few like to live more communally and have elected to stay there. Both Talins and humans are housed there in rooms of their choosing.'

He was startled by that information. Normally humans were housed in secure areas for their own safety. Although that was in places with large Talin populations where stealing a human could be accomplished relatively easily if the human wasn't properly guarded. He'd already experienced the vigilance of this colony and had to admit that stealing a human from here would be nearly impossible.

He still wanted to know how they'd realized he was there so quickly but knew no one would tell him. Instead he focused on Zia as she continued to point out buildings and give him explanations, uses, and their plans for future expansion.

Zia was well spoken and knowledgeable. It truly seemed she was in charge of this place, even though that was a ludicrous thought. A human in charge of Talins? A species with no homeplanet ordering around a species with one of the most powerful empires in the universe? Ridiculous.

Except, it was happening.

Kasi stayed by his side as the tour continued. He was walked through the dorms and allowed to look into several rooms. He noticed all the rooms were of similar size and well appointed. Then he was given a tour of one of the individual domiciles that was a standard size for young colonies. These types of homes came pre-made and could be erected in a single rotation. The limiting factor was that the company that made them had a waitlist despite having several manufacturing facilities on multiple planets in the empire.

They only looked inside three of the individual domiciles, but he saw smiling, healthy, and happy human families with all the items they needed to live a full life. One of the homes even had young cubs running around and playing.

The moment they walked in, everything stopped and the sire looked to Zia. "You said to return to normal, so we were about to take these guys over to the nursery," he explained, lifting one of the giggling human cubs up.

'Perfect,' Zia declared. 'We'll come with you.'

One of the children ran up to him and tugged on his belt. "My name is Della," she announced boldly, her dark brown eyes sparkling with eagerness and her short black mane a fuzzy mess around her head. "Will you carry me?"

He sounded an amused rumble and dropped to one knee in front of her. "My name is Ignatias. I'd be delighted to carry you, but only if your dam and sire are comfortable with that."

"Della is always looking for rides," the dam said with a little laugh that he thought sounded forced. When she reached out to pull her cub away Ignatias knew he was making her nervous.

She pulled the cub close and spoke gently. "This Talin is new here. Maybe we can ask again later."

Ignatias wasn't upset at the dam's caution. It was well known that human parents were protective of their offspring. Her protectiveness was a sign of a well-adjusted human.

"I'm sorry you can't carry me, Iggy," the cub said with far more volume than needed for the small space. Then she was off, running to her sire and tugging on him, demanding to be carried. When he refused, she ran to Oriscon who lifted her up with a loud purr.

"Don't feel bad," Kasi murmured. "Mathia will let you carry Della once you've been here a little while."

"I'm not upset, Pretty," Ignatias assured her as he stood up. "It pleases me to see the cub unafraid of strange

Talins, but the dam isn't wrong to be wary. She has good instincts."

The dam in question rolled her eyes and grinned at Kasi. "They're cute when they're clueless."

Before he could object and point out to Mathia that he'd read all the literature on human nature, they were being ushered out the door and down a well-trodden path. It wasn't long until he could hear the sound of laughing and excited chatter. They entered a large single room building and Ignatias's first impression was chaos.

Little bodies were running around in the center of the room, laughing and calling out to each other. The moment Oriscon set Della down, she rushed to join the other cubs.

Several Talins and humans were in the room, mostly ignoring the louder active cubs and speaking quietly to smaller groups of two or three cubs sitting or standing in other parts of the room. It reminded him a little of his younger days at the cresh. Before he lost his friend and nothing was ever right again.

No, he wouldn't think of that time. He couldn't because even thinking her name might send him into a dark place he might never come back from. He forced himself to focus on the cubs, noting how many and what ages he thought they might be.

There was so much going on that he didn't notice the cub at first. They were off playing with a small, blond human cub, taking turns stacking colorful blocks then knocking them down. At first, he didn't believe what his eyes were telling him. The sounds around him muted as the world narrowed down to a single offspring.

It was only when he tried to move away from his captors and was brought up short by Tisuran's hold on him that he remembered what was going on. He growled and tried to pull away from the warrior only to have Kasi step in front of him and place both her hands on his.

"I'm going to introduce you to Lamarin," she said. Her tone was soft but her expression fierce. "You're going to be nice to him. No loud rattles or harsh words. He's a sweetheart and just like all the other kids, he deserves only love and support."

Ignatias nodded his head, unable to speak. She let go of his hands and led him around the room to where Lamarin sat. He was young, probably not speaking in full sentences yet. The human cub he was playing with had to be several solars older because they were roughly the same size and humans grew much slower than Talins.

But then again, Lamarin wasn't a full Talin.

As they got closer, Ignatias could make out more of the boy's details. He had the hard keratin plating of a Talin, but he also had the prominent nose and facial movement of a human. His eyes were also distinctly human and yet he was missing the shell of the ear humans had that Talins didn't possess.

He'd heard this was possible but hadn't truly believed it; however, the evidence before him was irrefutable. He was staring at a Talin/human hybrid.

As he stood there, both children abandoned their game to look up and greet the adults. Someone called out a name across the room and the human child jumped up and ran off with an answering yell.

The hybrid remained seated, smiling up at them and showing off sharp, pointed Talin teeth.

"Kasi!" he declared, holding up his arms.

"Hi, Lamarin," Kasi said, dropping to her knees to give the child a quick hug. "Can we play blocks with you?"

"Yeah," Lamarin agreed and handed Kasi a big yellow block. "I'm building. Building with color!"

Kasi placed it on a smaller green block, and it promptly fell off, causing the rest of the stack to tumble down.

"I think you're going to need to show me how to stack them," she announced, picking the yellow one up and handing it back to him.

"Silly, Kasi!" he said with a very human sounding laugh.

Ignatias looked to Tisuran. "Can I sit on the floor and address Lamarin?"

Tisuran made a rumble of agreement. "Remember what Kasi said. I might not be allowed to kill you yet, but no one said I couldn't strip some plating off your hide."

Ignatias ignored the threat and dropped to a kneeling position next to Kasi and Lamarin. Other cubs and adults flowed around them, talking and playing games, but his entire focus was on the hybrid in front of him.

He watched silently as Lamarin showed Kasi how to stack the bricks and giggled when she pretended she didn't understand and placed the bricks so they'd fall down. The laughter blended in with the human cubs around them perfectly, but then Ignatias heard the distinct sound of a rumble of amusement. It seemed the child had a chestbox so he could express joy in several different ways.

Suddenly the boy turned to him and held out a bright purple brick.

"Play?" he asked.

Ignatias froze for a moment, unsure how to react. Lamarin's mouth flattened, a sign of unease in humans.

He saw Kasi reach for the block out of the corner of his eye, but he moved faster. Snatching the block from the child, he sounded a loud rumble of amusement. The child's smile came back as he dropped his hand away and watched Ignatias with interest. Kasi quickly introduced Ignatias to the child.

Lamarin pointed to the block he was holding. "Iggy, play!"

"Do I place it here?" he asked, putting the block on top of a precarious stack. The blocks tumbled down immediately and little Lamarin patted Ignatias's arm consolingly.

"No cry. I help," he said and started stacking again. Then he handed Ignatias another smaller block and pointed to the stop of the newly formed stack. "There! Put orange there."

Ignatias did as Lamarin commanded and was rewarded when the boy beamed up at him, sounding a rumble of agreement.

"Good job! Good, good!" he declared with a clap then swept a hand out to knock everything down.

There was a small commotion and Ignatias looked over his shoulder to see another hybrid entering the building. She was older than Lamarin, and the moment she could pull free of her human mother, she ran to the group in the center and started playing.

There were no full Talin children here, but he assumed they'd be treated in the same way as the humans and hybrids. They would learn, but they would also be allowed joy. Could he remember ever feeling joy at the cresh after he betrayed Darsinum?

"Iggy want?"

He turned his attention back to Lamarin. The hybrid was offering him another block. It was a simple gesture, but Ignatias was suddenly overwhelmed. His chestplates felt fused together. He couldn't make his lungs expand to pull in any air. He felt overheated but also numb.

He could tell Kasi was trying to talk to him, but he couldn't hear her over the roaring in his earholes. Darkness ate away at the edges of his vision as panic started to spread.

He had to get out of there.

Stumbling to his feet, he turned and fled, ignoring the surprised exclamation from Kasi. No one was expecting his flight, so everyone was slow to react. Tisuran tried to grab his arm, but he easily evaded the warrior. He leapt over a huddle of children sitting around a large data square and then sprinted out the door, his movements only slightly hampered by his bound wrists.

Once outside the building, he stopped and hunched over, trying desperately to pull air into his starved lungs. He was vaguely aware of a commotion behind him but was busy trying to force his body to breathe.

Then Kasi was in front of him, cupping his cheeks in both her hands and rubbing her fingers across his scent glands.

"Breathe, Ignatias," she whispered, her face close to his.

As if her words released the panic, he was able to take in a great breath of air. He filled his lungs, feeling weak and shaky. He tried to open his mouth to apologize but no words came out. How could he even ask for forgiveness after acting disgracefully? He'd let his emotions overwhelm him. He was a pitiful excuse for a Talin.

"Whatever you're thinking, stop it," Kasi demanded with a frown. "The only thing I want you to do right now is breathe with me, got it? I'm not going to leave you. You're not alone."

She kept rubbing her fingers over his scent glands and it was starting to wreak havoc with his already haywire body. Giving into impulse, he put his bound arms over her head and down her back until he could press against her backside and scoop up. He held her tight against his body and sounded a continuous comforting rumble. She gave out a little squeak of surprise but then wrapped her arms around his neck and nestled in close.

"It's going to be fine," she whispered, her mouth so close to the bare patch of skin on his neck that he could feel her hot breath.

He feared she was wrong and nothing would be fine ever again.

CHAPTER 9

Kasi

When Ignatias bolted out of the building, Tisuran had shouted that he was trying to escape but Kasi knew better. She'd seen him freeze up and then panic as he dealt with emotions he wasn't prepared to confront.

She'd scrambled to her feet to follow, thankful that the warriors had been slowed down by children running in front of them. Ignatias had broken the door to the nursery when he'd forced it to slide open faster than it was programmed to, so it stood mostly open and a little askew. That gave them all of a clear view of Ignatias standing outside, bent a little at the waist with his head hanging low.

It was pure luck that she was able to grab hold of Tisuran before he launched out the door and at Ignatias.

"Stop!" she demanded, throwing her weight back and pulling the male a little off balance. "Let me talk to him."

"Let go, Kasi," Tisuran said, trying to tug her hands off his arm without hurting her. "He's trying to escape."

"Then he's doing a really shit job of it!" she declared, lacing her fingers together to make it harder for Tisuran to peel her hands off. "Look at him! He's struggling. You knew about human pets and Talins falling in love from when you lived on Kalor, but he's finding all of this out now. Love, kids, families, everything. Think about how overwhelmed you felt at first."

"I didn't run away from a kind, happy child," Tisuran growled. Kasi noticed the other warriors had stopped short of the door and were watching their interaction with interest. As long as Ignatias wasn't trying to run, it seemed the others were willing to listen to her.

"But did you meet children first or were you able to interact with a bunch of human adults until you were comfortable?" she countered. "I bet there might have been years, I mean, solars before you were faced with a child, human or otherwise."

"What are you trying to say?" Tisuran asked.

"Talins are so emotionally repressed that walking into a building full of kids had to be overwhelming. Let me spend some time with him. He probably just needs to talk some stuff out."

She could tell Tisuran wasn't convinced but then Isla was there. "Let her talk to him," Isla urged. "Remember how I'd run away when I needed help? It might be the same with Ignatias. We should let Kasi help him."

"If he's unstable, he should be put down," Tisuran grumbled, but no one took his words seriously.

Just before Ignatias had his freakout, Lamarin's parents, Henni and Ianino, had shown up. Now, all of them were urging Tisuran to do as she asked.

"I agree with Isla," Henni said. "Give him the same patience you'd extend to one of us humans."

"Even I had moments of insecurity, and I grew up around all of this on Kalor," Ianino pointed out.

"Fine," Tisuran grumbled. "You and Ignatias can sit on the benches outside, Kasi. You have to stay in sight, and no going for a walk in the forest."

With a nod of agreement, she let go of Tisuran and rushed to Ignatias. His breathing was shallow and inconsistent, as if his lungs were damaged. Although Talins claimed they didn't suffer from anxiety or panic attacks, Kasi was pretty sure she was seeing one right now.

She put her hands on his face and leaned in close. "Breathe with me, Ignatias."

To her relief, he did as she asked and matched her deep breath. He met her gaze, his mouth opened but no words came out. A rumble that sounded a lot like a person rhythmically sobbing in the distance sounded from his chest. She'd never heard a Talin make this noise before. It sounded so desolate it broke her heart.

Rubbing her fingers on his face, she said the same words to him that had helped her in the past.

"Whatever you're thinking, stop it," Kasi ordered. "The only thing I want you to do right now is breathe with me, got it? I'm not going to leave you. You're not alone."

She was going to tell him to start counting his breaths with her when he moved with startling speed. One moment she was standing with her hands on his face, the next moment his bound arms were around her and she was pressed hard to his body.

She didn't fight but she might have made some kind of undignified sound while being scooped up. Once he was holding her, all he did was straighten up; he didn't try to run away or even take a step in any direction. He wasn't trying to carry her off, he wanted a hug.

Understanding the need for comfort, she only froze for a moment before wrapping her arms around him and relaxing into his hold.

"It's going to be fine," she promised. "I'm not going anywhere, and you can hold me as long as you need to. You're safe with me."

It must have been the right thing to say because some of the rigid tension in his body eased. She could hear movement around them and lifted her head to see Palforma, Zia, Henni, Ianino, Tisuran, and Isla watching.

'What can we do?' Zia tapped. Because of the way she was being held, Kasi had to use the simplified version of Norka.

'He needs some space and time,' she tapped. 'Let me take him to my domicile and stay with him.'

"No," Tisuran started to object but Zia hissed out a sound that made him look at her.

'Quiet,' she ordered, her motions sharp. 'Can't you see he's hurting?'

Relief hit Kasi as Tisuran went quiet. Zia was a powerhouse in a small body. No one was going to win an argument with her right now.

'Tell him you want to be alone in a familiar place,' Zia instructed. 'That will help him focus.'

'Good plan,' Kasi tapped, then put her mouth near Ignatias's earhole. "I don't want to be out in the open anymore. Will you take me to my domicile, please?"

She watched Isla move out of her field of vision and in front of Ignatias. "Let me show you where she lives," Isla offered.

Ignatias grunted, hugged her tighter, but didn't move. Pulling her head back, she craned her neck to look at Isla, who shrugged her shoulders. Kasi looked back at Zia, but it was Henni who spoke up.

"You want Ignatias to go with you, right, Kasi?" Henni asked, while giving Kasi an encouraging look. "You wouldn't want to be left alone."

Finally understanding, Kasi looked back at Tisuran and Palforma. "Can Ignatias stay with me?" Her voice might have been sweet, but her expression clearly told them if they didn't say yes, she'd make them pay.

Both Talins quickly sounded rattles of agreement, making their humans beam at them.

Ignatias's hold on her relaxed slightly. It seemed he was hearing what they were saying even if he wasn't responding.

"Come on, let me show you the way," Isla said. Tisuran disappeared from Kasi's sight when he rushed to stand at Isla's side.

She could hear footsteps, then Ignatias started to move. She breathed out a relieved sigh and let her forehead fall on his shoulder. Kasi was sure that getting Ignatias quiet time and a safe space was the key to helping him come back to himself.

The walk to her domicile was quick and soon Ignatias was passing by Tisuran and Isla as they stood next to her open door. Isla gave her an encouraging smile as they walked by.

Kasi flashed her a smile she hoped looked confident. The door slid shut, abruptly cutting off all the sounds and sights of the outside world.

Now the three of them were in the room alone: Kasi, Ignatias, and Ignatias's past trauma.

Ignatias

He wasn't sure how long he stood there holding onto Kasi, but by the time he started coming back to himself, his muscles felt fatigued and his joints were sore. Both were indications he'd held the same position for at least several marks.

Kasi felt like a dead weight in his arms. It took a few submarks to unlock his joints; then he shifted her weight. Her head lolled to the side, eyes closed and face relaxed. She was sound asleep.

Shame and concern filled him in equal parts. Had Kasi tried to get him to let her go and he'd ignored her?

As he stared at her and debated about waking her up, Kasi's eyes fluttered open. She started to smile and then her mouth turned down and she cupped his cheek.

"How do you feel?"

"Shouldn't I be asking you that question?" he countered. "I don't remember how I came to be in this room."

"You should probably set me down and give your arms and back a rest," she said, moving her hand from his face to grip his shoulder.

He didn't want to let go of her but didn't want to cause her worry by ignoring her request. Reluctantly he set her on her feet, and she ducked down as he lifted his bound arms over her head. She made a soft distressed sound at the sight of his chafed wrists.

"I'm going to ask one of the healers to come over," she said, resting her fingertips near the abused flesh and trying to keep the hard metal of the manacles from touching there. "And maybe I can talk the guys into taking these off."

"The pain is minimal," he assured her. "The healer should still be called to check you. How long did I force you to stay in my arms? Did you lose feeling in any of your extremities?"

She smiled up at him and shook her head, making her short mane brush her shoulders. "You were so gentle, I fell asleep. I can't believe you held me like you did. I'm so big."

He sounded a negative rattle. "You're the perfect size, Pretty. Your softness filled my arms and made the memory episode less severe."

"Memory episode, I've heard of them," she said. "Lakin said Dalt gets them sometimes. They're like flashbacks, right? You relive a traumatic event?"

He kept his answer deliberately vague. "Somewhat. Now, will you call the healer?"

"Only if you let her look at you too," Kasi said.

"That's acceptable," he agreed. There was nothing the healer could do for him since there was no medication or treatment for memory episodes. The best a Talin could hope for was that they happened in private so no one ever found out. It looked like this colony of lawbreakers now knew one of his secrets. Not that his secret compared to the enormity of what they were hiding on this planet.

"Where are Lamarin's parents?" he asked.

"Henni and Ianino are here, they showed up just as you ran outside," she explained.

"Ianino?" he repeated, a startled rattle coming out of him. "You don't mean Commandant Holian's son, Ianino?"

"Yup, that's him," Kasi answered easily, completely unaware of the power she'd just handed him. "From what I've heard, those two have been in love for ages, but Holian wanted Ianino to make a name for himself before settling down. Of course, he couldn't do that with a human pet in tow and there was the complication that Henni really wanted to have his kid so obviously they couldn't live in most places. Although I've been told that there are some hybrid children on Kalor. They must be really well hidden because I think it's illegal, isn't it?"

"Very much so," he agreed. "It's so illegal that if this got out, it wouldn't only ruin Ianino but also Holian. They could both be condemned and their family colony of Kalor could be seized. All Holian's assets, including his collection of human pets, would be redistributed to other families."

Kasi's mouth dropped open and her hands tightened on the manacles she was still holding up and away from the wounds. "What?"

"Did you not realize how serious this is?" he asked, then answered his own question. "That's right, you're wild-caught and have never been anywhere in the Talin Empire but here. Our laws are strict about relationships and children, Kasi. It's taboo for Talins to have intercourse with other species, and it's completely illegal to breed mixed-species children. There are Talins who've been condemned to death in the past for it."

Kasi let go of his wrists and took a step back, covering her mouth with both hands as she gasped. "What do they do to the children?"

"They are innocent so they're not going to be punished for the transgressions of the adults," he assured her. It was hard but he didn't reach for her. She'd already been patient with him. He didn't want to push her for more touching if she wanted space. "The offspring of illicit unions are sterilized and sent to live their lives out on remote colonies or stations, not dissimilar to here."

Kasi didn't look entirely happy with his answer but moved her hands to her cheeks to make it easier to talk. "That's not as bad as killing them but still, that's cruel. They aren't monsters. They're children."

"The Talin Empire sees them as both," he said. "They are the product of weak-willed Talins, and their very existence is considered an abomination."

"And you guys don't do live birth either, do you?" Kasi said with a sad shake of her head. "You have some facility grow your children in an artificial womb, then they raise them for you. Tisuran told me that parents aren't a part of the child's life until they're basically adults. That isn't what childhood is supposed to be like."

"Not for a human," he agreed. "But we are Talin. Our ways have allowed us to create one of the mightiest empires in the known universe. Isn't that why you and your human friends agreed to come here, to live within the safety of Talin-controlled space?"

She looked like she wanted to argue for a moment, then sighed. "I suppose you're right, but I still think the empire should change. Everyone should be more like we are here."

He couldn't help the rumble that came out of him.

"What does that rumble mean?" Kasi asked. "It sounded like two pieces of rotten fruit being smashed together."

He didn't want to tell her it was the sound of disgust, so he asked a question instead. "Do you mean the empire should let humans and Talins breed?"

She tilted her head to the side and narrowed her eyes. "I think they should let families be families."

A strong longing rose up in him, locking his throat and making it impossible to talk.

"Lamarin is really smart," Kasi continued, unaware of the tightening of his throat. "And he's the sweetest kid. He's going to grow up knowing he's loved not only by Henni and Ianino, but the whole community. Heck, he makes me want to have a kid just like him."

Her words made him imagine her round with a child. She'd probably talk to them constantly, murmuring words of love and devotion to her belly as if the fetus inside could understand her. The picture in his head was so real and visual he was suddenly desperate to see it happen.

"I'd take good care of you and your cub," he whispered.

Her expression softened. "I know you would. You were great with Lamarin."

"I meant a human cub," he insisted. He couldn't allow himself to think about a future where he was able to raise his own child. It was so illegal as to be ludicrous. It was hard to say the next words, but she needed to understand he wasn't one of the lawbreakers. He was a good, law-abiding Talin.

"I would find you a male to breed with. It might take some time, but now that I work for the Committee of Pet Welfare, I have more connections with families that own humans. I promise you would get to pick the male who breeds you."

"Yeah, no, that's not happening," she said, her words so quiet he might not have heard them if they weren't standing close. She had the same expression on her face as when she told him to let *families be families*. Was this how a human face looked when they felt pity for someone?

Kasi shook her head at him. "I can see we have a long way to go until you understand. It's a good thing I'm patient because I think you're going to need all of it."

CHAPTER 10

Kasi

Healer Joslum wasn't happy about tending to Ignatias's wrists and wasn't gentle either. Kasi tried to object to Joslum's rough treatment, but Ignatias assured her the healer wasn't causing him pain. The thing that bothered Kasi the most was that Joslum refused to have the restraints removed. Sandorian and Oriscon were stationed outside her door and Joslum could've easily asked one of them to take off the cuffs, but she wouldn't.

These Talins had all kinds of kindness to show humans but none for each other. It was maddening!

After the abrasions were dealt with, both Joslum and Ignatias insisted Kasi be looked over. She'd let Joslum do an exam, unsurprised when the healer declared her perfectly healthy and offered her one of the candies most Talins seemed to carry around specifically to give to humans.

It was both weird and endearing.

"Everyone is gathering for the evening meal," Oriscon said from the open door. "It would be good if you could attend, Kasi. There are a lot of people worried about you."

"Can't you tell them you've seen me and I'm fine?" she asked. She didn't want to go to the communal building for the evening meal. She wanted to stay in her domicile and work on getting Ignatias to tell her about his memory episode. He had a wound there she wanted to understand and maybe help him with, but he wouldn't be confessing anything to her surrounded by the rest of the colony.

"I could tell them, but it won't be good enough," Oriscon responded. "They want to see you with their own eyes. I'm sure you understand."

Unfortunately she did. If the roles were reversed, she'd want to be able to interact with the person who was carried off by an uncommunicative Talin. She looked over to Ignatias, but he remained silent. It was tacit agreement with whatever she wanted to do.

"I guess it won't hurt for Ignatias to meet more people," she agreed.

"Will you let me carry you to the evening meal?" he asked, his voice barely above a whisper. His question made her look down at his hands. They were opening and closing as if he was restraining himself from reaching out to grab her. Although she hadn't told anyone, she had a mildly painful crick in her neck from falling asleep in an odd position while being held by Ignatias. Being carried didn't sound like it would be good for her neck at all.

"How about we hold hands?" she offered instead, slipping one of her hands between his bound ones. He was quick to take the offer, holding her hand firmly but gently.

"I'll be better," he whispered as they walked out of her domicile, Oriscon in front of them and Sandorian with Joslum behind them.

"You don't need to be better," she responded. "You need to feel better."

He grunted an unintelligible word then remained silent for the rest of their walk. The village was still small so it wasn't long before they were walking into the communal building with long tables set up and bursting with food, people, and conversation. All eyes turned to them when they entered, and everyone stopped talking.

Kasi gave a little wave with her free hand and smiled at everyone. "See, I'm fine. Ignatias is fine. Everything's fine."

"Except now we have an outsider who knows all about us," someone said in a loud grumpy voice. "He could ruin everything."

"Nothing's going to be ruined," Kasi answered, trying to figure out who'd spoken. "I'm sure Ignatias will do right by us."

"Doubtful," someone else said. That was followed by general dissatisfied grumbling from both humans and Talins. Kasi pulled her hand free from Ignatias's grip and stepped in front of him with hands on her hips and a scowl on her face. Her heart was beating fast, and she felt a little dizzy from the anger that suddenly raged up inside her.

"We aren't like that!" she announced loudly. "We don't dismiss people before giving them a chance. Remember what happened to Lasha? She almost died because we didn't tell her enough that we loved her and wanted her to stay. She felt like a burden and was so pressed to find a job she ended up a virtual slave. If Tamerin hadn't gotten to her when he did, she'd be dead! Our sweet wonderful Lasha would be dead! I thought we'd learned from that. We give people the benefit of the doubt and we treat them with respect until they prove unworthy."

"He kidnapped you!" Joddy shouted.

Kasi rolled her eyes. "He was trying to save me. He thought I was being treated like Lasha was on Glakor. If anything, his actions should make us more forgiving, not less."

"Leave it to Kasi to turn a kidnapping into a virtuous event," Sandorian muttered behind her, then sounded a rumble of amusement.

Kasi ignored Sandorian and grabbed Ignatias's hands to lead him to a table with several empty seats. They sat down across from Isla and Tisuran.

"You look much better," Isla said with a smile for Ignatias.

"I'm sorry if my actions alarmed you," he answered without meeting Isla's eyes.

Kasi placed a hand on his thigh. "Isla wasn't alarmed, only worried for you."

"You missed the midday meal," Tisuran said to Kasi. "You should eat."

Ignatias stood up like he'd been shocked, making Tisuran stand up also, with a startled rattle. Ignatias ignored the other Talin and reached for a heaping platter of food. He set the entire thing on top of the empty plate in front of Kasi.

"Eat!" he demanded with a worried rumble.

Kasi laughed and picked up the platter. "That's a little too much for me," she responded as she dished some onto her plate and handed the platter to Isla. Tisuran slowly sat back down as Ignatias passed every platter within reach to her. She took some from each, even the foods that she wasn't fond of.

Once her plate was full, Ignatias sat back down and turned in his seat to face her, watching her with unblinking eyes.

"I'm not going to eat if you keep watching me like that," she said with a chuckle. "Why don't you fill your plate too? Or help yourself to some of this; I'm not going to be able to finish it all."

"If I consume some of the food, will you eat also?" Ignatias pressed.

"Yes, we can have the same deal as this morning. I'll eat if you eat," she agreed and watched Ignatias fill his plate from the closest platter. She got the impression he didn't even care what he ate, only that there was something to consume so she'd eat also.

Although Talins only needed to eat once a day, Ignatias probably needed a little extra food today. It wouldn't hurt him to have a second meal.

By the time both their plates were full, conversations had started up again, filling the room with the sound of voices. From beside her, Heginium asked a question about her field. Excited to talk about the project, Kasi launched into the current progress.

Between eating and talking, she didn't notice Ignatias had gone still until Heginium nudged her and nodded his head. A glance over found Ignatias staring with predatory focus at something on the other side of the table. Following his gaze, she tried to figure out what he was looking at but didn't see anything unusual.

Isla had moved to sit on Tisuran's lap, a common occurrence with those two. Actually, it was common with most of the Talin/human couples. It was never long before a human was picked up and cuddled by their Talin partner. After spending lifetimes without physical affection, these Talins were starved for hugs and snuggles.

As she watched, Tisuran kissed Isla. It started out as a peck on the lips, but Isla slid her hand behind his neck and held him in place to deepen the kiss. Next to her, Ignatias stiffened and an angry rattle came out of him.

"How many humans are being taken advantage of?" he growled. Tisuran and Isla separated as everyone went quiet, eyes all turning to Ignatias. Kasi almost groaned.

"No one is being taken advantage of," Kasi said. "They're a couple, just like Ianino and Henni, or Palforma and Zia. They love each other."

"This is unconscionable," Ignatias said, turning his gaze to her. "Humans are pets, not partners. They are to be cared for, coddled, and protected—not sexually abused!"

"We're not being sexually abused," Isla gasped.

"I picked Ianino," Henni said from further down the table. "No one forced me. Holian even tried to get us to wait longer, but I didn't want to."

Kasi could tell by the way he kept up the angry rattling that he refused to believe them. So much for making progress tonight. It seemed attending the communal evening meal hadn't been a good idea after all.

"Every Talin here brings shame to the empire, their clan, and their family," Ignatias growled. "There will be no Ancestors waiting for any of you!"

That must've been a serious insult because the Talins in the room all stood up, some so violently that chairs fell over backward. Deafening rattles of rage and challenge filled the room, making it impossible to hear any of the angry words being spoken.

Scared that this was going to turn into a brawl, Kasi got up and grabbed Ignatias's hand. When he didn't respond to her touch, she tried to pull him away from the table. "Let's go back to my place."

Even if he heard her over the din of rattles, he didn't respond. He was shouting something else to Tisuran and the others, and they were shouting back. Then Sandorian and Oriscon were there, nudging her out of the way and grabbing Ignatias.

Taking hold of an arm each, they dragged him away from the table. When he started to fight, Idrisan stepped in front of him and held up the same black device he'd used to knock Ignatias out in the woods. The sight of the device made Ignatias stop struggling, and he let the other men drag him roughly from the building.

Kasi hurried to follow. When she realized they were taking him back to the storage building, she tried to protest.

"Can't he spend the night in my domicile?" she asked, jumping in front of them and halting their progress.

Oriscon sounded a strong negative rattle. "Did you hear what he was saying, Kasi? He hates us. He sees every Talin here as dirty criminals."

"I know, but he just needs time," Kasi argued. "Not many individuals change their entire worldview overnight."

Oriscon didn't budge. "We wouldn't be able to secure him properly in your domicile and his escape means our death."

"He made it very clear that we can't trust him to keep our secrets," Idrisan added.

"Not yet," she agreed. "But making him sleep in the storage building isn't going to win us his favor. You could tie him to my bed. I think it's sturdy enough. It'll be safe, I'm sure."

Sandorian sounded a sad rumble she rarely heard from the Talins. "He would have us all put to death for breaking Talin law. Maybe even little Lamarin. He won't change his mind Kasi. He's too set in his beliefs."

"No!" she gasped. She refused to believe that Ignatias would do anything to hurt Lamarin. "He'd never do that. Would he?" A small bit of doubt made her stop arguing as Idrisan stepped up next to her.

"There's a bed and a heater box in there now," he said, urging her out of the way without touching her. "He won't be uncomfortable."

"It's also best for his safety to be in a room only I have the key for," Sandorian pointed out. "He angered many of us back there."

"You don't think…" Kasi couldn't finish her thought. The idea of anyone she knew hurting Ignatias while he was helpless was unthinkable. But then again, she couldn't imagine anyone being put to death for falling in love and wanting a family. She felt turned around and inside out. "Would they?"

Idrisan started purring and that seemed to break Ignatias out of his stony silence. He strained against the two Talins holding him, his quills flaring up and his backplates loud and challenging.

"Don't comfort her. Don't touch her. She's not yours!"

Kasi was close to tears. She hated conflict, and everyone was so angry and uncompromising. She knew in her heart of hearts that, given time, Ignatias would accept their way of life. Once he wasn't overwhelmed with the foreignness of it, he'd understand that Sorana was a place of love, not abuse.

Right now, she needed to get away from everyone before she broke down. She needed some quiet time to think.

Wrapping her arms around herself, she looked at Ignatias. "I'll see you in the morning."

He opened his mouth to speak but she turned, walking away before anyone could see the tears trying to escape her eyes. Tomorrow she'd try again with both Ignatias and the rest of the colony.

CHAPTER 11

Kasi

Idrisan followed her to her domicile. Standing in her open door, she turned to him and made a sweeping motion with her hands. "I want to be alone for a while. I don't even want you outside my domicile. Please go home."

Idrisan didn't leave. "Don't cry for someone like Ignatias. He's indoctrinated and rigid. He isn't worth your tears or pain."

She tried to smile but knew it probably looked more like a grimace. "They're my tears. If I want to shed them for Ignatias, I will."

"I'm sure you'll tell me it's your heart too," he murmured with a concerned rumble. "Be careful with your love, Kasi. Only give it to someone who deserves it."

"Who decides the most deserving?" she asked, then shook her head. "Don't answer that. I'm tired and I don't want to end up in a philosophical debate with you. You'll make me question if water is wet by the end."

"Conversation, not debate," Idrisan countered with an amused rumble. "Sleep well, Kasi. I'm on watch tonight patrolling the village so contact me if you need anything. Even someone to talk to about non-philosophical things."

"Sure," Kasi said with a smile and stepped back. The moment the door slid shut she got moving. It felt imperative to get out of her home and into the fresh forest air.

It didn't take long to change into her work clothes and sturdy boots. She had several walking torches she kept on charging ports in her domicile, so she grabbed them and opened the door. As expected, no one was there to keep her from heading to her field.

The early evening air was cool but not cold yet and there was no fog. Stars twinkled in the dark sky above her, but a combination of tears and bright walking torches kept her from seeing them.

For someone who cried easily, she hated it every time. Her first instinct was always to go off and hide until she had her tears under control. It was embarrassing to start crying around people who were calm and controlled. Her mom always told her it only meant she felt things more strongly than everyone else. Kasi was sure it was a sign that her brain wasn't wired correctly.

Whatever the reason was, times like this called for solitude and comforting activities. When she saw her field and the slow moving agricultural-bots, she started feeling better. Dotti was still shut down at the end of one of the rows, looking a little dusty and maybe slightly sad.

There was nothing she could do for the old bot, so she focused on other things. By the time she'd checked in with the two other bots and tested several samples, the tears were gone and she was feeling far more calm.

"You're looking so good," she said to the third row. They were growing better than any of the other rows. She took some detailed notes about the nutrients used in that row and continued. She pushed all thoughts of Ignatias and her friends out of her head, focusing only on her passion.

The walking torches dutifully followed her from row to row until she'd completed her measurements and notes. It was getting cold by the time she was done. Tucking everything away in the storage box, she gave her field a last look over then headed back to her domicile.

"I'm going to make myself a nice big mug of hot tea," she told the walking torch in front of her. "And you can have a comfy charging port all to yourself for the rest of the night."

When she got to the edge of the village, she shut down both walking torches and carried them over a shoulder. She wasn't worried about getting in trouble for being out late at night by herself. No one would dare to hassle her right now. It was more that she didn't want to talk to anyone. The time in her field had helped calm and relax her, but she still felt a little raw.

That was why she ducked behind a pile of empty shipping crates when she heard the familiar voices of Joslum and Sandorian talking to each other.

"We finally got a response from Holian," Sandorian said.

Joslum sounded an inquisitive rumble. "What did he suggest?"

"He's on his way, but we might have to act before he arrives," Sandorian answered grimly. "Ignatias didn't have a set schedule, but it will be noticed if he doesn't check in within a reasonable timespan. We can't afford for them to send out another inspector."

"I've already sent Holian my idea," Joslum said.

"I read it," Sandorian said. "Your plan has merit, but wouldn't they be able to detect the drugs in his system?"

Joslum made a negative rattle. "It would be easy to drug him with something that would mimic being poisoned by a faulty biosystem."

Kasi covered her mouth with her hand, shocked that they were already coming up with plans to murder Ignatias. It had only been a day and a half since he got there. Or maybe two days if she counted all the time he spent asleep the first night. How could they so callously talk about his death like this?

They moved out of range of her hearing while she stood there, stunned. Sagging against a box, she set the two walking torches on their feet so she could rub her hands over her face.

She'd thought Holian would be the voice of reason for the colony, but it seemed he might be the one who decided if it would be safer for everyone if Ignatias was dead. She couldn't let that happen.

She needed time with Ignatias—days, maybe even weeks more. But what could she do? She didn't have the resources to take him away from the colony and sequester him out in the woods. The colony was so new they didn't even have any "old" buildings that no one used anymore. Besides, if they stayed on the planet, it wouldn't take long for someone to find them.

"We'll need to go into space," she breathed, straightening away from the crate and grabbing the walking torches. Ignatias had a shuttle and a ship. If they could get out to the ship, no one could get to them. Then she'd have plenty of time to talk Ignatias into keeping Sorana's secrets. By the time Holian got here, she'd have Ignatias convinced and everyone would be safe!

Moving with purpose, she rushed home. She'd need to pack a bag for her time in orbit and leave detailed care instructions for her field because she didn't know how many days she'd be gone.

Ignatias

Laying there in the pitch dark and bound once again, Ignatias reviewed everything he'd seen and done that day. It played out like a vid in his head, over and over again.

All he'd need to do was keep himself calm and collected. After a sufficient amount of time, he plotted to pretend he was one of them and then leave the planet with Kasi. For all the threats they verbalized, he knew none of them wanted to kill him. They'd all been handpicked by Holian and approved by Prime Son Searin to live on Sorana. That meant each Talin here was highly honorable and killing a fellow citizen would go against their ingrained principles.

His strategy was a burned-out shell now. Instead of being calm and collected, he'd raged at everyone. The plan was ruined, but even worse, Kasi was probably scared of him now. He'd seen water leaking from her eyes when she'd rushed off. There was nothing wrong with her body, so it had to be from emotional distress.

Emotional distress he caused.

He hadn't even meant the words he'd said. He didn't think these Talins were sexually abusing the humans. It might not be legal or sanctioned, but it definitely wasn't abuse. By the time they'd taken him to the communal building for the evening meal, he'd understood that.

Then he'd seen the couple lip-pressing with each other. Blinding desire had swept through him. He wanted that with Kasi. But it was wrong, and he would be a disappointment to his species, clan, and family if he gave into the impulses raging within him,

To combat his desire, he'd lashed out. He'd shouted unkind words and caused a horrible disturbance. He wouldn't be surprised if Kasi didn't want to come near him ever again.

He would've welcomed retribution from the men who'd dragged him from the dining hall. It might have lessened some of his guilt. But all they did was secure him on his back and leave him in the dark without the heat box turned on. Hardly a fitting punishment for his actions.

When he heard noise at the door, he hoped it was one of the men coming back to physically reprimand him. What he didn't expect was to see a small human form standing in the doorway, backlit from powerful lights mounted on the eaves of the building.

"Kasi?" he whispered. The form stepped forward. Her face was still in shadow, but he could smell her unique human scent. He started up a soothing rumble and spoke in a soft voice. "Pretty, thank you for seeking me out. I'm so sorry for my cruel words. Please let me explain."

She made a shushing noise and knelt at his side. She was wearing the same strange clothing he'd seen her in when she was working in the field. The thick, durable fabric was worn and stained, completely inappropriate for a human pet's delicate skin. Why was she wearing these garments?

He sounded a worried rumble. "Kasi, why is your—"

She hushed him with fingers to his lips. He stopped talking and rumbling.

"No one knows I'm out here, so you have to be quiet," she explained.

When he nodded his head in agreement as the humans liked to do, she lifted her fingers from his lips and pulled something from her coat pocket.

"Why are you here?" he murmured. He didn't care what her answer was as long as she kept talking to him.

"I have an offer for you," she said, putting her face close to his. "I overheard some stuff that made me worried so I'm going to free you. But you have to promise me something."

He knew what she'd probably overheard because it was a logical avenue the other Talins on Sorana would take. He was a problem for them and needed to be eliminated, the only question was how. After tonight's drama he had no friends on Sorana except Kasi. Sweet, caring Kasi probably couldn't stand the idea of his demise and decided to help him despite the danger.

"What do you need from me, Pretty?" he asked.

"I'm going with you," she said. "If I free you, you have to promise we'll stick together. There's stuff I need to explain and make you understand, but to do that, you can't leave me behind."

As if he could leave her behind! "There's no question that you'd accompany me."

"That's good! And you'll listen to me?" she pressed.

"Of course," he agreed.

The Ancestors were favoring him because after a little tapping on what was in her hands, the manacles around his arms and legs released. Sitting up, he ignored the pain in his wrists and reached for her. She half fell, half climbed into his arms, and it was a struggle not to start up a soothing rumble.

"I was fearful I'd never see you again," he murmured, holding her tightly to his chest. Her warm, soft weight was a salve to his battered emotions. "I have so much to apologize for."

"We'll figure that all out later," she said, giving him a quick hug before pushing at his shoulders. He let her go and waited to see what she wanted to do. Standing up, she tugged at his hand, urging him to get up. "We don't have much time!"

He rose to his feet and let her lead him out the open door. The area within the village was so well lit it might as well be daylight. Kasi paused outside the door to reach for a bag laying on the ground outside the building.

Snatching the bag up before she could get a grip on it, he hefted it over one shoulder. It was large and heavy; she must have struggled under the weight. Kasi took his hand in hers again and rushed them around the building to the darkness beyond.

"There are walking torches in the pack," she explained as they walked briskly down an earthen path. "We can pull them out and turn them on once we are a little farther away. If we're lucky, no one will notice you're gone until morning."

"Where are you leading me?" he asked, unsure of their direction.

"If I take you back to the field where you found me, do you think you could figure out where your shuttle is from there?" she asked.

"Yes!" he assured her quickly. It was hard but he kept from rattling in enthusiasm. Pretty was helping him escape. They could leave this ancestor-forsaken colony together! "If I had my Ident, we wouldn't need to backtrack to the field first."

She stopped abruptly and let go of his hand. "It's in my bag," she said pointing to the pack hanging from his shoulder.

He opened the sack up as wide as it would go, only to find a jumble of items packed in no particular order or theme. To his surprise, Kasi reached in and was able to pull out the Ident without having to shift a single item. He hoped the dagger and pouch he'd been carrying when captured were in there also.

"Here you go," she said, holding it up.

He took it from her. Tapping it to life, he gave the tech a moment to orient before ordering it to locate and guide. Within submarks, the Ident had interfaced with the shuttle and was ready to give directions.

He pointed to a narrower path forking away from one they'd been following. "That way."

"Sure," she agreed and tried to take the pack from him. Not only did he close it back up and resume carrying it, but he also reached for her.

"Whoa," she said, stepping out of reach. "What do you think you're doing?"

"We'll make better time if you let me carry you," he explained, holding out his free arm and inviting her into his embrace.

She shook her head, her short mane dancing in the faint light. "Let's start with me walking first."

He grumbled but straightened up and let her set the pace. She walked with surprising speed for a small human and they covered ground tolerably quickly.

Several marks later, Kasi's speed started to slow. She'd lasted longer than expected, but it was clear she was starting to fatigue.

"We need to stop for a moment for the Ident to calibrate," he lied, putting an arm around her shoulder and guiding her to a small boulder. She leaned against it, breathing hard. He was startled to realize her entire face was damp, then remembered that was how humans regulated their temperature.

"Good," she said between breaths. "I could use the break. You landed really far from the village!"

"It was necessary if I wanted to observe before anyone knew I was planetside," he said as he ran a critical eye over her form. Other than the water on her skin and rapid breathing, she appeared fine. The literature said regular and brisk exercise was necessary for a human's optimal health, but these circumstances couldn't be beneficial.

"Will you let me carry you now?" he asked after her breathing had evened out.

"For a little while," she agreed. "But not like you did before."

"No," he agreed. "I was rough then. I'll be gentle with you now."

He secured the pack on his shoulder and held out his arms. She stepped up and wrapped her arms around his neck. He put one arm under her and straightened up. Her legs fit around his waist and her weight settled perfectly against him.

She was made to be carried in his arms.

"We should probably get one of the walking torches out of the bag," she murmured, her mouth close to his earhole. "Gorgs will be out hunting and simply having a light keeps them away. I can reach the pack and pull the top of one out so it can light up all around us."

He sounded a comforting rumble. "Do what you need to feel safe."

He waited as she opened the bag and pulled the top of a walking torch free. Soon the forest around them was brightly lit and the pack felt oddly balanced.

"I closed the top around the neck of the walking torch as best I could," she said, settling back in his arms. "If it shifts, I'll fix it again."

With a rumble of agreement, he set off at a run he knew was sustainable for the entire trip, even with her in his arms. Soon they'd be on his shuttle, and he'd have Kasi all to himself without fear of anyone taking her away.

CHAPTER 12

Kasi

The last few days caught up with Kasi by the time they reached Ignatias's shuttle. She should've been wide awake and excited. This was only the second time she'd been in space, a thrilling novelty!

Instead, she found it difficult to keep her eyes open after Ignatias buckled her into the passenger seat in his small shuttle. The craft was tiny enough that Ignatias was forced to duck his head and move carefully to avoid bumping himself as he settled down in his seat.

"This shuttle is perfectly safe but not well appointed," Ignatias explained as he tapped the display in front of him.

Resting against the back of the seat, she rolled her head sideways to watch Ignatias. "What do you mean?"

He started purring. "Our ascent will be loud and a little shaky. It's nothing to be concerned about. I promise, we're not in any danger."

"All the equipment we used back on Wimol was old and falling apart. I'm sure it'll be just like being back there and traveling between fields," she said.

"Indeed," he answered, distracted by his display. "I'm going to begin the startup and launch procedure; I'll need to concentrate."

"I'll sit here and be quiet," she agreed. She watched him for a little while, but all he was doing was pressing parts of the display. The engines started up, vibrating the shuttle and making a low humming sound. Letting her eyes fall close, Kasi relaxed into her seat. It turned out this shuttle did sound and shake a lot like the equipment back on Wimol.

She was asleep before they left the ground. It felt like only moments later that Ignatias was picking her up and settling her on his lap. Yawning, she snuggled against his bulk.

"Remain slumbering," he murmured. "It will be several marks before we arrive at the ship. You should rest until then."

She drifted back into a contented sleep feeling warm and safe, with the scent of caramel perfuming the air.

She woke up from her long nap to find Ignatias staring down at her with the intensity of a psychopath. If she didn't know that watching humans sleep was a favorite Talin past time, she would've been at least perturbed.

"You're awake," he announced before starting up a purr and loosening his hold on her so she could sit up.

"Are we close?" she asked, stretching her arms up and arching her back.

"We docked with the ship almost a mark ago," Ignatias admitted. "But you slept peacefully so I didn't want to disturb you."

The excitement that had been missing earlier sprung to life, making her eager to explore. "Do you have windows?" she asked.

The ship that had collected them from Wimol had been industrial. The facilities were comfortable enough, but the set up was practical, meaning no observation deck with large windows to watch the universe go by.

He paused, as if her question was strange. "Windows?"

"Um, I think they're called viewing ports on ships," she said.

A brief rattle of affirmation came out of him, sounding like water dripping on a piece of metal at a regular interval. "I'm afraid my ship isn't equipped with those. I can program a display to show you views from one of several angles outside the ship though."

Standing up with her cradled in his arms, he made his way off the small shuttle. The hatch was wide open, and they emerged into a tiny space barely big enough to house the diminutive craft.

"This ship was originally designed for exploratory and mapping missions when the Talin Empire expands into newly conquered territory," he explained as he carried her down a short corridor. "This one reached its military operating time limit and was decommissioned. I was able to requisition it as a personal craft because my duties for the Committee of Pet Welfare require travel to places outside normal shipping lanes."

"If it's too old for the military to use, is it safe for us?" she asked, looking around. Everything seemed shiny and new, but Talins had strict standards about what they used both commercially and militarily.

"The military must maintain the highest level of dependability, so they retire equipment before it's mechanically necessary," Ignatias explained. He walked them into what was obviously a bedroom and set her down on a neatly made bed. "Both the ship and shuttle have been thoroughly inspected and cleared for civilian use."

"Is this my room?" she asked, looking around the small space. The bed looked like it could fold up into the wall. There was a desk secured to a wall with a single attached chair that would swivel in and out from under it. Other than the bed and desk, there wasn't any other furniture or even personal items in the room. Everything was uniform and probably close to what it had looked like when it was a military ship. Even the bedding was steel gray and matched the color of the walls around her.

"This is my room," he explained as he opened up a cabinet and started pulling out bedding. "The other cabin on the ship isn't inhabitable, but I'll make you a nice nest on the floor, and if you wish, you can cling to me on the bunk in your sleep. Or I can join you on the floor in your nest."

She watched him put down several compression pads on the floor and tug the side straps so they started fluffing up. Then he piled pillows all around the pads. Finally, he covered the whole thing with several large, fuzzy blankets. By the time he was done, it looked exactly like what he was calling it, a nest.

"I'm not a bird," she said with a little laugh. Sounding the irregular beat of a confused rumble, he straightened up from where he was adding another round of pillows over the fuzzy blanket and looked at her.

"I'm well aware that humans aren't an avian species," he agreed.

"Then why are you–" she stopped talking, remembering something Tisuran had told her shortly after getting to Sorana.

Hundreds of years ago, when Talins first started collecting humans as pets, they came across an abandoned mine full of humans who'd been contracted to work there. To conserve their resources, they'd all gathered in one room so many individual rooms didn't need to be heated. Space limitations meant everyone's bed was a mat on the floor and families would gather their mats close to each other, resembling nests. The Talins who discovered them were under the erroneous impression that humans preferred living and sleeping this way.

Ignatias was simply trying to make her comfortable by creating the fluffiest nest possible. If she was honest with herself, it was looking pretty comfy! She could see settling down in it with a cup of tea to watch an Ugarian soap opera on an information square. She especially liked the idea of Ignatias joining her.

"That's a really nice nest," she praised. "You're more than welcome to sleep in it with me."

Ignatias purred loudly. "Thank you, Pretty. Would you like to try it now? You slept so soundly on the way here I thought you might wish to rest longer."

She stood up from the bed. "I feel much better after the nap. I'd really like to see more of the ship."

He sounded the many-hands-clapping rattle of pride and opened his arms up in an invitation to hug. "I can carry you."

She shook her head and placed one of her hands in his. "I'll walk."

The tour of the ship didn't take long. There were only two other cabins besides his and both were full of crates with markings in Talin on them. That was something else she'd noticed about Talins, they didn't write things in Universal. It was a clear sign of Talin arrogance. They expected everyone else to learn to read their language; they couldn't be bothered to learn a standard trade language like Universal.

But it was also proof of the Talin Empire's prestige and power.

"What's all this?" she asked, pointing to the second room filled top to bottom with crates.

"It was supplies for Sorana," he explained. "My original plan was to observe the colony unnoticed, return to the ship after taking detailed notes, and land at the port as if I hadn't been on the planet before. These were all items requested by the colony that I planned to deliver."

"We can drop them off later though, right?" she asked, eyeing the boxes. Could new agricultural-bots be in there? Or the sample testing station she'd requested? And the secondary comms array and supporting satellites were probably in there too. The colony needed those badly!

He went still, his grip on her hand tightening slightly. "We won't be returning to the surface. Once you're acquainted and comfortable with the ship, I'm going to plot a course for the nearest station with an interplanetary array powerful enough to reach Talarian. The authorities must be told about what's going on here."

Worry and alarm hit Kasi hard. "No, we're just going to orbit the planet. I got you off Sorana so you're safe. We don't need to leave the system!"

"You asked to come with me," he said, his tone half statement and half question. His purring stopped, replaced by the irregular confused rumble that sounded like a poorly tuned engine. "Why would you request that if not to escape your abusive owners?"

"So I can make you understand that there's nothing wrong with what's going on," she exclaimed. She felt like an idiot; she should've made him promise to stay in orbit!

"I'm sorry, sweet human," he said, going back to purring. "What's going on is illegal and it's my duty to stop it."

Frustration made tears gather in her eyes. She fought them for all she was worth. If she started crying now, he'd probably dismiss everything she had to say.

"How far away is the nearest interplanetary thingy?" she asked, proud at how even her voice sounded.

"About five rotations of travel," he said, dropping to one knee and trying to draw her closer to him. "You seem upset. Do you need to clutch and cling to me?"

"Five days," she murmured to herself. "I can work with that."

Accepting his offer for a hug she pressed against him and wrapped her arms around his neck. Ignatias didn't know it yet, but he was about to get the full force of Kasi's persistence. If she could grow plants that hadn't existed for hundreds of years from a piece no bigger than a speck of dust, she could persuade a single Talin to her way of thinking.

CHAPTER 13

Ignatias

He couldn't refuse Kasi so when she asked to send a message packet to Sorana so they knew she was fine, he agreed. He sat her on his lap in the cockpit and showed her how to work the controls for the recorder. She kept starting over because she would change her mind on what she wanted to say.

On the fourth recording she started to cry, and he stopped everything and pressed her gently against him. She didn't fight his hold and rested her cheek on his shoulder.

"They can't hurt you anymore," he reminded her. "You're safe here with me."

"I'm not worried that they'll hurt me," she said with a frustrated sigh. "I don't want them to be mad at me."

He almost sounded a confused rumble but managed to stop himself and kept up the soothing sound instead. "How is that different?"

"When you love good people, like everyone back on Sorana, you're not scared that they'll hurt you. You're scared that you'll disappoint them. One of the worst things is to feel like you let down those who rely on you. My friends and family are down there, worried about my safety and their own future. It's got to be horrible, and that makes me feel intensely guilty."

"Your actions were correct and commendable," he stated with authority. They were on the correct side of the law. What else was there to argue about?

She made a huffing sound, similar to the way Zia laughed. In this context he was sure the sound wasn't one of humor but of doubt.

"According to you they are. Everyone else will see my actions as foolish. I can only hope that I made the right decision."

He rubbed a hand up and down her back. "I can assure you that you did."

She put her mouth against the strip of exposed skin at the base of his neck. He'd seen vids of humans lip-pressing each other, and of course witnessed it between Isla and Tisuran, but he'd never experienced one himself. Her lips felt incredibly soft and warm, making him pull in a sharp breath.

Thoughts and emotions swirled through him. Humans lip-pressed for many different reasons that weren't necessarily romantic. Unwilling to reject her touch, he let himself assume this was a platonic kiss and gave himself permission to enjoy it.

"I really like your sweet caramel smell," she murmured, nestling her face more into his neck and breathing in deep through her nose. "It makes me want to rub all over you."

"It's good you find my scent appealing," he agreed. "I'm always available for clutching and clinging. You never need to worry about touching me. I'm yours at any time."

"Is this clinging?" she asked, her warm breath wafting across his exposed skin. It was hard, but he resisted the urge to move so that her lips were forced against him. Where were these impulses coming from?

None of the vids or literature warned that humans had an addicting quality. Or it might be only Kasi because she was such a unique and special human.

"This is clinging," he agreed, surprised at how deep his voice sounded.

"We call it hugging," she told him. "Or snuggling might be more accurate."

He liked the sound of her human word *snuggling*. It was soft and warm like the female in his arms.

"The humans and Talins on Sorana will know you're with me. You don't need to send them a message," he reminded her.

"It's still necessary," she insisted, rubbing her face against his neck. Then she sat back up and he immediately missed her warmth pressed against this chest.

"I'm getting it done this time!" she declared and tapped determinedly on the display. It only took her three more attempts before she recorded a message that she was satisfied with. After a short deliberation, she pressed the button to send it off. In a few submarks it would reach the planet.

This time there wasn't any water from her eyes, and a relieved look had replaced the tension in her face.

She smiled at him, but it didn't reach her eyes. "Zia will be so angry she might smack someone in the face while talking."

"What?" he asked with a brief confused rumble.

"Zia uses Norka to talk, remember? When she gets 'loud', she does it by making her gestures bigger," she explained with a small chuckle. "One of the pre-constructed domicile units arrived badly damaged and she was talking so loud with her hands she backhanded Palforma in the nose! He pretended she knocked him out and fell over. Then he played sick for the rest of the day and insisted she stay with him and attend to the injury she'd caused. Palforma wasn't hurt at all, he just wanted her to take a break. We'd all been working pretty hard for a while."

"Did she realize it was a ruse?"

Kasi shook her head with a chuckle. "Not until the next morning, but she laughed it off and promised Palforma she'd start taking more breaks."

"He should've forced her," Ignatias commented. "Harsh labor can shorten a human's lifespan."

Kasi snorted derisively. "Good luck making Zia do anything she doesn't want to do. She's probably the most stubborn person I know."

"But he's the owner," Ignatias insisted.

"In name only," Kasi said, then laughed. "Actually, she owns him too. There's paperwork filed in the Nimon records that state Palforma is owned by Zia."

"That can't be correct," he argued.

"It really happened," she insisted. "She was working for a trawler that pulled in his damaged shuttle. She had to claim him as her property or the captain would've probably shoved him back in the shuttle and left him in the middle of space to die."

Ignatias resisted the urge to dispute Kasi's outrageous claim. It was obviously one of the made-up stories humans were famous for. Humans liked to create fictional accounts all the time. They created fantastical records of people and beasts that never existed. It made humans an entertaining species, but also an unreliable source of information, even of their own experiences.

"That's interesting," he said, giving the most neutral answer he could think of.

She turned in his lap, maneuvering her legs until she was straddling his thighs and facing him. It shouldn't have felt as intimate as it did.

"I have questions," she said, leaning back against the dark display behind her.

Happy to change the topic, he sounded a brief rattle of agreement. "Ask anything, Pretty."

She covered her mouth to smile widely. Reaching up, he grasped her hand and drew her arm down. "You don't need to cover your smiles or laughter. I know showing your teeth is a sign of happiness, not a threat display. As I've told you previously, I'm well versed in human nature. What made you smile just now?"

"You call me pretty a lot," she said, her smile still there as she slid her eyes away. "I like it."

"Good, because it's the truth," he said. "Now ask me your questions."

Her gaze returned to his face, her expression curious. "I get that humans and Talins aren't supposed to be couples because we're considered pets and inferior. But what about Talins getting together? I heard Batium and Klorus talking about how they could have a child and hide the fact that Klorus gave birth instead of using an artificial womb. Why would they need to do that? They're both Talins, shouldn't they be allowed to?"

"They wanted to have offspring naturally?" Ignatias asked.

"Yeah," she said. "It's weird though, right? They shouldn't have to hide having a kid. Or are there strict laws about how many kids you can have? And why would they need to figure out how they'd be allowed to raise it on Sorana but still have them be a registered Talin citizen? It doesn't make any sense."

It was such a large question with many implications that Ignatias went silent, figuring out where to start his answer. When he didn't start speaking right away, Kasi started talking again.

"Was that too personal? You don't have to answer anything if you're uncomfortable." Her words rushed out of her as she cupped one of her hands on his cheek. Her fingers rested on his scent gland, sending a shock of pleasure through him.

It was difficult, but he reached for her wrist and drew her hand away from his face. With both her hands in his, it was easier to think.

"Your question isn't too personal, but the answer is complicated and has roots going back thousands of years in our history," he said.

Kasi nodded her head. "Go back as far as you gotta, I'm here for it."

Her genuine interest made him want to tell her everything, even if it involved history and politics that shouldn't concern a human. He decided to start with basic biology.

"There is an inconvenient aspect to our evolution. For a Talin to become pregnant, the couple needs to be scent-bonded. It made sense when we were a young species, only aware of our own world and having no understanding of the wider universe. If a couple is scent-bonded, they will be more successful at producing offspring. It was an excellent strategy while we were contained in small communities on a single planet."

"Scent-bonded is when you guys like to rub your oil on each other, right?" Kasi commented. "It's cute to watch you guys rub on us. Humans in relationships with Talins always smell a lot like their Talins."

A mental picture of rubbing his oil into Kasi's mane came to him with enough force to make his scent glands ache.

"No one should be scent-bonding with anyone." His voice came out sounding a little raw, probably because he was clenching his jaw tightly. "It's forbidden."

Kasi's eyes went a little wide and she nodded her head again. "That's right! I keep forgetting no one's supposed to be scent-bonding with anyone. Officially you guys think Talins can't scent-bond to humans, so you're allowed to rub bonding oil on us in public. I can tell you right now, that's totally wrong."

"If there are Talins able to scent-bond with humans, then they are genetically inferior," he responded with an angry rattle. Kasi flinched at the sound, and he slapped his back plates down, ashamed at his loss of control. Kasi's experience with Talins was limited to the rulebreakers that had owned her. He had to give her allowances for being incorrectly educated.

"Let's get back to the explanation," Kasi pressed, her voice tense. "You guys need to scent-bond to have kids. What's wrong with that?"

"Although it was inefficient, there was nothing 'wrong' with it until we became a space-faring species. Scent-bonded partners can't be separated for long periods of time, or they will suffer from Collapsed Scent disease."

"That sounds horrible," Kasi breathed.

"The nickname for it is Ending because the end is always the same. Both partners will suffer great pain and die," he explained. "There's no treatment or cure. There have only been a few individuals in recorded history who survived, and they were shells of their former selves."

Kasi sucked in a breath. "I knew you guys didn't like to be away from your partners for long, but I didn't know it was this bad. How long can they be separated before Ending starts to happen?"

"Every individual is different. One could start to suffer the effects within rotations, another might last almost a solar."

Kasi shivered and grasped his hands with hers. "That's scary. I can see why you might be reluctant to scent-bond if either one of you has to travel."

"You're a clever human," he murmured. "That's exactly why scent-bonding started going out of fashion. Many couples were being separated by great distances and any little problem with a schedule might result in their death. When we started to expand and colonize other planets the problem became worse. War was a common result of our expansion, and it caused deadly unpredictability. At first, only unbonded Talins were allowed to serve in the military or even leave the homeworld. That quickly caused a population drop that might have been catastrophic given enough time."

"I can see how that would cause a negative feedback loop," Kasi agreed. "But it seems counterintuitive to outlaw scent-bonding if you need more kids to be born, not less!"

"It wasn't outlawed at the time, only frowned upon," he assured her. "We aren't an irresponsible species. Our leaders and scientists understood the issue and worked diligently to solve it. What made our empire truly successful was the development of artificial wombs. Two Talins could decide to enter into a marriage contract and have a child without scent-bonding to each other. It was the answer to all our needs. It took several hundred years, but our society developed protocols for breeding and raising children in centralized locations by well-trained, professional staff."

"You're talking about creshes," Kasi said.

He sounded an affirmative rattle. "Yes, you're correct. Over time, fewer and fewer Talins scent-bonded and raised their children, and at the same time, our empire expanded. The evidence was clear, this new way was superior to the old. Laws started to be proposed and passed that encouraged families to use cresh facilities. Eventually the laws demanded the use of artificial wombs and creshes."

"And that's where you are today," Kasi said. "A powerful, love-starved empire."

"Love is a human emotion we Talins never suffered from," he corrected her gently. To his surprise she rolled her eyes at him, a common human indicator of disagreement or even outright disbelief.

"I think love and scent-bonding are the same thing," she stated, then hurried to continue before he could object. "But we can talk about that another time. Tell me what happens if someone's caught scent-bonding or having their own kid these days?"

"The minimum punishment for scent-bonding would be banishment from their family and clan," he explained. "They'd be stripped of their wealth and probably forced to leave the empire."

Kasi's response was both naive and romantic. "At least they'd get to be together. It'd be tough, but they could find jobs at the same station or planet. They wouldn't have to go more than a work shift without seeing each other."

"They wouldn't be banished to the same place," he explained. "They'd be separated and shipped to different locations far away from each other. Even if they found out where the other one was, they probably wouldn't get to them in time to keep from dying. Once someone starts suffering from Ending, they're quickly debilitated by pain."

Kasi's eyes welled with water. "That's unnecessarily cruel. Why couldn't you take away their things but let them have each other?"

"We are not meant to think of ourselves," he answered, falling back on the mantra he'd been taught in the earliest days of his childhood. "First our people. Then our clan. Next our families. For ourselves, only last or not at all."

"That sounded rehearsed," she commented, a single droplet of water falling from her eye to streak down her cheek. She didn't seem to notice or care.

"It's a saying we learn young to teach us that we don't live for ourselves," he explained. "Our ways might seem cruel to you, but they've made us powerful. Many species beg to broker trade deals with us or even the right to travel through our territories. We haven't lost a war in over a thousand years. Save your pity for a species that deserves it."

"I have enough empathy for all of us," she murmured. Hands still entwined, she leaned forward until their lips were almost touching. "And I'm determined to teach you that love isn't a weakness."

CHAPTER 14

Kasi

After their conversation, Kasi was emotionally exhausted. She had more questions but didn't have the energy to ask them. It was still the middle of the night for her, and it was a relief when Ignatias suggested they go to bed.

After taking turns in the cleansing and elimination room and changing into her night clothes, she stood staring at the nest taking up most of the room's floor. Ignatias stood behind her, looking at it over her shoulder.

"You don't like it?" he asked without a purr or trying to touch her.

She turned and grabbed his hand. "It's perfect, but I want you to sleep with me. I want to cuddle with you, but I don't want to make you feel obligated."

He wrapped his arms around her shoulders and drew her back against him. "I'm always available for clinging and clutching. I've told you that, Pretty."

"I know, but I thought that was while we were awake. Everything feels a little different now that I know more about, um, your taboos and stuff. You don't have to snuggle with me if it makes you uncomfortable because of the way you were raised."

His arms tightened around her, and the smell of caramel got stronger. "Touching you could never make me uncomfortable."

His low voice and strong purr combined with his caramel scent made gooseflesh break out on her skin. She imagined licking him all over and rubbing her sex against his purring, vibrating body.

He might retract his invitation if he knew what she was thinking!

"That's good," she murmured, tugging his arms off her and stepping into the plush nest. He willingly followed her gentle tugs, only pausing long enough to take off his belt and set it out of the way.

It took a little awkward maneuvering before Kasi ended up as the little spoon almost completely engulfed by Ignatias's much bigger body. She thought it would be uncomfortable, but instead she felt safe and secure. The warmth was perfect for the girl that was always getting cold, and his purring filled her ears and vibrated against her back. It made her think that Ignatias was singing her the Talin version of a lullaby.

It wasn't long until she drifted off to sleep. Unfortunately, it didn't last long.

As was common, her eyes popped open a few hours later, her brain buzzing with thoughts. At least she didn't feel the anxiety that normally accompanied these inconvenient moments of wakefulness.

Being snuggled up to Ignatias made her whirring thoughts mostly bearable. Her new knowledge of Talin culture made her reassess when Zia showed up at Wimol with Palforma in tow.

After the initial celebrations at Zia's return, she and Palforma made all the humans an offer. All they had to do was pretend to be helpless pets during the rare inspection in exchange for safety and resources in abundance. They were offering a dream life, so saying yes was an easy decision.

There'd been some information sessions about Talin culture on the trip to Sorana. Everyone had attended, but like Kasi, most of them only paid minimal attention. If Kasi was honest with herself, she'd thought they were exaggerating the restrictive nature of their society to keep the Wimol humans in line.

Ignatias was making her realize how naive she'd been. Love wasn't taboo; it was illegal! What kind of civilization outlawed love and affection, especially toward children? It made her want to rush to Talarian, steal every child, and take them back to Sorana so they could be kids instead of good little citizens of the empire.

Being loyal to your species was one thing, but this was extreme.

The other disquieting thought was her own lack of self-determination. She hadn't realized the implications of being a pet before because it was never an issue. When she and the Wimol humans agreed to Zia and Palforma's terms, the trade ship Bountiful had picked them up and taken them straight to Sorana. There was no chance to experience the darker side of being a human among Talins.

Within the Talin Empire, she was considered a possession with no ability to do anything beyond what her owner wanted. It was a sobering thought, and for the first time since this whole adventure started, she felt vulnerable.

If she was separated from Ignatias, she could lose her independence. The only reason she could move freely around Sorana was that no one was really treated like a pet. Something as simple as locked doors and a collar she couldn't remove herself would keep her confined and a prisoner for the rest of her life.

"You've started breathing hard," Ignatias whispered. "Are you suffering from a sleeping terror or are you awake and thinking fearful thoughts?"

"I'm awake," she said, grateful that he'd woken. "We call them nightmares, but I wasn't having one. Sometimes I wake up in the night and my thoughts go a little haywire. It can make it hard to go back to sleep."

"I'll make it a priority to find you a competent healer," he announced with a concerned rumble.

"Don't say that," Kasi moaned out with an annoyed sound. She wiggled around until they were facing each other. "Joslum is a very good healer. This is just something weird about me."

"I'm sure your affection for Healer Joslum is clouding your judgment of her skills," he said. "You'll never be neglected again."

Kasi gave up on convincing Ignatias that Joslum was more than competent at her job. Changing tactics, she burrowed into him, tucking her head under his chin.

"I'm sure I'll fall back to sleep soon enough," she lied. "Your purr is very soothing and you're a great snuggle buddy."

"Snuggle buddy?"

"What we're doing is snuggling," she explained.

"That means someone you snuggle with is a buddy?" he asked, the unfamiliar human word sounding strange coming out of his mouth.

"Yup," she agreed.

"What else does a buddy do to give comfort?" he asked. His question was innocent, but her dirty mind buzzed off in a naughty direction.

That also made her notice his intoxicating scent of caramel had faded. Blindly, she reached up and found his cheek with her fingers. She rubbed until she felt oil and then brought it down to rub on her lips. She didn't expect the oil to make her lips tingle and then get warm. It was a pleasant sensation and only strengthened her growing ardor.

Thinking about what the bonding oil would feel like rubbed in other places distracted her, which was why she didn't notice how stiff Ignatias's body was for several minutes.

"Ignatias?" she murmured, trying to move her head back so she could look up at his face. His tense arms tightened around her as his purring changed.

The new rumble was a lower, thrumming version of a purr. She'd heard it a few times when Talins thought they were alone with their partners. It was the sound of desire.

It seemed her lust wasn't one-sided.

"Be still," he ordered, his voice low and gruff. "I'm struggling with my…"

His voice trailed off and Kasi felt a distinct bulge against her belly. There was no mistaking it for anything else but a mating shaft trying to swell enough to escape a flesh pouch.

Back when she'd read about Talin anatomy, those words and medical images had stuck with her, probably because her humor hadn't changed much since she was sixteen. She never thought she'd take a Talin partner, but now she was thankful she'd read the educational material provided by Joslum.

"You make me feel things too," she offered. "Things I thought I'd only feel with another human."

"This is not…we can't…" he made a lot of noises with his mouth that sounded like they were meant to be words but came out as a jumble instead.

"I'm an adult," she reminded him.

"I'm well aware," he said, voice harsh. "But I won't act inappropriately."

"But you want to," she taunted with a grin. "And it wouldn't be inappropriate if I wanted it."

With a growl, he sat up and lifted her away from him. His movements were quick but controlled. He sat her on the edge of the nest while he put several pillows in the center.

"Bad pet," he grumbled as he moved pillows around.

Biting her lip, she tried really hard not to laugh. "I'm sorry?"

After arranging the pillows to his satisfaction, he raised his eyes to her. It was hard to see him in the dim room, but she could hear his brief annoyed rattle.

"This is a test of my *stellian*," he grumbled and reached for her again. "I'll conquer this test because I'll comfort you while maintaining control."

She let him move her around until she was facing away from him with the pillows between their spooning bodies. His arms caged her upper body, keeping her from moving her hands to touch him.

"There," he declared with a brief triumphant rattle. "This is acceptable."

"I remember Tisuran grumbling about *stellian* during the last Twelve Nights of Halloheen celebration. It means something like willpower, right?"

"Yes, it is similar to your concept of willpower, but more significant."

She gave up the fight and giggled. "This pillow wall will totally protect you from me!"

He grumbled something about naughty humans, then pulled in a deep breath and started purring again. "I think you're teasing me. That's a good sign. It means you're calm and perhaps ready to slumber again?"

"I'm wide awake," she warned him. Moving her hands in the limited space he allowed, she found one of his hands and tangled her fingers with his.

"Then we can converse until you're ready to sleep," he offered. "We could talk about your childhood."

"Only if you're willing to talk about yours," she countered.

"Perhaps another time." His tone made it clear that his real answer was *no,* but he didn't want to upset her with an outright refusal. "What about your adulthood on Wimol?"

"I can tell you some fun stories, but we have to trade."

A questioning rumble interrupted his purr for a second. "Trade?"

"Story for story," she explained. "I'll tell you about something that happened to me, and you have to tell me about a similar event in exchange."

"What if there are no comparable events in my life to yours?" he asked. "I'm a decorated warrior with prestige within my clan and family. You're a human and a pet. We've led very different lives."

"Very different," she agreed, biting back another chuckle. He'd probably be insulted if he heard her laugh. "But I believe there are universal things that everyone experiences: work challenges, community drama, or disappointments. Stuff like that happens to everyone."

"You make a good point," he conceded. "If you tell a story, I will find one suitable from my own life to share in return."

"Deal!" she agreed, then launched into a detailed retelling of the time she, Isla, and Zia got drunk at a Twelve Nights of Halloheen celebration when they were teenagers. There was a heatwave and one hundred percent humidity at the time so they decided to go for a swim in a nearby reservoir.

The only problem was the reservoir turned out to have been emptied the previous day so it was mostly mud. It was dark and they were drunk so they all stripped and jumped in without pausing to take a closer look at the water.

They ended up covered head to toe in stinky, boggy mud. They didn't want anyone to know what they'd done so they thought they'd use the industrial water tanks to clean up. Except they were treated with a chemical to help the plants grow, and that dyed their skin a bright purple!

It wasn't a long story, but it was funny, and by the end, Ignatias's purr was interrupted by rumbles of amusement.

"Why would you think that was a good plan?" he questioned after she was done.

"Lots of dumb things seem like great ideas when you've had one too many spiked holiday drinks," she explained with a laugh of her own.

"It's surprising none of you were injured," he murmured, going back to purring.

"We were injured," she retorted. "We were all really hungover the next day, and it was miserable. Isla swore she'd never drink again, and Zia couldn't even open her eyes. She said it hurt too much so she was going to be deaf-deaf for the rest of the day and we all needed to leave her alone if we wanted to live long lives."

"Deaf-deaf?" he asked.

"That's when she won't look at you to see what you're tapping," Kasi explained.

"What about you? Did your head hurt also?"

Kasi grimaced at the memory. "Sure, but my stomach was what did me in. First, I threw up everything I had consumed that night. When that was all gone, I started throwing up my will to live."

He sounded a distressed rumble. "What do you mean?"

"It was a joke," she explained, squeezing his fingers with hers. "I only mean that I kept throwing up even though there wasn't anything in my stomach. It's not the type of ab workout anyone wants."

"Being ill is never pleasant," he agreed. "Even if it's self-inflicted."

She made a humming sound of agreement. "Now it's your turn. I told you a story from when I was younger, so you have to do the same."

Ignatias was silent for a full minute. Was he going to refuse? Maybe she should give him some parameters so he knew his story didn't need to be funny, like hers.

"You could talk about—"

At the same time, Ignatias finally started to talk. "I could speak of—"

They both stopped at once.

Kasi chuckled. "You talk, I'll listen."

"I was going to tell you about my first week in general training for the military," he explained. "However, I'm afraid it might bore you."

"I promise I won't be bored," she encouraged. "Now that I'm out here with you, I'm eager to learn all the ins and outs of Talin culture and government. What's general training?"

"Serving in our military is considered prestigious, and they are picky about who they accept. But there is a program that allows any Talin to do basic military training, even if they plan to pursue civilian careers. We're encouraged to be battle ready even if we don't plan to be professional warriors."

"That sounds like some civilizations that existed on Old Earth," Kasi commented. "They were small and vulnerable, so they encouraged all their citizens to train and be ready in case they were attacked."

He sounded a gentle affirmative rumble. "Your example is apt. This philosophy is a holdover from when we weren't as powerful a species as we are today. Still, it's a good practice for us to maintain. My parents were eager for me to start a military career, so they pushed me to enter general training when I was still an adultlette."

"Adultlette," Kasi murmured. "That's when you guys are around nineteen human equivalent years old, right?"

"Roughly," he agreed. "We're usually not quite fully grown yet but soon will be, and we often need to practice our *stellian* a lot at that age. I found myself often rattling, even when I wasn't feeling a strong emotion or speaking with someone. It was embarrassing and something I should've outgrown long before then."

"Did it limit what you could do?" Kasi asked.

"It didn't keep me from activities, but everyone would stare at me when I rattled at inappropriate times."

"Some humans laugh when they're nervous," she pointed out. "It doesn't mean anything. It's a stress response, that's all. Maybe it's the same thing with Talins and rattling."

"Stress response or not, to the other Talins, it meant I wasn't as dedicated as they were," Ignatias explained. "No matter how much I concentrated, I was still rattling. I grew so desperate I decided to glue my back plates down. I thought it would be better to not rattle at all than to keep doing it at the wrong time."

Kasi sucked in a sharp breath. "That sounds like it could be painful, and maybe even dangerous!"

"It wasn't dangerous and only a little uncomfortable. The problem arose at field practice that day where we were doing drills with an ancient, edged weapon. Although we don't use them in battle any longer, the military still uses them for ceremonial purposes, and everyone was expected to learn how to wield them."

"What does that have to do with your back plates?" Kasi asked.

"We were supposed to sound the loudest war rattle we were capable of before doing a certain move," he admitted. "I was only able to rip two of my back plates free, so my war rattle was a mewl."

Kasi burst out laughing. "I'm sorry, I shouldn't laugh. That had to be really embarrassing!"

"It was, but I recovered," he said with a rumble of amusement. "I can see the humor of it now. The incident also led one of the instructors to take me aside and help me work on my *stellian*. I learned from her that it's like a muscle, you have to grow it in increments. Soon I had full control of my rattles without the use of adhesive."

"Tell me another story about general training," she demanded. "I find your voice soothing."

"Certainly, Pretty," he agreed. "This one isn't funny, but it is an interesting insight into learning as an adultlette."

Halfway into his next story, her eyes started getting heavy and her mind kept drifting off. Then she was asleep and dreaming of giant caramels that purred.

CHAPTER 15

Ignatias

The first thing Ignatias noticed was the secondary emissions control unit was registering outside normal parameters. He was concerned but not worried. After running diagnostics on various systems, he was moving toward worry. By the time the display showed him results of a third ship-wide diagnostic, he knew there was a problem.

Turning his gaze to the co-pilot seat, he saw that Kasi was still engrossed in the Ugarian soap opera episodes she had saved on the information square she'd packed for the trip. Although the bag had been heavy, most of the weight had been unnecessary items like food.

His little human had packed with the belief she'd only be gone for several days and assumed he wouldn't have food she'd be able to eat on the ship. She'd only brought a single change of clothes and nothing appropriate. It was the same type of outfit she was wearing now.

She needed all new clothes and a proper omnie. It would be a pleasure to see her wearing outfits made of soft fabric instead of the drab, rough things she was currently dressed in.

She must have sensed him looking at her because she raised her eyes to his and smiled. "Torfor's family unit found out he was eating even though it was Ascension Day. He's going to be in so much trouble, especially because his elder mostly-brother doesn't like him. He should've told everyone he's sick but is afraid they won't let him marry into the Osof family unit. This is the best story arc yet!"

Her enthusiasm for a fictional Ugarian show didn't make it easier for him to tell her the bad news.

"I believe we might have a serious problem," he stated. Turning his seat to face her, he opened his arms. She set down her information square and accepted his invitation to sit on his lap.

"More serious than not getting to marry into the Osof family unit?" she asked.

"Far more. It seems the ship's systems are malfunctioning."

She stared at him, her smile disappearing. "Which ones?"

"Most of them," he admitted. "This shouldn't be happening. Not only was the ship thoroughly inspected before being decommissioned, but I had independent techs and engineers go over it before I left on this trip."

Kasi put a hand to her chest and shook her head. "We didn't do it."

"That didn't cross my mind," he assured her. "The logs would've recorded anyone accessing it since I launched from Talarian."

"Then that means the tech and engineers didn't do their jobs very well," Kasi stated with a frown.

"Or one of them did a job other than what I hired them for," Ignatias said, no longer able to ignore the glaring point all the information on the display was indicating. "This is a clear case of sabotage. Even the emergency pod and long-distance distress beacon are non-functioning. If all that wasn't evidence enough, this all happened within submarks of each other. Talin ships don't fail like this naturally; this had to be deliberate."

Kasi moved her gaze to the display and spoke in a soft, fearful tone. "This is messed up. I thought I was saving you, but now we're both going to die. I didn't think it would end like this."

Sounding a loud comforting purr, he hugged her to his chest. She didn't resist and even tucked her head under his chin, a position she seemed to favor.

"We aren't going to die," he assured her. "Some of the equipment that didn't get offloaded to the colony will keep us alive, and the ship will continue on the same trajectory it was on before the engine shut down. The beacon is offline, but the regular transmitter is still working. Our momentum will send us into a busy shipping lane where someone will respond to our request for aid."

She straightened away from him so she could meet his gaze. Her eyebrows were lifted, and her mouth was slanted in a half-grin. "I guess things aren't so dire. Sorry I got all dramatic. This is only my second time in space, so I assumed the ship shutting down around us would be a big deal."

"Normally it would be, but we're lucky that this happened right after the ship performed a last course correction. Even a mark earlier, and we'd be heading right into a planet instead of a shipping lane."

"How long until we get someone's attention?" she asked.

"A minimum of four rotations."

"That's not too bad," she reasoned. "I requested agri-heaters; if they're in the supplies you're carrying, then we could keep our room warm."

"Heat isn't the only issue," he warned her. "Even the galley equipment has shut down, so we'll have to subsist on caloric-packs."

Kasi wrinkled her nose. "Those things taste like packing foam, but it's better than starving."

"Do you eat packing foam often?" he asked, sounding a worried rumble. "Those aren't meant for consumption; they could be harmful for you."

Kasi's mouth dropped open before she covered it with both hands and laughed loudly. He'd never heard such raw, unencumbered joy from an adult before. Even though he didn't know what she found so humorous, he found himself rumbling in amusement with her.

Wiping her eyes, Kasi grinned up at him. "I don't eat packing foam, I promise."

Dropping the subject, because sometimes humans just didn't make sense, Ignatias turned to more practical matters. "We should prepare our room before the ship starts to cool down."

"Sure," Kasi agreed and jumped off his lap and headed out of the room. "I'll start looking for the agri-heaters."

Ignatias was quick to follow her. "Don't eat the packing foam, even if you're very hungry!"

Her laughter echoed down the hall and through the ship.

Kasi

By the time they'd unpacked an agri-heater and several powerpacks, the ship was getting cold. Her heavy coat dealt with the mild chill of Sorana but not the freezing temperatures of outer space. Kasi didn't notice the cold at first because she kept getting distracted by finding more and more items she'd requested. Every other crate was filled with goodies she couldn't wait to use once they got back to Sorana.

She was so excited about all the items that if Ignatias hadn't been there, she might not have found the agri-heaters before she froze to death! By the time he was lugging the agri-heater to their room, she was shivering, and her sigh condensed white in the air. What she wouldn't give to have one of the nano-infused omni's right now!

Ignatias set the agri-heater down in the corner with a solid thump. Kasi hurried over with the power packs.

"Are you familiar with this type of equipment?" he asked.

"I've used the older version a lot," she explained as she ripped open the power pack and cracked the separator tabs. "It won't take me long to get this one up and running, I promise."

He sounded a rattle of affirmation. "While you do that, I need to check something and gather a few more things. Call out if you are in need of my assistance. I'll hear you and rush back."

"I'm good," she assured him. "Wow, this is a nice design. Look at the output coils. They have trisoridum sheathing. That had to be expensive. When I use this on Sorana, there won't be any singed plants."

"I'm glad you're pleased," he said with a rumble of amusement.

She ignored him. Ignatias wasn't the only one who found her horticultural obsession funny and odd. Most of the humans back on Wimol thought she was strange to enjoy working in her garden after spending all day in the fields, but they'd always appreciated when her garden provided supplemental food. It didn't matter that others didn't understand, as long as she was allowed to keep doing what she loved.

This newer agri-heater was similar enough to the old one for her to be able to set it up without needing to run the instructional vid. Soon, gentle heat was radiating from it. Standing close, she let the heat soak into her clothing and warm the room before she moved over to the nest.

If they were going to be stuck in here for a few days, it was a good thing she'd brought a bunch of episodes of her favorite Ugarian soap opera with her. She could make Ignatias watch them all as punishment for being so stubborn about denying the sexual tension developing between them.

That made her think about ways she might be able to push him. She needed to be careful, or he'd stack pillows between them, or worse–make her sleep by herself!

Maybe what was happening with the ship was a stroke of luck. This gave her extra time to help him understand that what he felt for her wasn't an evil impulse to be ignored, but a natural feeling to be enjoyed.

One thing she did know was that more skin was better. The agri-heater had brought the room's temperature to a more manageable cold, but she was still shivering violently by the time she changed into a loose pajama top. She didn't bother with the matching pants.

It wasn't lacy lingerie, but it was the most skin she could show without stripping down naked. Going naked would probably push Ignatias too far, but this would let her rub her legs against him, and maybe her bare butt if she planned it right.

Snuggling down in the nest, she pulled the fluffiest blanket around her shoulders and started going through the menu on her information square. The agri-heater had raised the temperature enough for her nose to stop feeling cold by the time Ignatias came back through the door, letting in all the cold air from the rest of the ship.

"Akk!" she cried out, startled. She had gotten absorbed in an Old Earth novel she'd forgotten was on the information square. The square went flying, and she winced when it cleared the nest and hit the hard metal floor with an ominous crack.

Ignatias started purring and dumped all the items he was holding on the floor next to the nest while, at the same time, sinking to his knees.

"Are you well?" he asked anxiously.

"I'm fine, but I think my square might be mortally wounded," she lamented, leaning over the edge of the nest to retrieve the square. She tapped it, but it gave one burst of color and an impression of shapes, then went blank. She'd saved forever to afford this square. She'd treated it carefully all these years only to ruin it because Ignatias walked through a door.

"I think this might symbolize my entire life," she muttered. "Breaking precious things because I'm a high-strung, clumsy idiot!"

"You are none of those things," Ignatias stated with a loud decisive rattle. She'd noticed Talins tended to do that when they were trying to make a strong point. He crawled into the nest and took the square from her. "Accidents happen to all species. This square appears quite old; how long have you had it?"

"About seven years, uh, solars," she answered. "Or I guess six solars because your years are a little longer than Old Earth years."

"Considering how difficult your life on Wimol was, it's a testament to you that the information square lasted as long as it did." he turned it around and pointed to the maker's stamp on the back. "This one is from an inferior manufacturer and would've been prone to damage given the slightest provocation."

Kasi only heard the insult in all of that as she snatched the square back. "It was all I could afford."

Ignatias started purring and pulled his legs out from under him to sit more comfortably in front of her. "I'm not dismissing the effort it took to purchase the item, only that you did well in keeping it running for so long."

He opened up his arms, an invitation for a hug. Kasi hesitated a moment, still feeling the sting of the earlier comment about her square being cheap. Giving in, she dropped the square on the floor and crawled between his legs and into his arms.

"I'm sorry I snapped," she murmured, snuggling into his warm body. The agri-heater was humming softly in the corner, warming the room again, but it would take a while. Talins didn't feel cold like humans did, but she'd never expected them to be so warm. As with the night on Sorana, Ignatias was acting as her own personal heater.

"I'm sure you felt great pride in owning the square," he commented. "It was a sign of accomplishment."

"It was," she agreed, thankful he understood. "And now it's gone and all the stuff I had on it might not be recoverable."

"I will make it a priority to get you a new one," he promised. "And if we can't transfer the data from the old one to the new, then we'll purchase as much as we can to replace it."

Although it was greedy of her, Kasi felt relief at Ignatias's offer. "I don't want you to think my affection can be bought, but I don't want to have to live without a square."

"I never thought I could buy your affection," he said with an amused rumble. "After all, I had nothing to offer and yet you stayed with me in the storage building. I know you have nothing but the most honorable intentions toward me."

Kasi hid her wince against his neck. Were her intentions honorable? She had rescued him but also plotted to seduce him. That wasn't dishonorable if the seduction was for his own good, right?

Wait, was it just her or did that sound creepy? Was she acting like a sexual predator?

Kasi was saved from sliding down a spiral of self-doubt when Ignatias's Ident pinged. Holding onto her with one arm, he unclipped the cube with his other hand and looked at it. After some skillful tapping with the same hand holding it, Ignatias let out a surprised rattle.

"What happened?" Kasi asked, afraid it was more bad news, and started down a completely different spiral of panic. "Are we about to be attacked? Is an engine going to explode? Are we about to hit an asteroid?"

Ignatias re-clipped the Ident onto his belt and held her with both arms, rocking her slightly as he purred. "Calm yourself. We are saved. It seems a ship received our distress broadcast and is coming to our aid."

"Already?" she asked, relaxing back into his hold. "That seems fast."

"A merchant ship is on their way to Portalie station, so they deviated from the shipping lane early to take a more direct route. They will be here soon."

"How soon?" she asked, realizing this was both good and bad. She'd been prepared to rough it for a few days until they drifted into the shipping lane. With no tasks to perform, it would've been time dedicated to getting to know Ignatias without fear of interruption. With almost guaranteed rescue, she had been able to ignore the fear of death by starvation or cold. Now she didn't have to worry about dying, but their bonding time was suddenly cut short.

"They should be here in less than a mark," he said. "You'll be warm soon."

Kasi wrapped her arms around Ignatias's neck and realized she'd just gotten pussy-blocked by a rescue. That had to be a first!

CHAPTER 16

Kasi

Even though it represented warmth and comfort, Kasi was reluctant to get onto the shuttle and make the short trip to the merchant ship, Ever Prosperous III. If Ignatias noticed, he didn't say anything. All he did was assure her over and over again that they would be back on their way soon and this was only a temporary displacement.

It was a short trip from Ignatias's ship into the tight quarters of the Ever Prosperous III's bay. She didn't know what to expect when the door to the shuttle opened, but it definitely wasn't the entire crew of the ship all packed tightly in the small shuttle bay and staring intensely at Kasi. Even Ignatias was stunned into stillness at the sight.

The crowd's simultaneous rumbles of comfort filled the space with noise, made worse by everyone seeming to talk at once.

"Oh, you're such a pretty human!"

"Are you hungry? I've got food."

"Why is she wearing those clothes? They aren't what humans are supposed to wear!"

"Where is her collar? Is she stolen?"

"She might be wild-caught, that would explain both the clothes and short hair."

"Do wild-caught humans know how to talk?"

"Come over here, little human! I have some sweets that humans like, you can have one."

"I have a sachie squeeze, would you like it?"

All the voices got louder as they vied for her attention, making all the words blur together. Kasi had never suffered from social anxiety or shyness, but she'd also never been mobbed before. Stepping back, she came up hard against Ignatias, who wrapped a strong arm around her and sounded a threatening rattle that sounded like many feet stomping. She'd only heard a Talin war rattle once and that was in an open field. Within the confines of a bay only big enough for two shuttles, it was deafening.

It was all too much!

The shuttle they'd come over in might be cramped and without any kind of bathing or elimination facilities, but she decided she was spending the rest of the journey in there, thank you very much!

She tried to pull away from Ignatias and disappear into the safety of the small craft behind her. Ignatias tightened his hold on her, effectively keeping her in place. She couldn't get away, but she still wanted to hide, so she turned in place and pressed her face against Ignatias's chest.

"She's not used to Talins and all of you are frightening her badly," he roared, dropping her bag to the floor. Bending at the knees, he lifted her up with one arm under her butt and the other supporting her back. She wrapped her arms around his neck and buried her face against him, pressing her lips against the soft strip of exposed skin at the base of his neck. The smell of caramel filled her nose, and Ignatias's warm body chased away the last of the chill from time spent on the disabled ship.

"Quiet!" an authoritative voice shouted. Those words were accompanied by a challenging rattle that had everyone shutting up. "Report back to your stations. If you're not on shift, you will vacate this area immediately and return to quarters until further notice."

The next thing she heard was the sound of feet rushing out of the small bay, then a respectful, inquisitive voice.

"Captain Solmance, I'm working in this bay right now," someone said. "Should I still leave?"

"No, Kilmanum, I need you to stay, but keep a respectful distance and don't speak until I give you permission."

"Yes, Captain," Kilmanum agreed with an affirmative rattle.

By now the sound of feet had faded to nothing, and Kasi felt brave enough to lift her head and look around. The small bay was empty except for the four of them, but she could see several Talins trying to look busy in the hall beyond.

"May the Ancestors grace you with wisdom and loyalty, Captain Solmance," Ignatias said and shifted her weight around a bit so he could smack his fist on his chest.

"And lead you to honorable actions," Captain Solmance responded and smacked her own chest, making Kasi wince. For such a refined species, Talins had a harsh greeting style. Of course they were covered in that keratin plating. If she tried to hit her chest that hard, she'd end up badly bruised instead of making a nice, loud impact sound.

Kasi studied the confident Talin curiously. Female and male Talins looked very similar except the women didn't have full quills. Instead they had little nubs running up their forearms.

Someone on Sorana had mentioned that quill extensions for women had started to become popular and she could see why. Solmance had shiny silver-colored extensions on her quill-nubs that looked even more deadly than Ignatias's natural ones. Kasi found herself transfixed by them and desperately wanted to touch one.

To be honest, now she wanted quills too. But she wanted them in an iridescent-blue metallic color.

"You're welcome on my ship, General Ignatias," Captain Solmance said. "I'm Solmance of the Tand family within the Anize clan. We've never met but you served with my cousin, Baniforum."

"She was an excellent warrior; I was glad to hear she retired to her family's estate on Mopa colony. I must correct you though. I'm no longer a general," Ignatias said. "I'm Committee Citizen Ignatias, working for the Committee of Pet Welfare now."

Solmance sounded a rattle of affirmation. "Ah, that explains why you're in possession of a wild-caught human."

"Indeed," Ignatias said. "It was fortuitous you found us."

Although Solmance was technically correct about Kasi being "wild-caught," there was a lot more to their story than that and Ignatias wasn't sharing. For all his bluster about revealing all the rulebreakers on Sorana, he was being surprisingly quiet now. It was a good sign.

"The Ancestors must have guided us," Captain Solmance said. "We were delayed at our last stop by several marks, which put us in the exact perfect location to find you."

"By the will of the Ancestors," Ignatias murmured.

"We don't have the ability to diagnose or repair your ship," Solmance warned him.

"I didn't expect you to," Ignatias said. "I'm simply grateful to have safe passage to the nearest place I can have the ship seen to."

"Whykeen Station is on our way; we can drop you off there," Solmance explained. "It's a medium-sized station that has the facilities to assist you. We'll be there in about three rotations."

"I can pay for our accommodations on this ship," Ignatias said.

"No need," Solmance assured him with a dismissive rattle. "Bringing this human to us is payment enough. No one on board has ever met a human before. If this one becomes more comfortable with us, I'd like to interact. Are they a female or male?"

Kasi had to fight to keep from snorting out a laugh. She half expected Solmance to echo the "does she know how to speak" question from earlier.

"Kasi is an adult female," Ignatias said. "She's normally a friendly and happy human. Given a little time to adjust, I'm sure she'd be willing to interact."

"Excellent," Solmance said. She raised a hand and gestured to the other Talin in the bay to come over, her metal quill extensions gleaming in the bright artificial lights. "Kilmanum, join us."

He rushed to them. "Yes, Captain?"

"You're the only one on board with a spare bunk," she explained. "I'm going to give that bunk to Committee Citizen Ignatias."

"May the Ancestors grace you with wisdom and loyalty!" Kilmanum said with more volume than needed as he faced her and Ignatias. The eager Talin didn't realize he was still holding a tool in his hand, and tried to thump it against his chest, sending the tool flying.

"Let their wisdom guide us," Ignatias responded with an amused rumble as he smacked his chest also. It was hard, but Kasi kept from chuckling. She remembered being young and awkward too. It was nice to see Talins went through the same phase!

"Do humans thank their Ancestors?" Kilmanum asked. "Should I greet her also?"

"Give her a little more time," Ignatias instructed. "Thank you for sharing your accommodations, Kilmanum."

"But what about the little human?" Kilmanum asked with a worried rumble. "Where will she be housed?"

"She'll probably want to share the bunk with me," Ignatias said. "She's been very insistent on staying close to me, even in her sleep."

"It sounds like she might have already formed an attachment to you!" Kilmanum explained. "The Ancestors favor you greatly."

"This is the exact reason why it's so hard to get jobs with the Committee of Pet Welfare," Solmance pointed out. "It's often a fast track to getting a pet of your own."

Kasi expected Ignatias to get upset at Solmance's comment since he was so strict about honor and protocol, but he didn't even comment. Instead, he focused on Kilmanum.

"Which shift do you work?" Ignatias asked. "I don't want to disturb your rest period."

"You won't," Kilmanum assured him. "This ship is old and noisy; I've learned to sleep through anything."

"Including safety alarm checks," Solmance added dryly.

Kilmanum ducked his head and sounded an anxious rattle. "It was only that one time, Captain."

"It only takes one time," Solmance responded.

"Don't feel bad, Kilmanum," Kasi said, surprising herself by speaking up. "I wish I could sleep that deeply!"

Kilmanum started purring and took a small step closer. "I could help you slumber! Maybe I could hold you and sound a consistent comforting rumble. I read humans like that."

Ignatias sounded a loud, angry rattle. "Do not!"

Kasi jumped at Ignatias's sudden aggression. She rushed to calm him down before they lost their ride to Whykeen Station!

Ignatias

"Easy, Ignatias. He's only being friendly," Kasi said, petting the side of his face. He ignored the pleasure that came from her palm rubbing over his scent gland.

"The young upstart should know his place," Ignatias growled but stopped rattling.

The young crewman stumbled over his words. "Forgive me, General…uh, Committee Citizen Ignatias!"

"Leave Kilmanum alone," Solmance ordered with an amused rumble.

"I won't—"

Kasi covered his mouth before he could finish telling Solmance he wouldn't let Kasi be in a room with Kilmanum. He couldn't trust the young Talin around Pretty. Her heart was too soft and kind. Kilmanum would take advantage of her and maybe even touch her.

Hold her.

Rub his bonding oil on her.

The thought enraged him to the point where he almost set Kasi down to launch himself at Kilmanum. It was Kasi's hands on him that helped keep him calm. The last thing he wanted to do was frighten her with a display of violence.

"Thanks for sharing your room with us, Kilmanum. I don't need to be comforted by anyone else but Ignatias. He's my, um, Talin, and I'm happy with him."

"It's nice to see a wild-caught human becoming tame so quickly," Solmance commented. "From what I hear, it's not a surprise to see a Talin being so possessive of a pet human. Though I would think you'd have better *stellian* than this, Ignatias."

Solmance's chastising forced Ignatias to realize he was acting without his normal control. Of course Kilmanum wasn't a threat. Pulling in a deep breath, he relaxed his quills and looked at Kilmanum.

"You've generously agreed to share your space, and I've acted poorly. I apologize."

Kasi made a happy encouraging sound at his words and petted his face again. If she kept doing that, bonding oil was going to start leaking down his cheek, but he didn't stop her. It felt too good.

"You don't need to apologize," Kilmanum rushed to say. "I overstepped. I shouldn't have talked to your pet like that. It was rude. If I had a pet as pretty and friendly as Kasi, I'd be possessive too, so I understand. Come this way. I'll show you the room. I started my shift only a little while before we picked you both up, so you'll have the room to yourself for many marks before I need to rest."

Kilmanum sounded sincere and Ignatias briefly considered letting Kasi give him a hug, then dismissed it. If he was honest with himself, the most he'd be able to tolerate was the two of them talking.

"I'll be in the control room if you need me," Solmance said. "I expect you to join me at tomorrow's meal, with the human." Without waiting for a response, Solmance turned on her heels and left.

"Follow me," Kilmanum said, leading them out of the bay and down a series of narrow corridors. "You missed the meal for this rotation, but I'm sure the galley tech could put something together if we asked. Do you think Kasi is hungry? We must have something she can eat. Or we could ferry food from your ship. It will be hard to get in and out now that it's secured to our hull, but I'm sure we can manage."

"I can wait to eat," Kasi said. "And I'm sure I can eat some of what you guys eat. No need to do anything dangerous yet."

As they walked, the young Talin pointed out the communal elimination and bathing facilities and gave them suggestions about the best times to use them. Then Kilmanum led them into their temporary accommodations.

It was the standard size for a ship like the Ever Prosperous III, which meant it was going to be tight quarters for the three of them. The room only had two bunks on opposite walls and a small table attached to the far wall with only one chair. There were several wall cubicles to store items and only two of them were full, testament to Kilmanum's lowly status on ship. The higher the status the more items a crew member was allowed to bring on a journey. It was a surprise one of the least senior crew members got a room to himself.

Setting Kasi on the bunk with no bedding, Ignatias noticed it was slightly smaller than regular sized. It would be a tight squeeze for him and Kasi to share. Or perhaps not if she slept on top of him like she'd done that first night on Sorana.

Standing at the open door, Kilmanum spoke up. "I'll be right back with bedding."

He was gone before Ignatias could say anything. Setting Kasi's pack on the floor at the foot of the bed, he took the spot next to her.

"I guess this is home for a little while," she murmured.

He wasn't sure what to say, so he remained quiet. Kilmanum and another crew member returned, their arms loaded with far more pillows and blankets than could ever be used. After dropping them in the space between the bed and the table, both left quickly with comforting rumbles.

Once they were gone, Kasi bounced off the bunk and picked up a few pillows, eyeing the large pile with obvious amusement.

"You guys sure are fascinated with bedding," she murmured. "I thought I liked a comfy bed, but you guys are over the top with your soft blankets and fluffy pillows! It's kinda cute."

Remaining on the bed while Kasi chatted and moved, he tried to understand why he suddenly felt distinctly odd. Everything felt both equally real and unreal at the same time.

Could this strange mood be due to the extreme number of things that had happened in the last few rotations? It wasn't everyday he uncovered a plot to hide the mistreatment of humans that had ties to Prime Son Searin himself.

Then he'd been captured and expected to accept his captors' illegal activities. While in captivity, he'd met a hybrid child that caused a memory episode, something that hadn't happened for many solars.

On top of all that, there was talk of murdering him. Rescue came from the same frail creature he meant to protect. He and Kasi escaped the planet only to find his ship had been sabotaged and they faced potential death again.

Now Kasi was acting as if this was a normal day for her as she fluffed pillows and shook out blankets. Something broke in Ignatias. He could feel a memory episode trying to manifest. Desperate to hold it off, he grabbed onto the one thing that he knew would ground him.

Snatching Kasi up, he cradled her to his chest and started to rub his scent glands into her hair. She'd gasped when he grabbed her but didn't resist. Once he'd emptied both scent glands, saturating her with his bonding oil, he breathed in deep. The tension in his chest loosened and the pressing memory episode retreated.

"Are you okay?" Kasi asked.

"I believe so," he answered honestly. It was a near thing, but he hadn't lost control of his mind. Fear of having another memory episode made him want to sound a desolate rumble and hide his face in Kasi's hair. Shame filled him. What kind of owner needed to use their pet for comfort?

"Hey, stay with me," Kasi said.

"I haven't left," he assured her.

"Then it's time to talk, handsome," Kasi commanded gently, her mouth near the strip of exposed skin at his neck.

"What happened just now, and why does it feel similar to what happened with Lamarin?"

It appeared it was time to reveal to Kasi that he was a broken Talin unworthy of caring for a human. He wished this moment had never come.

"I'm flawed," he croaked out. "Deeply, irrevocably flawed."

When Kasi raised her head, he expected her to pull away with visible disgust. Instead, she stretched up to place her lips on his. Surprise made him open his lips, allowing her warm tongue to sweep into his mouth. The feel of it sent blood pouring into his mating shaft.

He knew he should halt this intimacy, but he was helpless to stop it when the scent of Kasi's blossoming desire hit his nose. He no longer had control of his actions; his instincts were in control.

CHAPTER 17

Kasi

Kasi had only meant for the kiss to be comforting. A quick press of her lips to his. Then he'd opened his mouth, inviting her to deepen the kiss. Unable to resist, she accepted his invitation and parted her lips further.

She'd never felt or tasted anything like him. Talin lips were thin but soft and his tongue gentle. Moaning, she cupped his face in her hands. Her hair was saturated with his bonding oil but the glands in his cheeks weren't empty. More warm, fragrant oil coated her palms.

His oil was to blame for all this! It smelled heavenly and did weird things to her. She wanted to rub it all over her body, especially between her legs.

The thought of him touching the part of her that was needy and throbbing gave her the strength to pull away from the kiss. He was slow to lift his lids, and when he did, his eyes were slightly unfocused. He looked as dazed as she felt.

"I want you," she stated so there'd be no confusion. "I think you want me back, but I don't want to take advantage of you."

Later she might see the hilarity of the human pet making sure the Talin owner was consenting, but all she could think about was getting naked with him. She'd stop if he said no, but she really hoped it would be a yes!

He blinked a few times, as if trying to process her words. Then his gaze snapped into focus, and he sounded a sexy, slow, thrumming rumble. "You speak of rutting. You want to have intercourse with your owner."

"No, I want to make love to my Talin," she argued, rubbing her fingers a little harder over his scent glands. He shivered from her touch, his eyes rolling back a little.

"Pretty," he breathed out, his voice needy. "I've never felt this way before."

She went still, then pulled her hands away from his face. "Are you a virgin?"

He made a soft whimpering noise at the same time he sounded a negative rattle. "I've been with other Talins before but never any other species."

That was a relief. She didn't want to think she was pressuring him to have sex for the first time. "Then what do you mean you've never felt like this before?"

"This feels different. Significant," he said, stumbling a little over his words. "You feel important, Pretty."

"I am important," she answered. She meant it to be a joke, but her words came out breathless instead. Then the real answer came to her. "We're important."

His deep, thrumming rumble filled the room and vibrated against her skin. She was straddling his thighs but the needy parts of her weren't touching him. Gripping his shoulder, she moved her legs a little further apart, allowing her to press her sex against his. She could feel the bulge there and rubbed against it.

"Pretty!" he moaned.

"This would be better without clothes," she whispered.

"We shouldn't—" he started to say, but she cut him off.

"Don't throw up limits or objections. This is a yes or no situation." If he said *no,* she might scream. She'd abide by it, but she'd still scream!

"Yes," he growled. "Ancestors forgive me, but I can't live another submark without tasting you!"

Relief made Kasi open her mouth to utter words of relief, but Ignatias covered her lips with his. She moaned into his mouth as his hand slid under the hem of her shirt and then under the strained fabric of her bra. His hand closed over her breast and squeezed gently. It felt so good, she pressed into his touch.

Both of them were breathing hard when he broke the kiss off. He pulled his hand out from under her shirt. She reached down to tug the garment off, but he growled and grasped it at the neckline. He violently ripped it down the center and drew it off her arms. No one had ever been so aggressive or forceful with her during sex.

It made her sex flood with slick!

"That was sexy," she whispered, quickly removing her bra before he could destroy it. Shirts and pants were easy to replace, but most species didn't even understand the concept of a bra let alone make them. Zia and Isla were small enough that they didn't bother with them, but she was a big girl and needed the support.

While she removed it, Ignatias watched her every move like a predator waiting for his prey. He licked his lips and rumbled out that strong thrumming that vibrated deliciously through her body.

Never breaking eye contact with him, she tossed the garment aside. She reached for his belt, but he was faster. He nearly tore the thing off in his haste. He flung it out of the way, uncaring of the sound of the Ident and pouch hitting the ground hard.

"Need you," he said in a low, throaty voice.

"Finish stripping and you can have me," she promised, reaching for her boots.

He ripped his pants off, and she only managed to get her second shoe off before he was on her. Grabbing her hips, he stood her up and roughly pulled off her sturdy work pants.

"Need you in my hands. In my mouth. I need to feel all of you."

Now that she was naked, she expected him to throw her down and cover her body with his. Instead, he backed away a little and ran his eyes over her form. Her confidence lasted all of three seconds before she started feeling self-conscious. Wrapping her arms around her chest to cover her voluptuous breasts, she looked around for a control panel or display to dim the room's lights.

"Every part of you is perfect," he breathed.

She whipped her head back toward him. "What?"

His eyes roved all over her body. "You don't possess a single flaw."

Frowning, she looked down at herself. "But I'm heavy, and I have that stupid dark birthmark all over my right thigh. The scars from when I was a kid and fell from a planter-bot never entirely went away. I have—"

He grabbed her around the waist and pulled her down onto his lap, making her gasp and stop talking.

"How can you be speaking both truth and lies at the same time?" he asked. "You say you're heavy, but how can that be true when you feel perfect in my arms? You point out the different colors of your skin, but the plating on my shoulders isn't the same as my chest. Do you find that ugly?"

"No, of course not!" she replied.

"Then why would it be less than wonderful on you? You talk of scars as if they don't prove you've lived a life full of purpose. How can anything you've said be a bad thing?"

"I…but, uh…" Kasi was at a loss for words.

Cupping the back of her head, he held her still and brought his lips close to hers. "You are gorgeous, Pretty," he whispered against her mouth. "No one I've ever met can compare to you."

He moved his lips against hers, feather light and teasing, then moved away. She begged. "More, please!"

His hand slid down from her head and neck to rest between her shoulder blades, supporting her body so he could urge her to lean back. Ducking his head down, he sucked a peaked nipple into his mouth. Fire shot through her.

"Ignatias!" she cried, arching her back and pressing her nipple harder into his mouth. The hand supporting her back was the only thing keeping her up. His free hand cupped her other breast, kneading the flesh.

She didn't realize she was grinding her sex against him until pleasure spiked up her spine from between her legs. She could feel his mating shaft pressing hard inside the flesh pouch. She wasn't simply eager to feel him emerge from the protective flesh pouch, she was desperate.

Blindly groping for the edge of the pouch, she sank her fingers in and stroked her fingertips across the head.

Ignatias pulled away to cry out. "Ancestors be praised, that feels amazing!"

Moving her hips back a little, she looked down to see what she was doing. Talin flesh pouches were covered in keratin to protect them. Unlike the plating on the rest of their body, this keratin was more in the shape of beads than plating. This different type of plating allowed the skin to roll back for access to their cock and ball.

Yes, a singular ball. Only one for these guys, and they called it a seed sack. It wasn't inaccurate, but it had made Kasi think of farming when she'd first heard the term. Now that she was getting to touch her own Talin, she realized the educational literature hadn't done them justice. It hadn't mentioned how silky the skin of their mating shaft felt or the soft and velvety texture inside their pouch.

Before now she hadn't thought hidden away genitals could be sexy. Now that she was playing with him, she realized the fact his cock was tucked away was enticing. Kind of the alien version of sexy lingerie. The way it was hidden only made Kasi more desperate to draw it out.

"Please don't stop," Ignatias rasped when she shifted her body.

"Not stopping," she promised. The new position allowed her to lower her head and lick across the head of his emerging dick.

He cried out and his entire body jerked. She was going in for another lick when his pouch snapped down, allowing his mating shaft and seed sack to emerge. It was so sudden she startled, then almost giggled. The way his cock was bobbing in her face made her think it was waving at her. Unable to resist, she took it in her hand and shook it once.

"It's nice to finally meet you," she whispered before letting go.

Ignatias's sexy rumbling abruptly stopped. "Did you just greet my mating shaft?"

Kasi stifled a laugh and ignored him in favor of lowering her face to suck the head into her mouth.

"Sweet souls!" he yelped. His hips rose slightly, pushing his cock a little deeper into her mouth. She gagged and drew back, annoyed that she couldn't take even half his shaft into her mouth. Maybe if she used her hand with her mouth, she could cover the whole thing.

Correction, she was going to need both hands because she could see he was still getting bigger! It was a good thing she liked a challenge!

Before she could get a grip on his cock, he lifted her and moved both of them. The room twirled, and suddenly she was on her back with Ignatias crouched between her legs.

"I have better *stellian* than this!" he growled. "You will not make me spill my seed like an untested youth. You will climax first, Pretty. I demand it!"

She wanted to laugh at his haughty attitude but was too busy pulling air into her lungs when he pushed her legs further apart.

He ran his fingers down her sex, parting her labia to reveal the most intimate parts of her. "Look how your body weeps for my touch."

He pressed fingers into her core. It felt good, but it wasn't enough. She lifted her hips, but he didn't change the depth of his fingers inside her.

"Do you want more of my touch, Pretty?" he asked, then leaned over and licked a textured tongue across her nipple. "Tell me exactly what you want."

It was hard to gather her thoughts enough to speak, but she managed. "I need you inside me!"

To her horror, he denied her. "No, Pretty, not yet. You have to wait for that, but you can have this."

He brought his thumb up to rub on her clit. He pressed gently, teasing the nub.

"Yes, there!" she agreed.

"Does my Pretty like this?" Ignatias asked. With dexterity she didn't expect, he started rhythmically stroking with his thumb while massaging his fingers in and out of her. It was wonderful and horrible all at the same time.

"More! Faster!" she ordered. To her frustration he slowed down. "Ignatias!"

"I find it fascinating that even though you know it will feel better if I draw it out, you want to race to orgasm," he drawled.

"But it's right there!" she cried out. "I can feel it. I'm on the brink and I want to come!"

"You'll get to come, Pretty. But only when I let you."

He sucked a nipple into his mouth, careful to only tease her with his sharp teeth and not hurt her. The graze of his teeth made this feel a little dangerous and a lot more forbidden. He alternated between licking, sucking, and scraping his teeth across her sensitive flesh, working his way from one breast to the other.

She started moving her hips against his hand, desperate for more pressure. Thankful he didn't stop her from thrusting onto his fingers this time.

"So good," she moaned.

"You are," he agreed before returning to tormenting her with his mouth.

Grabbing his head, she pressed his mouth down hard when he was over a nipple. He bit gently, sending sparks of pleasure down her spine. The rhythm against his hand became more frantic, sending jolts through her body. He pressed his thumb down, letting her get the pressure she desperately needed.

Her orgasm hit her hard, making her scream and let go of his head so she could grab the bedding on either side of her body. She gripped it in her white-knuckled fists and pulled hard, her entire body going tense and stiff as the climax washed over her.

Then it kept coming. She'd never experienced anything so powerful or long lasting before. Was there such a thing as too much pleasure? Could someone die from orgasm?

When the waves of orgasm finally subsided, she let her body go lax and wheezed out a pathetic moan. Ignatias pulled himself back and sat up, staring down at her with a critical eye as his rumble of arousal was replaced by one of concern.

"Are you well?"

"Oh yesssss," she said, drawing out the word with a sigh of happiness. Slitting her eyes open, she gave him a lazy smile. "Really yes. Big yes. So much yes."

"Then it's my turn!" he growled and flipped her over on her belly.

She gasped. "What are—"

He interrupted her. "Tell me no if you want me to stop, otherwise I'm using your body for my needs."

Gone was the gentle careful lover, and in his place was a male driven by desperate need. Grabbing her hips, he forced her up on all fours. Using one of his knees, he pushed her legs apart and fitted himself against her.

"I'm going to take you like this," he warned her. "Tell me now if you don't want this."

She didn't object but she also braced herself for it to be uncomfortable at first. He was a big guy, and she wasn't a Talin.

Despite his strong words, he pushed himself inside her body slowly. Her wet, ready sex gave way to him with no pain. He eased himself inside until he bottomed out, making both of them gasp.

"Your body is gripping me." His voice sounded like he was speaking through a clenched jaw. "I won't last long, Pretty. Your body is too hot and tight. You feel like we were meant to fit together."

He pulled back then pushed forward again. His size was intense and almost too much. Thankfully she was so turned on that his giant dick felt amazing. He stroked all the right spots, making that delicious tension start to build again.

Was it possible that there was another orgasm in her? Moments ago, she would've said no, but here she was—body quivering and breathless.

He started increasing the pace. The movements were so forceful, he had to hold onto her to keep her in place. It seemed her body liked both versions of Ignatias. It felt so good, she was having a hard time thinking. She was nothing but pleasure and sensation.

"I'm never letting you go," he said, voice guttural and determined. "You're my Kasi. My Pretty. You will never truly understand how special you are. How amazing and wonderful. I'm going to spend our lives worshiping you, my human."

His pace was starting to become frantic. A combination of his pre-com and her slick was flowing down the insides of her thighs. Lowering her head, she pushed her hips up and changed the angle of her pelvis a little. His cock started hitting just the right place, and she sucked in a sharp breath.

"I'm going to come, Pretty!" he warned her. She wanted to tell him she was orgasming already but couldn't.

Instead, she cried out wordless nonsense. His vibrating, sexy rumble got louder as his body started to quake.

"By the Ancestors!" he cried out.

She trembled under him, pleasure short circuiting her brain. Her limbs turned to jelly, and the only thing holding her up was his grip on her hips. Jets of hot cum filled her in time with his shudders.

The next thing she knew, he was wrapping his arms around her and rolling them both on their sides, keeping himself firmly inside her.

"We'll stay this way," he declared. His voice didn't sound steady, and his body was shaking.

Unable to talk, Kasi hummed her agreement. Clean up could happen later. Remembering how to speak and move was going to be the first task. But only after some cuddle time. Ignatias's rumble went from sexy to purring as Kasi closed her eyes and let her dazed mind drift off.

CHAPTER 18

Ignatias

If someone had informed him before meeting Kasi that sexual relations could expand his understanding of the universe, he would've scoffed at them.

Now he knew differently.

He felt as if he was a part of everything. Beyond the ship's hull, he could feel stars burning, planets spinning on their axes, black holes swallowing light and bending space-time. He could feel it because he was part of it. He'd touched the stars when he'd come inside Kasi.

It was profound, enlightening, and exhilarating.

This new mindset was going to require a shift in worldview. There were implications he wasn't comfortable examining yet so instead he focused on practical things. He'd give Sorana a glowing review to the Committee. That should go a long way in being forgiven for taking Kasi off planet. Then he'd beg Holian to let him settle on Sorana with Kasi.

One thought kept interrupting his careful planning—his children.

He had two children being raised in a cresh back on Talarian. They were children of obligation and duty that he hadn't seen in over a solar.

He and Jacilius were both from the same clan and had attended general training together as adultlettes. When it came time to marry, it made sense for the two of them to enter into a marriage contract. He felt as much affection for her as any other member of his family, which was pleasant but distant. What he'd had with Jacilius was nothing compared to the fiery passion and sense of union he experienced with Kasi.

He'd only been married a short time before his wife died of Fading. He'd wanted to rush to her side so she wouldn't die alone, but the military refused to release him from his post. He'd booked passage anyway, determined to be with her even if he had to disobey orders and receive harsh punishment. He got word of Jacilius's death only moments before he was going to board a ship.

In the end, he'd gone back to his duties, but that was when he understood that some things were more important than orders. Before his wife died, they'd done their duty and donated genetic material to a family approved cresh. That was six rotations ago, and he was ashamed to admit he didn't even know what skill levels his children were working at. He'd accepted the role of distant Talin father and visited them only once a solar.

He'd wanted to do so much more, but feared being labeled as a troublesome parent that interrupted their children's growth and education. After seeing the children on Sorana, he longed to let his children learn and play like that. Wanted to interact with them and share in their joy.

If he was honest with himself, he'd always wanted to break rules, even as a child. His life had been a constant battle between his natural impulses and Talin social norms.

"What are you thinking about?" Kasi murmured. She was draped on top of him with her head on his chest. He thought she'd drifted off to sleep and was content to be her bed until it was time to clean up and hide their activities from Kilmanum.

"I'm thinking about my children," he admitted.

"What?" Kasi said, her voice halfway between a shout and a cry of disbelief. She scrambled off him to sit on the bed and stare at him with wide eyes. "You've got kids? Wait, are you married? Did I seduce a married man?" She buried her face in her hands. "I'm a monster."

Sounding a soothing rumble, he sat up and drew her into his arms. "You are guilty of nothing, I'm a *maldom*."

"What's a *maldom*?" Kasi asked, dropping her hands away from her face and looking up at him expectantly.

"Someone who's lost their partner," he explained.

"Lost, as in they left you?" Kasi asked.

"That can happen. Occasionally partners will dissolve their marriage contracts," he answered. He didn't want to tell her all of it but knew she wouldn't stop asking until he gave a full answer. "But in this instance, the partner died."

Kasi looked up at him with a grief-stricken expression. "Oh, Ignatias, I'm sorry!"

"It was long ago. She and I never shared the same closeness that you and I have," he assured her.

"Do you miss her?"

"Of course," he answered easily. "She was a loyal friend and brilliant Talin. Her absence was felt by all those who enjoyed her company."

"That sounds so cold," Kasi muttered with a shake of her head. "What about your kids? Are they with her parents?"

He placed a hand on the back of her head and tried to tuck her under his chin. "They are in the cresh that created them."

She resisted the pressure and pulled his hand down, holding it in both of hers. "I forgot about those damn creshes. We need to get your kids. Bring them to Sorana. Then we can all live there. Wouldn't that be perfect?"

"That's not possible," he said with a negative rattle, even though he'd just thought about it himself.

Her brows wrinkled and her body tensed. "Not possible because you're still going to report us?"

He sounded a shocked rattle. "Of course not! I meant that it's not possible because several separate committees have to be notified or petitioned before a child can be withdrawn. Permission is usually only granted for older children."

"That sounds hard but not impossible," she argued.

"Pulling them out of their cresh could cause them irreparable harm," he argued. It wasn't common, but occasionally Talin parents wanted to move their children from one cresh to another, especially if they were starting a new colony. It was considered high risk for a child and most families and clans looked down on parents for wanting to move their children for anything but the most dire of circumstances.

"I doubt we'd do more harm than what's being done to them right now," Kasi countered, her mouth pressed into a straight line and her brows furrowed. "The Talin Empire might be powerful, but they got that way by crushing your spirits as children."

The truth of Kasi's statement was like a physical blow, making the air rush out of his chest.

Memories assaulted him. They weren't clear or sequential. Images, voices, moments, and actions filled his head in a jumble of impressions. Buzzing started in his ears, then a roaring, as if he was standing in the same room as a vumincator engine.

He felt frozen in time, unable to distinguish between memories and the present. He felt someone touch him, but was it a touch from his days in the cresh or was it happening in real time?

Reality was impossible to distinguish.

He was in a bubble where time existed all at once and the pressure was building. It was squeezing in on him, threatening to suffocate him. He'd felt this happen before and once again was helpless to stop it. He couldn't even tell if he was breathing.

"Ignatias? Come back to me, please!" a voice filtered to him. She sounded frantic but distant, as if she was calling to him from far away.

Kasi. That was Kasi. A sensation of warmth accompanied her name. She represented comfort and kindness.

"Open your eyes, Ignatias," Kasi begged. "You're scaring me here."

Kasi's distress started to break through to him. He needed to care for her. She'd be helpless without him, at the mercy of anyone who took her.

"Rattle or rumble for me," Kasi requested. "Make any sound. I need something. Please!"

He wanted to tell her he was working on it, but that was beyond him yet.

It took an intense amount of concentration, but he focused on the sensations of his body instead of the memories assaulting him.

The first thing he became aware of was pressure on his face. It was Kasi's fingers rubbing over his scent glands. Her touch was gentle, so it wasn't causing him shocks of pleasure. Instead, it felt like she was petting him, trying to give him comfort.

"I think you're coming back," she whispered, her voice coming to him more clearly now. "Keep moving this way. Lift those lids so I can see your gorgeous, vermilion eyes."

There were several failed attempts before he was able to move his eyelids. Kasi was up on her knees, which put her face right in front of his. Her copper-colored eyes were sparkling with unshed tears, and she was grimacing as if in pain.

"There you are," she breathed, her face relaxing into a smile. She sniffled a little and leaned in close to give him a quick lip press. "You had me worried."

He opened his mouth to speak but couldn't get the words out. His brain wasn't ready to talk yet.

"Take it slow," she advised. Letting go of his face, she scrambled off the bed. "Stay here, I'll be right back."

She was leaving him? A sad, desolate rumble drifted out of him.

"Okay, I guess I'm not going anywhere," she muttered, getting back on the bed and settling her smaller body between his legs. She rested her hands on his thighs and met his gaze. "I was only going to put on some clothes and get a cleaning cloth from the bathing facilities. I thought you might like it if I gave you a kind of bed bath."

He didn't care if he was filthy. She needed to stay. He wouldn't be able to breathe if she left the room even for a second.

"Don't leave me."

She made a soft, soothing sound. "I wasn't going to leave you. It's good you're talking. Is there anything I can do for you?"

"Don't leave."

"I won't leave," she promised. "Why don't you work on breathing with me? It might help you feel better. Watch me breathe in, do it with me. Good! I'm going to count and then we'll breathe out. Can you do that with me too?"

It seemed like an exercise for an overly emotional adultlette, but he found it was more difficult than expected. His mind kept trying to drift back into the past. It was hard work to stay present and match his breathing with Kasi's.

He had no sense of time, but eventually he started to feel the muscles in his body loosen. The first thing he did was stretch his jaw wide and then snap it closed. That helped release his neck plates, letting him bend his head forward and roll his shoulders.

"I made you yawn; I'm going to take that as a good sign," Kasi declared.

Ignatias raised his head and met her gaze. "I'm no longer trapped within the memory episode. How long has it been?"

Kasi slid her eyes to the side and shrugged. "A little while."

His belt with his Ident still attached was on the floor. He reached down to tap it and noticed many marks had passed. Some of that time would've gone by while they'd been engaged in intimate activities, but the rest was time lost due to his slipping into a memory episode.

Shame hit him. He hadn't suffered from them in a long time, and now he'd had two within a handful of rotations. What was wrong with him? Even worse, both times he'd caused Kasi distress. This was inexcusable.

"There's nothing wrong or shameful about what happened," Kasi said, making him sound a rattle of shock.

"How did you know what I was thinking?" he demanded.

She chuckled and rolled her eyes. "It doesn't take a genius to know where your logic would go. You're probably calling yourself weak, right?"

"Perhaps," he answered.

"Well don't," she ordered. Putting both hands on his chest, she pressed. He let her push him until his back was resting against the bulkhead. Then she arranged herself in his lap, tucking her head under his chin. Finally, she drew his arms around herself, then gave a happy little sigh.

"There, that's perfect."

"Is it?" he questioned, unable to give in to the comfort she was trying to share.

"Absolutely," she answered without hesitation. "I'm sorry you're having flashbacks, but I'm not sorry I saw them and was here to help. No matter what you think, this isn't a sign of weakness, it's a sign of trauma."

Ignatias wasn't sure they were two distinct concepts but kept that to himself.

"Both times involved kids," Kasi continued. "That first one back at Sorana happened while we were playing with Lamarin. This one was during a conversation about your kids and creshes. That's a pattern."

He remained silent, unsure he could voice any objections to Kasi's reasoning without sounding like a petulant child.

Kasi wasn't daunted by his silence. "You don't have to tell me, but you can't simply ignore it and think the flashbacks will magically go away. You need to talk to someone about how to treat them. We might not be able to ever get rid of them entirely, but I bet there's stuff we could do to help you cope."

Revealing his inner torment to a fellow Talin was a terrifying thought. He must have tensed up because Kasi reached up and started petting his face.

"Easy, I'm not going to make you do anything. I'm only talking about it now because I'm worried about you."

Perhaps it was time to tell someone what had happened so many solars ago. If anything was going to drive Kasi away, it would be this.

"Her name was Darsinum, and we were pulled from our artificial wombs on the same day. We were laid next to each other on a communal table for infants. My first clear memory is seeing her deep-orange eyes watching me and hearing her try to rumble with curiosity. From that moment, we refused to be parted. Death took her away and it's my fault. I didn't try hard enough to keep her here."

CHAPTER 19

Kasi

When Ignatias started to talk, she'd expected a story associated with his time in the military, but no. He hit her with childhood trauma involving death.

This was going to be so much more complicated than she first thought, and that worried her. She really wished she was more like Lakin. She'd only met the human woman once, but that single visit impressed Kasi. Lakin was intensely intelligent and emotionally intuitive. She'd know exactly what to say to Ignatias. Unfortunately, Lakin wasn't here. Kasi was simply going to have to do her best.

Before anything else, she needed a little clarification. "Can I assume we're speaking of death as a personification?"

"As opposed to what?" he asked.

"As opposed to someone in your society that goes around murdering children?" she answered, then winced. She could've been more diplomatic with her word choices.

He sounded a burst of surprised rattles. "We don't murder children!"

"Easy," she soothed, petting his arm. These Talins were so dramatic! "I'm trying to understand. I'm wild-caught, remember? I don't know much about how things work on Talarian, or anywhere else that isn't Sorana."

Ignatias went back to purring. "I shouldn't have snapped at you. For all you know, we routinely cull children. The answer is no, we aren't like that."

"Actually, I'm curious, what happens to children who aren't like everyone else?"

"The healers and techs in charge of reproduction are very careful to only grow children with flawless genetics. On the rare occasion a child is born with a deficit, they're tagged and won't be allowed to have children themselves. They're educated as best as possible and usually end up working for their family or clan. The parents are then expected to finance another child to make up for the one that will not be able to have a family."

"That sounds, uh, very organized," she commented. "Given how much oversight you had as children, I don't see how you could be at fault for Darsinum's death. How old were you when it happened? Could you translate it to human equivalent years, please?"

"Six solars, I believe," he answered. "Talin offspring mature far faster than humans so our intellectual age might have been closer to a human child of nine or ten."

Kasi gave a little encouraging sound. "Most species mature faster than us. I'm surprised that you have memories from birth though."

"The memories weren't as sharp as I was able to retain later," he explained. "But we start to form memories a few days before we're born."

That bit of news distracted Kasi. "You remember being born?"

"Only some sensations. Talin births happen over the course of several days and are a gentle process. The artificial wombs simulate the gradual movements that press us out of the birthing folds."

"Birthing folds?"

Ignatias pointed to his belly. "Talin females develop a crease during birth where the layers of plating and skin slowly draw apart to allow passage of a child. Artificial wombs mimic this process."

That was fascinating! Kasi wanted to know all about Talin births, but that had to wait for later. "It's romantic that you and Darsinum met the moment you were born. Was it love at first sight?"

"Talins don't love like humans do," Ignatias corrected. His haughty tone made Kasi grin. There was the Talin arrogance she was used to!

"Fine," she said with a suppressed snicker. "It was best friends at first sight then."

"Yes, that might be an accurate term," he agreed. "We became devoted companions. Our birth numbers were sequential, so we were always next to each other in every queue or activity. She was talkative, and because language skills are such an important part of our species, she was encouraged to speak with the other children. At least until the caretakers and instructors noticed she liked to make up stories."

"Don't all kids make up stories?"

"We were encouraged to relay facts, not fiction," Ignatias explained. "Some inaccurate extrapolations are expected, but not to the imaginative extent Darsinum did. By the time we were several solars old, she was being routinely reprimanded for it."

There weren't enough cuss words in her vocabulary to fully express how she felt about this aspect of Talin childrearing.

"What kind of punishments?" Kasi asked. "Did they kill her by accident because of the punishments?"

"The punishments weren't physical. We don't believe in corporal punishment for children," he assured her. "Darsinum simply had to do extra tasks or wasn't allowed to participate in her favorite activities for a set amount of time. We are strict with our children, not cruel."

Kasi didn't agree but kept that to herself. "Did she stop telling the stories?"

He sounded a negative rattle. "She stopped sharing them with our caregivers and teachers, but she continued to tell me. Late at night, we would huddle together on the floor, hidden between our beds. We'd stare up at the skylight, studying the few stars we could see. She'd make up fantastical stories about foreign planets and exotic species. I was always asking her questions and demanding details. I would try to find a part of the story she hadn't considered, but she always had answers."

"I wish I could've heard her stories," Kasi commented. She didn't point out that many species prized those who had active imaginations. She instinctively knew Ignatias wouldn't be interested in knowing what other species valued.

"You would've been awed by her brilliance," Ignatias assured her. "The worlds she made up were as vivid as the one we lived in. I'm ashamed to admit I don't remember all her stories, but I have clear memories of the strong feelings they'd invoked: wonder, excitement, interest, and amusement."

"I'm glad you kept listening," Kasi murmured.

"I did, for a while," Ignatias said. His purr faded and then went quiet. "But we were almost caught once, and I became afraid. I didn't want the adults to voice their dissatisfaction with me. Darsinum seemed unbothered by their disapproval, but I was very fearful."

Kasi was starting to see where this story was going. "Did you stop listening to her stories?"

"I refused to leave my bed and join her on the floor. I wouldn't respond when she crouched next to my bed and whispered to me. After several rotations, she stopped trying and would remain in her bed through the night. I thought I was relieved."

"But you missed it," she guessed.

"I felt like I was hungry in a way I couldn't satisfy," he admitted. "There were so many times I almost gave in and slid out of my bed. I saw the urge as the first test of my *stellian*. It never got easier to resist. Each night was a struggle."

He went silent, and Kasi gave him a few minutes before asking another question.

"Did she talk to you during the day?" Kasi asked.

"We would still converse, but she limited our conversation to appropriate topics. Our teachers praised her, and the punishments stopped, but she changed. Her speech slowed, and she reacted without enthusiasm. Everything about her started to dim. It worried me, and eventually the caregivers and teachers noticed also. She was seen by the healers multiple times, but nothing changed."

Kasi's heart broke for both children. "Did you try to get her to tell her stories again?"

Ignatias heaved out a heavy breath. "No. I was afraid if I asked her to share, I wouldn't be able to keep myself in bed at night. I craved her stories that much. I told myself that she would be fine. That this was only a little thing and she'd be lively after a while."

"She didn't get better, did she?" Kasi murmured. "She got more depressed, and no one would help her."

"Depression is a good word to describe her lack of enthusiasm. It got to the point where she wouldn't eat much at mealtime, and eventually, she stopped eating all together. I heard one of the caregivers mention Fading. The next day she was sent to the room where only the very sick were housed. When the healers stopped visiting her, I became fearful. If she was getting better, they'd put her back in her own bed, but they were leaving her in that room."

"I've heard the term Fading, but I don't have any context for it," Kasi said.

"Officially it's called Catatonic Withdrawal Disease, but everyone simply refers to it as Fading. It's considered the disease of the weak willed. The authorities claim it can't be cured and those that die of it are doing our species a favor. Families will go to great lengths to cover up a death by Fading. I even heard of them launching crafts into a sun with the dead body on board to hide the cause of death."

Kasi was struck speechless by the level of cruelty. She clung to Ignatias and fought her tears. Crying right now wouldn't help him and might even make him stop talking. When she was sure she had her emotions under control, she asked another question.

"What happens to Talins when they get Fading? I mean physically."

"They shut down," he explained. "The few that have survived describe the world becoming muted. Colors, sounds, smells, and taste all no longer function as they once did. They stop craving food and have to force themselves to eat. Eventually they lay down and withdraw into their minds. They waste away."

It didn't sound like the worst way to die, but it also sounded like a disease that could be treated. "Did you know all that at the time?"

"I didn't. When I asked the adults if Darsinum would be back soon, they told me that she wasn't suffering but she was dying."

Kasi gasped and hugged him tighter. "They were that blunt? You were a kid!"

"It was considered a kindness to tell me the truth. They didn't want to give me hope that my friend would return when she was clearly not going to recover."

"Did they let you see her?" Kasi asked.

"They refused my request, but I did sneak in one night. I debated for marks about doing it but finally thought if anyone could help, it would be me. I knew all her secret worlds, and I was sure she'd gotten lost in one and didn't know how to find her way back to the real world. I thought simply speaking with her would make her all well. It was very childish logic."

"No, it was the logic of someone who wanted to help a loved one," Kasi argued. "Was it hard to get to her?"

"Not at all. Gaining access to her was as simple as opening the door to her room and walking in. There were very few locked rooms at the cresh. We were all expected to honor the rules without physical reinforcements. The room was completely bare except for the bed and a single dim light. At first, I thought the bed was empty, but then I realized the bundle at the foot of the bed wasn't bedding, it was her."

Kasi made a soft encouraging sound and hugged him tightly. "What did you do?"

"I rushed to the bed and pulled the bedding off. I planned to shake her and demand she speak to me, but I wasn't prepared for what I saw. She was lying on her side, eyes open but unfocused. In only a few rotations, she'd shrunk horribly. She was small and frail looking, with sunken eyes and keratin plating sloughing off in big chunks. My first instinct was to run from the room. I was afraid I'd catch Fading from her, even though I knew it couldn't be transmitted. It was hard, but I didn't leave."

"You were a brave kid," Kasi murmured.

"If I'd been brave, I would've acted sooner," he whispered, then spoke up. "I tried to touch her but couldn't. I was scared I'd do damage or cause her pain. She looked so unimaginably fragile."

"Did you talk to her?"

"Yes, until I was hoarse. At first, I demanded she respond to me. After that didn't work, I tried to bribe her by saying I'd listen to her stories if she would only respond in some way. It took me most of the night to realize I was too late."

"She died that night?"

"Yes," he answered, voice thick. "I watched her take her last breath. I made sure she had a pillow clutched to her chest to offer the Ancestors a traditional gift. I begged the Ancestors to welcome her into the Domicile of the Souls. I stood there praying to them until I went hoarse. I failed her in so many ways, I didn't want to think her soul was left homeless."

"You didn't fail her," Kasi argued. "Every adult in your lives failed both of you. Your kid brain was able to make the connection between her imagination and thriving. Why couldn't they? They literally killed her with rules!"

He briefly sounded a frustrated rattle before speaking. "You don't understand. They were only trying to make her a good Talin. I was the one who knew she needed to tell her stories. That they were as vital as her lungs and heart. I'm the one who stopped listening at night. I'm the one who let fear rule me. If I'd only been braver, she would've survived."

"That's a whole lot of guilt to be carrying around for so long," Kasi said, trying to figure out the best way to approach this. "It was such a messed-up situation that now I feel like I need therapy!"

She shouldn't have tried to joke because Ignatias sounded a worried rumble. "Have I damaged our relationship by revealing my cowardice? Have you lost faith in me as a protector?"

"No!" she adamantly denied. "If anything, I feel closer to you. You had to trust me a lot to tell me. That's a gift. Thank you, Ignatias."

"It's you who've gifted me," he responded. "I feel strangely at peace after telling you all this. I don't have the normal pain I suffer after a memory episode. You have a healing effect on me, Pretty."

"I think—"

She was interrupted by a chime that sounded from Ignatias's Ident. The sound made him jerk and then rattle with urgency.

"Shift change is close," he explained as he picked her up and set her on her feet next to the bunk. "Kilmanum will be back soon. We need to be dressed before he returns."

"Yeah, we wouldn't want anyone to find out what kind of naughty things we've been up to," she teased as she reached for her clothing. She would've liked to bathe, but maybe that could come next. She couldn't go streaking down the hallway naked on this crowded ship.

"Having sex with a human pet isn't just taboo, it's against the law," Ignatias reminded her grimly.

"I wasn't talking about that," Kasi said, her vision briefly obscured as she pulled her shirt on. "We were sharing feelings!" she made an exaggerated gasping sound.

Ignatias paused for a moment. He'd been about to buckle his belt around his waist but stopped to regard her, then sounded a rumble of amusement. "That's doubly illegal!"

Kasi burst out laughing. Ignatias cracked a joke, there was hope for the Talin yet!

CHAPTER 20

Ignatias

Eating with Captain Solmance and a small selection of the crew after having several profound emotional experiences back to back felt surreal. It also felt strange to sit there, eating and conversing with Solmance and the crew while having committed a major crime only a few marks earlier.

The most incomprehensible part was that he felt no guilt, not for sex with Kasi or revealing his poor conduct as a child. He didn't even feel shame at having not one, but two memory episodes in front of her.

"What do you think, Committee Citizen Ignatias?"

Realizing he had no idea what they were talking about, he looked at Captain Solmance and tried to formulate a response that wouldn't reveal his lack of attention. Kasi came to his rescue.

"Does this station grow any food?" Kasi asked, drawing everyone's attention, and rumbles of comfort. "Do any stations grow food? I've never been on a space station before. This is only the second time I've been in space."

"A few of the very large stations will have grow rooms where fresh items are produced, but it uses up a lot of resources," Solmance told her. "Most use fresh-packs. They're as nutrient rich as freshly grown. If they're prepared correctly, they are indistinguishable."

"Almost all stations have green rooms or green areas though," Tamerous added.

"What's that?" Kasi asked. It seemed Pretty had successfully distracted everyone from whatever Solmance had been asking him. He knew she was doing it on purpose. His clever human was being protective of him.

"They're rooms or sections set aside and filled with plants from our homeworld," Tamerous explained. "The station we're traveling to has a very large area on their main floor. I've been there many times. I could show it to you. I know most of the plants."

"I doubt we'll be docked long enough for you to do that," Solmance commented. "I have several vids that go over the most commonly cultivated plants on Talarian if you're interested, Kasi. I could watch them with you and answer any questions you have."

Tamerous's and Solmance's offers weren't a surprise. Every Talin in the room had tried to tempt Kasi into spending time with them. She had a small pile of candy they'd given her the moment she sat down. He saw items sitting on the floor next to chairs and knew that most of them were probably gifts to attract her attention.

He couldn't blame any of these Talin. If the circumstances were different, he'd be doing the same thing.

Sitting on his lap, Pretty covered her mouth with a hand to hide her smile. "That's a nice offer, but Ignatias is still teaching me things. I'm not sure I could add more subjects to learn right now."

"What kind of tricks is Ignatias teaching you?" Isthmus asked.

He could tell by the way her eyes went wide that Pretty wasn't prepared for that question and was probably thinking of the illegal things they'd been doing earlier.

"I, uh, we are, um," she stumbled over her words, making Ignatias rumble with amusement.

"Pretty wants to learn how to read Talin," he offered.

The others responded with encouragement while also warning her not to get upset if she didn't learn very quickly. Kasi handled all their comments with grace. He could tell she found their reactions amusing instead of insulting.

"There are two shops on Whykeen that will carry human items," Isthmus told him while Solmance explained the intricacies of writing vowels in Talin. "You'll probably need to visit both to get everything since she has so little. The station has some funds set aside to outfit wild-caught pets if you don't have enough wealth. I know none of us would want to accept charity, but it's more important to consider the well-being of the pet than our personal pride."

Ignatias felt too relaxed to take offense at Isthmus's clumsy conversation. "I have plenty of funds to pay for all the things Kasi will need but thank you for reminding me."

Isthmus wasn't finished. "You also need to take her to the healers there. She could be very ill and not showing any signs. Humans are prey animals and have evolved to hide their weaknesses."

Ignatias couldn't explain to Isthmus that she'd been thoroughly examined by a healer without going into details he'd rather not share. Instead he sounded an affirmative rattle and lied. "I plan to."

"Is her human name Pretty Kasi or Kasi Pretty?" Wuelum asked. She was deliberately flashing her iridescent gold-colored quill extensions. It seemed Captain Solmance had noticed Kasi's interest in her extensions and mentioned it. Every female at the table was wearing bright, showy extensions and some of the males had decorated their quills with eye-catching paint.

"My nickname is Pretty," Kasi answered for him. "You should call me Kasi because only Ignatias is allowed to call me Pretty."

"Ah, it's an affection name," Wuelum responded with a comforting rumble. "I've heard humans develop different names for everyone to show affection. Have you decided on an affection name for Ignatias?"

Kasi tilted her thoughtfully. "Ignatias is really important to me, so he needs a good name. Iggy would be too obvious."

"Why is Iggy obvious?" Ignatias asked. He was eager for Kasi to develop a special name for him.

"It just is," Kasi responded with her familiar amused quirk of her lips. "You call me Pretty, maybe I should call you handsome. No, that's not right either."

"Kasi, have you tried jol?" Tasium asked from across the table. He stood up to set the platter closer to her. He flared his red-dyed quills as he set the platter within reach.

"I couldn't eat anymore," she responded, leaning back against his chest and patting her stomach.

"I'm surprised you look so healthy," Isthmus commented. "Except for the short mane of course. Healthy, well-adjusted humans grow their mane long."

Kasi tugged at a lock of her shoulder length mane. "Some of us like to keep it short."

"Only because you were probably forced to do harsh work you weren't suited for," Tamerous said with an angry rattle.

Sitting back down, Tasium spoke up. "There are so few of your species left in the universe that it's a tragedy every time one of you dies, especially in circumstances we could easily protect you from."

Kasi's mouth turned down into a frown. "We aren't all that fragile."

Tamerous sounded a comforting rumble. "I'm sure you're very strong for a human."

She turned her gaze back to Isthmus. "Why did you say I look healthy?"

"Because you're round," he explained.

Her eyes went wide but her mouth continued to frown. Ignatias thought she might be displaying outrage. "I'm what?"

"You have a healthy round body," Isthmus continued.

Then everyone else jumped in to explain to Kasi why she looked healthy to them.

"Humans can store energy in the form of fat," Tasium added. "Humans who don't have enough fat have been starved."

"Talins can't store energy in this way, but it's good when humans do," Wuelum said. "Humans are meant to be soft and round, like you. I've seen images taken of the first humans discovered hundreds of years ago and they looked very sickly. They'd been living on very little food for quite some time. The documentation from that time period is easily accessible on the Talarian Unibase."

Solmance sounded a rattle of agreement. "Everyone knows round humans are happier too. Look at how quickly you've adjusted to being with Ignatias. Your generous body shape has helped you adapt to being a pet. You should be commended for being able to maintain this body despite your circumstances."

"This is the first time I've been complimented for being overweight," Kasi muttered. Despite the low tone of her voice, everyone at the table heard her. There was a general angry rattle that cut off when Captain Solmance slapped her hand down on the table.

"You're not overweight," she snapped, then sounded a soothing rumble. "I know what that term means, but it isn't true or accurate!"

"I've always been the fat kid," Kasi explained. "And I stayed that way into adulthood. You can't tell me you guys think this is good."

Ignatias was shocked by her words. Grabbing her under the arms, he lifted her and turned her around so she was straddling his thighs and facing him, "Do you honestly think you're not a beautiful human?"

Kasi's eyebrows squished together, and she gave a little shake of her head. "I'm not beautiful, at least not my appearance. There were guys on my old colony who were willing to date me but only because there weren't that many of us. They always went after Isla or one of the other girls first. I was everyone's last choice."

"If other human males didn't pick you, it was because they lacked intelligence," Solmance declared.

"They had to be dumb even for humans if they didn't appreciate your beauty," Wuelum assured her.

"You were probably the smartest one of them all," Isthmus added. "You're a perfect little human. Anyone would be proud to own you!"

"I know Ignatias must feel as if the Ancestors have given him an immense blessing," Solmance continued. "You're a rare and lovely treasure."

As they'd talked, Kasi's expression had gone from agitated to surprised. "You guys aren't making fun of me. You really think I'm pretty."

"We'd never tease a human in that way," Ignatias assured her. They both had past trauma to work through, and Kasi's revolved around her appearance. "I named you Pretty because that's what you are. I could've used Utterly Gorgeous and Without Flaws, but I worried that would be too long for a name." His words were met by a chuckle from her and a few rumbles of amusement from others at the table.

"You can't mean that," she murmured shyly, a small smile starting to lift one corner of her mouth.

Ignatias sounded an affirmative rattle. "From the first moment I saw you, I could tell you were magnificent, even wearing these clothes and covered in dirt."

"I wasn't covered," she argued, but her smile reached her eyes now. "I was only a little dirty."

Running gentle fingers down her face, he cupped her cheek. "You were, and are, the picture of human beauty. We'll find you better clothing, but it's only to showcase an exquisite female."

"Well said, Ignatias," Solmance commented. "One of our home-bred humans would never be in doubt of their value. I'm sorry you were raised in circumstances that led you to believe you weren't lovely. I can assure you, we Talins know quality, and all of us would be quick to claim you as our pet."

The skin of Kasi's face darkened—perhaps from embarrassment? She might not be used to so much positive attention. His guess was proven correct when she reached up to wrap her arms around his neck and nestled her face against him. Her lips rested near the exposed patch of skin at the base of his neck, her warm breath making him want to shudder.

"I think she might be a little overwhelmed," he explained to everyone. They all sounded either rumbles of sympathy or comfort.

"Poor thing," Solmance commented. "Do you think she'd like some Delorta tea? I've heard humans find it a comforting beverage."

"Perhaps later," Ignatias answered. He ducked his head down and put his mouth to her ear. "Are you well?"

The meal wasn't over yet so leaving would be considered rude and everyone would be disappointed to be deprived of Kasi's company earlier than expected. Still, he was willing to mildly offend everyone at the table if Kasi needed a break.

"I'm fine," she whispered. "But you guys can be really intense."

"When it's important, yes," he agreed. "And you are important."

She mumbled something under her breath he couldn't make out but was forced to raise his head when Tamerous started speaking.

"I hesitated to mention this before, but perhaps it could help Kasi feel more secure. One of the families in my clan has a male human of breeding age," Tamerous said, sounding an excited rattle. "I haven't met him, but I've heard he's very kind and gentle. I'm sure they'd be thrilled to introduce him and Kasi. Humans do well when they can live in bonded pairs, and he can help Kasi understand how desirable she is. She might even have offspring! Human cubs are so adorable."

The thought of anyone touching Kasi caused a wave of rage to wash over him. If Kasi hadn't been clinging to him, he might have leapt over the table and taken Tamerous to the ground. He would've pounded the male until his head was nothing but pulp.

With Kasi's safety to consider, he hesitated, although the desperate need for violence made his heartbeat kick up and his quills flair.

Kasi must have sensed his change in demeanor because she let go of his neck to sit up and blinked up at him with raised eyebrows and a questioning tilt of her head. "Ignatias?"

It was hard to talk because the muscles of his jaw were so tense. "Do not be concerned. I have no interest in introducing you to any other humans for breeding purposes."

"I wasn't worried," she answered, reaching up to run her fingers over his scent glands. "I trust you, remember?"

Yes, of course. Not only did they share profound secrets, but they'd been as intimate as two individuals could be. Kasi's words and touch calmed his fury as quickly as Tamerous's words had raised it. She might not realize it yet, but Kasi had a lot of power over him that had nothing to do with laws or taboos and everything to do with the way his scent glands were rapidly filling to the point of pain.

"You have my trust as well, Pretty," he whispered to her.

She gave him a tired smile. "I think I've had enough visiting for today. Can we leave yet?"

"Absolutely," he agreed.

Ignatias looked up to find that no one noticed their exchange because Tamerous's suggestion had sparked a heated discussion. It seemed everyone knew someone who owned a human and they wanted to put their candidate in front of Ignatias and Kasi. They were so adamant that everyone was standing and starting to shout. He and Kasi had been so wrapped up in each other, they hadn't even noticed!

Taking advantage of their disorderly conduct, Ignatias wrapped his arms around Kasi and stood up. "I believe Kasi needs quiet."

Captain Solmance was the first to recover. Straightening up, she cleared her throat and voiced a formal goodbye. "Our time together has been of great value. Thank you for gracing me with your company."

Ignatias gave her the expected response. "It is I who must thank you for the pleasure of your conversation. I look forward to more exchanges in the future."

Although it would be polite to repeat the process with everyone else in the room, it wouldn't be considered rude to recite the formal farewell with the highest-ranked person and then leave. Ignatias ignored the formal words from everyone else and strode out of the room, holding Kasi tenderly against his chest.

The last of his tension dissipated as he carried her back to their shared accommodations. If every meal was like this one, it was going to be a long few rotations.

CHAPTER 21

Kasi

Kasi knew Whykeen Station was going to be big, but because she had no frame of reference for space station size, she'd pictured it being like a large ship. She couldn't have been more wrong.

When they got close, Captain Solmance invited her and Ignatias to observe the approach and docking from the command center. Kasi was thrilled to be so close to the action only to find out it was actually pretty boring.

Noticing her yawning, Solmance had images from an outside vid capture put on a large wall display. At first, Kasi thought they were approaching an oddly shaped, slowly rotating, colonized moon. She'd audibly gasped when she realized the entire shape was the space station. Her comment about how massive it was led to educational lectures from everyone in the command center about space stations and the Talin Empire.

She mostly ignored them as she watched the station get closer. Whykeen was shaped like a moon with two big bites taken out of it on either side. Each "bite" was lined with ships of all sizes. Brightly lit bots that looked like large bugs flowed all over the outside of the ships and the station. While she watched, an automated tug-ship slowly guided a vessel away from the station.

There had to be an entire city on that station, with interesting things to see and do. Ignatias seemed ready to indulge her and she might never get another chance.

"I want to experience everything!" She'd tried to whisper those words to Ignatias, but they ended up coming out much louder and everyone heard. There were a few rumbles of amusement followed by many suggestions on where they should go while they were there.

It took longer than normal to dock because they had to make arrangements for the tug-ships to take Ignatias's ship to the repair bay on the far side of the station. After that was done, another tug-ship took control of the Ever Prosperous III and guided them to their assigned dock.

Once they were secured to Whykeen, Captain Solmance turned to face them. "You're free to stand now. I've instructed the crew to remain at their stations until given permission. I didn't want them inhibiting your exit from the ship."

Ignatias shifted her in his lap so he could keep her in his arms even after he stood up. "You have my deepest gratitude for both the rescue and accommodations."

"Meeting you and your pet, Kasi, was a blessing from the Ancestors," Solmance replied. She plucked something from her seat and held it out. "This is a gift for you, Kasi."

She wiggled in Ignatias's hold until he grumbled and set her on her feet. She accepted the gift with both hands, excited to see what it was. "You didn't have to!"

"It's not particularly expensive," Solmance said. "I hope it will remind you of your time with us."

Deeply curious, Kasi flipped open the plain box and pulled out a perfect miniature of the Ever Prosperous III. Kasi held it up so she could marvel at all the details. "This is amazing!"

"I used one of our small-parts fabricators to create it," Solmance explained. "It took some time to get all the features correct, but I'm pleased with the results."

"I love it!" Kasi exclaimed, then lunged at Solmance. Wrapping her arms around the woman, she gave the captain a hug. "Thank you, you're a sweet Talin!"

Solmance sounded a startled rattle and went stiff. Kasi laughed and let go of Solmance long enough to draw the Talin's arms around her. "This is how you hug, or uh, clutch with a human."

After a slight hesitation, Solmance squeezed Kasi gently and purred. "I didn't realize you'd feel so soft," she whispered with wonder and tightened her hold slightly when Kasi tried to pull away.

"Captain." Ignatias spoke the one word with clear warning.

Solmance reluctantly let go of Kasi and stepped back. "You're a good human, Kasi. I hope to find one like you someday."

How did you respond to something like that? *I hope you buy a happy human that makes you feel loved because you obviously don't know how to love yourself or each other.*

Yeah, no, that didn't seem like a good idea. Instead she pressed her back against Ignatias and held the little ship in her hands. "I hope you have a happy life."

"Happy life?" someone behind Solmance murmured. "Humans say the strangest things. Shouldn't she want us to be successful and make our empire proud?"

"Humans value joy, not duty," someone else answered. "She probably thinks that's the most important blessing she could give."

Kasi bit her lip to keep from laughing. Now she understood why Zia was always so reluctant to leave Sorana. Talins could drive a human crazy with their odd assortment of beliefs and values.

"I will strive to be happy," Solmance agreed, and slapped a fist to her chest. "I'll walk you to the outer doors.

You'll want to hurry, a large passenger ship is docking and will be unloading many individuals who will clog the hallways and terminals."

With that, she led them through the ship and into Whykeen. She walked so fast that Kasi almost had to jog to keep up. Once they were at the ramp leading from the Ever Prosperous III to the station, Solmance stopped and stood to the side to let them pass.

Kasi stopped and looked up at the captain. "Could you say goodbye to Kilmanum? I thought I'd see him before we left; I didn't realize we wouldn't." Kasi thought of something and turned to Ignatias to request her bag. He held it up so she could rifle through it. It took some looking, but she found two of the seed satchels she'd packed for good luck. She didn't have any money, but experience taught her that sometimes other species would barter for exotic seeds.

"Here's one for you and one to give Kilmanum," Kasi said. "It isn't much, but maybe you could trade them for something you want."

Solmance accepted the satchels with a curious rumble. "You don't need to give away your things, little human."

"They're seeds," Kasi explained. "I collect them, and I want you and Kilmanum to have them as gifts. But you probably don't use seeds so you can trade or sell them for something you really want."

Solmance clutched the satchels so tightly Kasi thought they might burst. "I'll carry this to the afterlife with me, and when I meet my Ancestors at the Domicile of the Souls, they'll welcome me for bringing them such an excellent offering. You've given me something precious. Thank you, Kasi."

Kasi blinked, unprepared for her meager gift to be received with such enthusiasm. "Great?"

Ignatias slung her bag back over his shoulder and took her hand in his. "We should be going. Thank you for your gift of time and skill, Captain Solmance."

"Have a fruitful rotation, Committee Citizen Ignatias, and take good care of this human. I'll hear of it if you don't." With that, Solmance turned on her heels and hurried back into the ship.

"What was that about?" Kasi asked as Ignatias led her down the short hallway and into a larger corridor filled with Talins, hover carts, and various types of bots carrying cargo and luggage.

Thankfully Ignatias paused to let her take it all in as he explained. "When we die, we are interred with items that we think will please the Ancestors so they let us enter the Domicile of Souls. The most common items are bedding, seeds, and a piece of iron ore. If you ever pull apart any Talin pillow, you'll find a little packet containing a few seeds and iron dust. That's why ships will always carry extra pillows, even though the crew will all bring their own. Your gift of seeds was deeply meaningful to Solmance. I'm sure both the captain and Kilmanum will treasure them. They might even use your seeds to replace the ones in their personal bedding."

Kasi had unknowingly given a couple of Talins part of their grave goods. She was happy the presents went over well, but she also felt odd at having accidentally given them a deeply religious gift. Before she could ask another question, someone's loud exclamation distracted her.

"Human!"

The single word caused a flurry of movement, and then next thing she knew, they were surrounded by Talins, all pressing in and speaking at once. It was similar to what happened when she first boarded the Ever Prosperous III, but worse. There were a lot more Talins here, and they were louder and more insistent.

Ignatias shoved her behind him and sounded one of his loud war rattles. His quills flared and his claws slid all the way out.

"Back away!" he roared. "I'll gut anyone who touches her!"

Many in the crowd sounded the metal-tools-dropping-on-the floor rattles of alarm and all of them moved a small distance away. Kasi clutched at the back of Ignatias's belt, not sure what to do. She'd expected visiting Whykeen to be exciting but not in a scary way!

Unfortunately, Ignatias's attempt to disperse the crowd didn't do much. If anything, more Talins gathered to see what everyone was looking at. Someone even tried to sneak up and touch her. When Ignatias shifted to fend off that Talin, it left her vulnerable for other sets of hands to grasp at her arm and hair.

She could hear many of the same comments the Ever Prosperous III crew had made coming from this crowd, but the words seemed more threatening, and the situation was on the brink of devolving into chaos.

"There is no reason to congregate in this corridor!" a voice boomed out, making everyone but the passing bots go silent. "Unless you can provide me with a legitimate reason to linger, I'll be issuing citations."

That got the crowd moving, and within minutes, foot traffic was flowing again. The large male Talin who'd gotten everyone to leave stepped up and addressed Ignatias with a thump of a fist to his chest. "I'm Lead Volormus, head of the station's law keepers."

Ignatias thumped his chest in return. "I'm Committee Citizen Ignatias and this is my human, Kasi."

Volormus sank down to one knee and addressed her. "I'm sorry they scared you, Kasi. I'm going to escort you and your master. No one will bother you again."

Coming out from behind Ignatias, Kasi waved a hand at Volormus. "You've got good timing. Thanks for coming to our rescue."

Volormus examined her critically then looked up to address Ignatias. "I assume the first place we're going is the healers?"

"I don't need the healers!" Kasi said quickly. If the healers on Whykeen were anything like the ones back on

Sorana, she'd be stuck in medical for at least a day while they "made sure" she was healthy. She didn't want to waste all that time. "There's nothing wrong with me. Tell him, Ignatias!"

Volormus sounded a rumble of amusement as he turned his attention back to her. "You're obviously wild-caught and need to be examined. It's for your own good."

Kasi worked very hard at not replying to Volormus with sarcasm. "I've seen healers already. I'm perfectly healthy. They all said so. Well, except for that one tooth, but Joslum got that all fixed and it's good as new now."

Ignatias wrapped an arm around her shoulders and drew her against him. "Kasi has seen healers, but they didn't have proper clothes for her there. I'm hoping to visit some shops here and buy her all the things she needs to be comfortable."

"That explains her poor garments but healthy appearance," Volormus said, but still didn't stand up. "I'll escort the two of you to the shops and then to registration."

Relief that he wasn't going to make her spend time in medical combined with excitement over getting to see the station. She did a little dance in place, too happy to remain still.

"Look at how joyful you are!" Volormus exclaimed with an amused rumble. "The mere thought of receiving a few trinkets has delighted you. I can't wait to see how you'll react when you're able to choose many new items."

"Probably more dancing," Kasi said with a laugh, deciding not to be offended by Volormus or any of the Talins that treated her like a low-intelligence species. The joke was on them because Kasi could do happy dances wherever she felt like it and they were stuck smacking their chests with their fist anytime they were meeting each other. Out of the two, she liked her dancing better.

Standing up, Volormus addressed Ignatias. "Your human is adorable. I can see she'll need everything. The station has funds to provide for wild-caught humans if you need help purchasing items."

"I've been informed," Ignatias answered. It was cute that he was more annoyed by Volormus than she was! Tangling her fingers with his, she pulled his arm off her shoulder and turned to face him.

"This is mostly your fault," she reminded him. "Now you have to literally pay the price by buying me stuff!"

Ignatias started purring. "At the moment, I can't think of anything I'd want to do more."

CHAPTER 22

Kasi

Volormus led them into the station, his imposing presence and warning rattle keeping them from getting mobbed again. Even with all that, many Talins stopped to watch her go by. A few tried to interact, but either Volormus or Ignatias were quick to intercept them.

All of it made Kasi feel like a celebrity. With Volormus there to help Ignatias keep her safe, she wasn't concerned about getting grabbed or handled by strangers, and it was a lot less scary. She even started waving or saying hello to the occasional passerby who halted their activities to stare.

Soon the corridors of the docking area gave way to the main area of the station, and it was Kasi's turn to stop in her tracks and gape. The place was enormous, and she was probably only looking at a small portion of it. A massive dome covered an area bigger than all the farmland back on Wimol. There had to be hectares of area all illuminated by a nearby star shining through the semi-transparent dome.

Under the dome were layers of balconies stair-stepping up, each layer bright and active with shops and foot traffic. Bots were everywhere, moving on invisible networks of wires from balconies to balconies to ferry goods. There weren't any shops on the lowest level. Instead, the place looked like a park with many different sized planters full of greenery everywhere. A lush clover-like plant covered the floor except for narrow foot paths winding their way through in serpentine patterns.

At regular intervals around the perimeter there were stairs next to exposed lifts to take people up to the balconies. The lifts were simple platforms that ran continuously at a slow, steady pace. As Kasi watched, a Talin carrying several boxes stepped up to one, paused long enough for a new platform to emerge, and stepped onto it. The moment he was high enough, the next platform appeared and the Talin behind him got on. The same process repeated for those wanting to descend.

It was a good thing she wasn't afraid of heights because there wasn't a rail to be seen anywhere!

"This way," Volormus said, pointing to the closest moving platform. "The first shop we'll visit is on the fifth tier."

"Can we look at the garden first?" Kasi asked, gazing at all the unfamiliar plants in front of them.

There were several that looked like they were about to flower. Another plant didn't have any leaves, only a trunk the thickness of her wrist reaching almost all the way to the next tier level with what looked like tiny round fruit covering it in an irregular pattern.

Her hands itched to touch leaves and stems while her mind filled with questions.

A female Talin carrying several monitoring tools stepped around a planter. "Back before we were able to construct stations like this one, we would set aside a single room and fill it with native plants from Talarian. It was a place we could go to connect to our homeworld. Having a single room is out of fashion. The new goal is to incorporate Talin flora in a more impactful way."

Kasi tried to take a step toward her to ask questions, but Volormus was quick to move between them.

"May the Ancestors grace you with wisdom and loyalty, Botanical Specialist Harquias," he said with a smack to his chest.

"And lead you to honorable action," Harquias replied to Volormus before looking back to Kasi. "Do you like plants?"

Volormus sounded a negative rattle. "We don't have time to delay. As you can see, this human is in desperate need of personal items."

"I wouldn't say desperate," Kasi argued. "Can't we spend a little time here? I'm not going to get sick because I wore this outfit a little longer."

Volormus looked over his shoulder at her and purred. "The clothes you're wearing might be doing damage to your delicate skin. It's imperative we get you better garments. This green space will be here when we're done."

"We're really not that delicate," Kasi muttered to herself.

If Henni were here, she'd be rolling her eyes at Kasi's request to look at plants instead of shops. But Henni was raised among the Talins and familiar with getting new items. For the majority of Kasi's life, clothing was bought in bulk, in one size, and distributed to everyone in the community as needed. It was up to the individual to take the items to a tailor machine to get them fitted or do it themselves with an old-fashioned needler.

Some of the other humans on Wimol learned to wield the needler with skill and would make their standard issue clothing fancier, but not Kasi. She'd always felt too self-conscious to draw attention to herself with decorative or distinct outfits.

Maybe that was one of the reasons she dug in her heels when Ignatias tried to walk her away from Harquias and the plants.

"No really, I want to stay here for a while." She was surprised to realize she sounded like a toddler ready to have a meltdown, but she did finally get both men's attention.

Volormus sounded an inquisitive rumble. "Exploring the green space is that important to you?"

"It really is!" Kasi answered with a dramatic nod of her head that made her hair fall into her face and obscure her vision for a moment. After she'd pulled a few strands out of her mouth, she looked up to find Volormus and Harquias holding their Ident's and speaking in low tones.

"He's arranging a time to cordon off most of this floor so Harquias can show you around and answer all your questions without anyone bothering you," Ignatias explained. "It seems I'm not the only one who plans to spoil you while on Whykeen."

Finding out that she was going to have Harquias's undivided attention went a long way to alleviating her disappointment that they weren't staying. When the two Talins were done speaking, Harquias hurried away without even looking at her.

"This way," Volormus said and continued to lead them to the nearest lift.

Instead of letting her get on the lift, Ignatias picked her up. Cradling her against his chest, he stepped on the lift. It was big enough for all three of them to share, but Volormus waited for the next lift plate to appear and followed.

Taking advantage of their close proximity, Kasi pressed her face to Ignatias's cheek. The familiar sweet scent of caramel filled her nose and silky bonding oil covered her lips. Ignatias's purr dipped lower into a sexual rumble before he remembered they were in public and pulled his face away from hers.

"Don't test my *stellian* like that, Pretty," he admonished with an amused rumble. "I don't think it will ever be strong enough to resist you."

"Sorry," she murmured, settling back down and rubbing her fingers over her lips to spread his oil evenly. The other humans said Talins got addicted to how the scent of a human changed when bonding oil soaked into the human's skin. That might be true, but she was getting addicted to Ignatias's at the same time.

Without jostling her at all, Ignatias stepped off the lift and waited for Volormus. Ignatias didn't set her down and she didn't ask him to. It felt good to be held and carried, especially because she was starting to get overwhelmed by all the noise and business of the station. She'd never been in a place so crowded before. Even if she only counted the bots, there were more of them than any gathering of people she'd ever attended on Wimol or Sorana.

How did anyone get used to the commotion and movement?

It was a relief when they stepped into a shop and the noise abruptly cut off as the doors slid shut behind them.

"The Ancestors have led you to my establishment so I can serve you," a Talin said as he rushed up to them. "I'm Olahenus of the family Orf within the clan Anize." He looked at Kasi and made a slight distressed rumble. "I can already see why you're here. Come this way, I'll show you everything we have in stock for this poor little pet."

"Now my *stellian* is being tested," she whispered to Ignatias. "You guys act like my work clothes are made of sandpaper. I swear, they're nicely worn-in and perfectly comfy!"

"The key words in your statement are *work clothes*," Ignatias pointed out. "Humans shouldn't be laboring. It shortens your lifespans and deprives you of the joyous part of your natures."

Kasi shook her head. "We are so much tougher than you think we are."

"I know humans can endure a great deal. Prime Son Searin bought a human named Sora, which is how your colony came to be called Sorana. She managed to survive slavery for ten years before she became Searin's beloved pet. Just because you can endure doesn't mean you should have to."

"My friend Lasha told me Sora is a sweetheart," Kasi said.

Ignatias made a brief rumble of surprise. "You have a friend that met the Prime Son's pet? That's uncommon. I thought I was fortunate to meet them while they were out shopping. This was when he'd only had her a short time, before he became so protective she's almost never seen out in public anymore."

"Lasha lives on your homeworld now with her Talin, Tamerin," Kasi explained. "They were trying to get support for a clinic on Talarian when Lasha bumped into Sora. Now they're friends and hang out together sometimes, and they'll even have dinner with Searin occasionally. Lasha sends me messages with all kinds of interesting information."

"I have so many questions," Ignatias stated as he set her down in the corner of the shop Olahenus led them to. "But most of all I'm impressed by the human's knowledge network. You might know more than I do about some things."

Kasi pretended to pat his arm reassuringly. "It's okay. I'll tell you when I think you should know something."

Ignatias's rumble of amusement was loud enough to fill the shop.

By the end of their time at the store, Kasi had to admit the stuff they'd bought was nice. Even nicer than her clothes back on Sorana.

The wraps in the shop were all in the same basic unisex shape as the ones at home. The difference was in the details. These had all kinds of elaborate frills. A few were even decorated with crystal beads all around the neckline and down the sleeves! Not even Henni, who had the most impressive wardrobe on Sorana, had anything like them.

"We design and make these ourselves," Olahenus explained. "The humans' simple minds are delighted with shiny things, so we thought they'd enjoy the way these crystals refracted light."

Kasi held up one in a gorgeous teal with double rows of complementary crystals around the neckline. "Can we get one of these for Zia? I know she'd really like it."

"Of course," Ignatias agreed.

"Thanks!" Kasi said, already picturing the delighted expression on her friend's face when she saw the decorated garment. Zia liked all things sparkly and would probably hang this in her domicile as a decoration when she wasn't wearing it.

Thinking about Zia made Kasi contemplate where she and Ignatias would go after they were done on Whykeen. Did Ignatias need to travel back to the Talin homeworld before they returned to Sorana? She really hoped they wouldn't need to leave Sorana permanently to live on Talarian. At least she already had a friend there, and it would be good to see Lasha again!

And there was still the question of who'd sabotaged Ignatias's ship! Kasi had deliberately avoided that topic, but they should really talk about it!

Anxiety roared to life inside her, tying her stomach in knots. She'd never been in a situation where someone was being targeted like this. Her mundane life on Wimol never prepared her for attempted murder. What if the mysterious person or people who wanted Ignatias dead decided to do it directly by coming at him with some kind of deadly weapon? She would be no help!

"Kasi?"

She focused on Olahenus to find everyone was looking at her. "I'm sorry, what?"

"It seems we've overwhelmed her with choices," Olahenus commented. "That happens sometimes."

Kasi looked down and realized that Olahenus had pulled a bunch of slippers off a nearby shelf and piled them on a small table for her to look at.

"I was just lost in thought for a moment," Kasi said, slinging the wrap for Zia over her shoulder and reaching for a pair of slippers.

Volormus sounded a concerned rumble. "Lost in thought. Is that like a memory episode? Is your past trauma bothering you?" He looked up at Ignatias. "There's medication that might help alleviate the symptoms. Perhaps I was wrong letting the two of you talk me out of visiting the healers first."

Kasi dropped the slippers and grabbed Volormus's hand before he unclipped his Ident. Volormus sounded a surprised rattle and went still.

"I wasn't having a memory episode. I was simply thinking about how much my friend will like the wrap," she explained. "Nothing more was happening."

"You're touching me," he said, his voice soft.

Kasi snatched her hand back. "Is that bad? Did I break a rule?"

"You must trust me very much to voluntarily touch me," Volormus said, sinking to his knees.

Kasi drew back a little, confused by Volormus's actions until he opened his arms and purred. Realizing he wanted a hug, Kasi grinned and stepped up to wrap her arms around the Talin's neck.

Behind her, Ignatias sounded an angry rattle. "You don't have to clutch everyone who offers you open arms."

Kasi looked over her shoulder and gave Ignatias a small frown. "Don't be jealous. I'm not going to pick another Talin over you, but everyone needs a hug sometimes."

While she spoke, Volormus wrapped his arms around her so loosely he was barely touching her. "You're a good little human," he murmured.

"You're a nice Talin," Kasi responded, not sure what else to say. Were all Talins touch starved? The anecdotal evidence was pointing to a yes!

Ignatias must have decided they'd hugged long enough because he pushed Volormus away from her and drew her into his arms. She wasn't upset; Volormus's smell was starting to give her a headache.

Instead of standing up, Volormus sat back on his heels, clasping his hands in front of him. "I'd like to buy you something, Kasi."

"As I've said, I have enough funds to pay for any item she wants," Ignatias said with another annoyed rattle.

Kasi petted his arm. "Calm down, Nace. He's trying to be nice to me, not insult you."

Ignatias stopped "Nace? Have you finally given me an affection name?"

"Yeah, I guess so. Is it okay?" she asked.

"It is perfect," he said with a purr. "Thank you, Pretty. I'm honored."

Kasi was about to tell him it really wasn't that big of a deal and nicknames could change or morph over time, but then something caught her eye.

Olahenus was holding up a silver belt with little dangling things all around it. It made a clear and pleasing sound as he held it out for her to see.

Pulling away from Ignatias, she cried out, "Bells!" and grabbed it. They tinkled cheerfully as she wrapped the belt around her waist and wiggled her hips. This was going to amp-up all her happy dances.

How great was this trip turning out to be!

CHAPTER 23

Ignatias

Ignatias expected Kasi to balk at the selection of collars at the second shop they visited on Whykeen. Once again, his little human surprised him by selecting several to test and choose from. None of them were of the traditional style, but they would still be recognizable as collars to any Talin.

"Are you sure this one isn't too expensive?" Kasi asked, holding up the one she seemed to be favoring. It was longer than most collars and had a bright dormin crystal on the locking mechanism.

"What a considerate pet!" Milous, the Talin helping them, commented. "Don't worry yourself. All collars are paid for by the station."

"I told you I didn't require the station funds," Ignatias reminded her.

Raising her gaze to his, Milous sounded a negative rattle. "This isn't about your wealth. It's a station requirement. There was a short while when quite a few newly bought humans were coming through here. That's when the fund began. The station director at the time also instituted the collar program as a way for us to gift the new pets."

"That's nice of the station," Kasi commented as she tried on the dormin collar again. The bright artificial lights in the shop made it sparkle. She tapped the crystal. "This is the same color as your eyes, Nace."

"Nace?" Milous asked.

"That's her affection name for me," he explained and wasn't surprised when Milous sounded an excited rattle.

"She already has an affection name for you? That's most excellent," she exclaimed.

"Yes, she only picked it a little while ago," he answered.

As he spoke, he saw Kasi roll her eyes, a human expression of amused annoyance. He didn't blame her. They'd basically had the same conversation several times and would probably have it more times as they met other Talins on the station.

For the first time, Ignatias saw how burdensome it could be to be a human among Talins. He'd always been so focused on getting one of his own he hadn't considered what their popularity meant for the individual pet. If Kasi wasn't so comfortable with meeting new people, she might be suffering from anxiety to the point of causing severe distress.

"Yup, I want this one," Kasi announced, setting the other collar back in the case Milous had brought out.

"It's a good choice," Milous complimented, then pointed at the locking mechanism hanging at the hollow of Kasi's throat. "If you would be so good as to press any of your digits to the back of the lock, it will program to you, Committee Citizen Ignatias."

Kasi frowned as Ignatias reached for the lock on the collar. He knew she didn't like this, but he'd seen her wear a collar back on Sorana when she was trying to pretend everything was being run according to Talin law.

She didn't protest but she also didn't look pleased as he pressed his second thumb to the underside of the mechanism until it gave a faint beep.

"There now, all done," Milous announced with an enthusiastic rattle. This was the last item they'd needed. There were three cargo-bots loaded down with all the items they'd purchased from both stores. It was more than he'd planned to buy, but it had been hard to stop selecting items as he saw them. At one point Kasi tried to put a few things back, but he'd snatched them away from her and added them to the purchase selection. He'd never felt so much joy from shopping as he did with Kasi.

"I'm glad I was here to see you properly outfitted, Kasi," Volormus said. "I wish I could spend more time with both of you, but I must resume my duties. You shouldn't have any trouble any longer. A station-wide announcement has gone out from the station director regarding Kasi. Talins can stop and look, but they aren't allowed to approach. Only you and Kasi can initiate an interaction."

Ignatias had heard of this being done before, but usually only when a member of the royal family or one of the Apogee Assembly was visiting. It was a shock that a single human could warrant such an order from the station director.

Volormus continued speaking. "I've already arranged a cabin for your stay here. After you told me what happened, I instructed the repair bay that your ship is top priority. They might be able to start as soon as the next work cycle, so you should expect a progress report by fourth or fifth mark tomorrow."

Ignatias sounded a surprised rattle. "I never expected to be pushed ahead in the queue."

"I'm not doing it for you," Volormus said. "A station is no place for a human. They need real sunshine and fresh air. I know some stations let owners keep their pets and even have areas designed for them to gather and play, but I don't approve. Humans haven't evolved to do well in space."

"Unless you can breathe in a vacuum, you haven't evolved for it either," Kasi muttered, but only loud enough for Ignatias to hear.

Stifling his rumble of amusement, he slapped his fist to his chest. "Thank you for your gift of time and skill."

"May the Ancestors guide us in all things," Volormus responded with a slap of his own. Looking down at Kasi, he went to his knees again and started to open his arms up for a hug. Ignatias got between them and rattled out a warning. "No."

Volormus got to his feet without sounding a single rattle or rumble. "Perhaps I could join the two of you for a meal before you leave the station."

"Perhaps," Ignatias said.

"Sure!" Kasi responded at the same time.

Volormus pointed at her. "All I heard was Kasi's affirmative response." Then he turned and strode quickly from the store.

Kasi pulled his attention back by sliding her hand in his. "You don't have any reason to worry about Volormus or anyone else. You're my Talin."

"She sounds like she owns you instead of the other way around!" Milous commented with an amused rumble.

He couldn't imagine life without Kasi, and if she was ever ripped from his life, there was no question he'd suffer a painful death. He was scent-bonded to her. Addicted to the way his bonding oil changed once it soaked into her hair and skin.

In a real way, Kasi did own him, and he had no regrets about it.

Their cabin was one in the area reserved for those staying for up to a solar as temporary labor on the station. That meant it was a bit larger than the shorter-term accommodations and boasted more amenities. At the most they'd only be here ten or so rotations, so he shouldn't have qualified for the nicer cabin. This had to be Volormus's doing.

"This is nice!" Kasi exclaimed as she explored the cabin. The three personal cargo-bots they'd rented stopped in the middle of the main room and waited patiently for instruction.

Kasi disappeared into a separate room. "Look at the size of our cleansing unit. It's huge!"

While Kasi examined every aspect of the cabin, Ignatias checked his Ident for information. He was being charged a pittance of the going rate. He could only assume the infamous station fund for pets was at play here. The station personnel running the fund must be desperate to spend it if they decided paying for a room was an appropriate expenditure.

Before he could send a request for information, there was a chime at the door. With Kasi safely in the bedroom area, he felt confident in opening the door without checking. Waiting on the other side was a food delivery bot.

The display indicated it was to be delivered to *Committee Citizen Ignatias & Human Pet Kasi*. He'd never seen *human pet* used as a title, but it didn't surprise him. The list of food was both expensive and fit for both humans and Talins. The display also indicated everything was paid for.

He was going to feel a lot better once they were on their own again. All these gifts were nice, but they also felt oppressive.

Stepping aside, he let the bot into the room. The thing wheeled over to the other carrier bots and settled down to wait for further instructions. Kasi came out of the bedroom to see the additional bot.

"You ordered food?" she asked.

"Another gift for us," he answered.

"Too bad we ate that big meal before leaving the Ever Prosperous III," Kasi said.

"The bot is designed to keep the food for several marks. We can eat it later without worry of it growing cold or becoming contaminated," he assured her.

"Great, because I want to use the cleansing room," she said and started digging through one of the cargo-bots. "It's huge and all ours!"

The communal cleansing rooms on the Ever Prosperous III had been cramped and in constant use because there were only four for the entire crew. He and Kasi were quick when using them. The limited availability and no cleansers for Kasi meant neither ever felt truly clean. Spending an extravagant amount of time in a large, private cleansing unit sounded like the height of luxury.

"I can't wait to try some of the products we bought." Kasi moved to another cargo-bot and started going through those purchases. All the boxes were marked with Talin labels that Kasi couldn't read.

"I think they're in this one," he said and reached for a package on a different bot. Opening it up, he showed Kasi the various bottles they'd bought for her hair and skin.

She grabbed the packages from him and then grasped his wrist and tugged him to follow her. "Join me. The cleaning room is big enough for both of us to fit and even move around."

He sounded an amorous rumble. "Will you let me bathe you?"

Kasi's smile curved up in a slow, sensual grin. "Only if I can do the same to you."

The thought of having Kasi's soapy hands all over him proved too much for his composure. Kasi gasped when he snatched her up, cradling her against his chest. Going around the bots would've taken too long so he vaulted over them. Kasi laughed loudly as he sprinted the short distance to the cleansing room.

"All surfaces set to warm," he ordered the room. The floor and walls heated to create a room warm enough to keep his perfect human comfortable.

Setting her down, he tugged off his belt and tossed it out of the still open cleansing room door. Then he pulled his pants off so fast they ripped a little at the waistband.

After he was naked, he reached for Kasi and growled, "Need you now!"

CHAPTER 24

Kasi

Ignatias's eagerness was both flattering and adorable. She winced when he carelessly tossed his belt and it bounced off a wall and out the door. She covered her mouth to keep from laughing when she heard his pants rip.

Then she saw the bulge under his flesh pouch and didn't feel like laughing any more. Suddenly her skin felt hot, and she wanted to touch him again. She wanted to feel his cock get hard and watch it emerge from his flesh pouch. Did anyone else have an emerging-mating shaft kink or was it just her?

Deciding to get naked before she lost herself in his body, she reached for the ties on her brand-new wrap. He didn't give her a chance to untie it. With a hungry growl, Ignatias came at her. He leaned over and slid his arms between her legs and lifted until her splayed thighs were resting on his forearms. He straightened up and put her back against one of the heated walls. Her wrap bunched around her waist as her thighs ended up on his shoulders.

"Ignatias!" she gasped. There was nothing to grab but his head and she didn't want to accidentally hurt him. "Put me down, I'm too heavy for this!"

"No!" he growled. "You're the perfect weight. Need to taste you!"

He pushed his head into her crotch. She felt his teeth graze her panties and then he whipped his head back. There was tugging and the sound of ripping clothing. She felt the flimsy, soft garment drop away, and then his breath was on the curls at the apex of her legs.

"Did…did you just tear my panties off?" she whispered, both stunned and turned on by his controlled violence.

He didn't answer, probably because he was too busy burying his face between her legs. Moving his head side to side, he opened her labia to his mouth, then buried his tongue in her pussy.

"Nace!" she cried out. Sparks of pleasure shot up her spine, making her squirm against his face.

"I'll never get enough of your taste," he said, voice muffled. Then he went back to moving his tongue deep inside her, as if she was a delicious exotic meal.

How could something feel wonderful but horrible at the same time? It made her want to flail and scream but also hold his head in place and press him harder against her.

He pulled his head away to speak. "Say you're mine, Pretty. Say it!"

"I'm yours," she gasped. "Please, I need to come."

"Again," he ordered, then teased her by lightly stroking his tongue over her weeping pussy and throbbing clit. "Say it again."

"I'm yours!" she screamed, her hands scrabbling against the smooth wall over her head. She wanted to cling to something, but there was nothing for her to grab. She didn't think it was possible to feel more pleasure than the first time they'd had sex, but she was wrong. The way he was holding her in the air with startling ease made her feel small and petite. His adoration of her flesh made her feel desired.

His demand for obedience made her feel hot!

"Again!

"I'm yours," she repeated. "Your human. Your Kasi. Entirely yours."

His throbbing rumbling was loud in the small room. "I'm yours as well. Your Talin. Your Ignatias. All of me will always belong to all of you."

It was romantic and she was going to make him repeat those words later, but right now, she really needed him to move that tongue!

"Please lick me," she begged.

"Anything my human wants," he agreed. After another few long deep strokes into her, he moved his mouth up to her needy clit. He sucked the nub into his mouth and Kasi fell apart. Her body arched back against her will, and her legs tightened over Ignatias's shoulders. She might have screamed, but she wasn't sure.

Ignatias kept sucking on her, and the waves of pleasure continued crashing through her, making her brain fizzle.

It wasn't until she sobbed from being too sensitive that Ignatias stopped. Like a puppet with its strings cut, she sagged forward.

"You're a perfect human," he murmured as he lowered both of them to the warmed floor. "A gorgeous human. My human."

She blinked up at him as he laid her on the smooth ground. He ran his extended claws over the front of her wrap, then hooked them in and pulled in opposite directions. The garment was no match and ripped easily. Thankfully she'd decided to go without a bra today and use the tank-top like binding garment that was more common. The way he was acting, she knew he would never have given her time to remove the hard to find item.

He pulled in a sharp breath as her breasts spilled free of the torn fabric. "Splendid," he whispered, and dropped his head down to nuzzle her chest.

The orgasm had been so powerful it left her dazed and limp. She didn't think she could move any of her limbs. The self-warming surface of the floor felt good against her back and Ignatias's touches were wonderful. She was content to lie there and let him nuzzle, stroke, lick, and kiss her until he was ready to come.

It turned out he wasn't going to let her get away with not participating.

"I'm going to feast on you every rotation," he said as he kissed from one breast to the other. "Your taste sustains me."

She thought about trying to speak. Saying something sexy or romantic in response to his erotic proclamations, but her pleasure-soaked brain couldn't form words yet.

"I'll run my tongue over every part of you," he continued, then licked the underside of her breast. "Kiss your delicate skin and worship all of you."

As he talked, he licked and kissed a circuitous path down her body. Occasionally he'd throw in a gentle nip that made her skin come alive. His words and actions started to bring her back. She shivered from his touches and moaned when he paired gentle licks with harsher nips and bites.

"I'll take every opportunity I'm given to venerate your body." His hands roamed over her, kneading and massaging her flesh. Tension was coming back to her muscles, and her pussy was starting to weep again. Widening her legs, she tried to wrap them around his torso and draw him down onto top of her.

Reaching back, he captured her ankles and drew her legs up and apart, exposing her sex to him. His eyes fixed on the most intimate part of her, as if taking in a painfully beautiful work of art.

"This flower tastes as good as it smells," he murmured. "Our culture treats sex like a transaction. It's a race to orgasm, and often the female partner will leave the male in need once she's climaxed. It's meant as a service to each other, not a way to grow close. With you, it's a form of worship. You make me feel transcendent."

It wasn't every day that someone said having sex with you was similar to a religious experience. It was flattering and a little intimidating. It was especially weird because her legs were still spread wide, exposing her to his intense gaze.

"This is what it's like to be with someone who loves you," she whispered. "Now, can we do something else besides talk?"

His head snapped up to meet her gaze.

"Love," he said, voice low and powerful. "Yes, you love me. You'll never regret this. I will treasure you always."

Did she find the only guy who turned poetic during sex instead of after? She wanted to scream at him to get on with it but didn't want to hurt his feelings. Thankfully, he finally took the initiative.

His cock was jutting out with liquid dripping from the head. Letting go of one of her legs, he palmed his dick, stroking it a few times. "I'm going to bury myself deep inside you and fill you with my seed. I'm going to mark you as mine."

"Yes!" she breathed, lifting her hips a little in invitation. "Please!"

He fitted the head of his cock to her entrance, but didn't thrust in. Slowly easing forward, he moved at a glacial pace. Starting to feel half crazed, Kasi tried to wrap her free leg around him.

"No," he growled, grabbing her ankle and forcing her leg into the same position he still held the other one in. His dominant attitude made heat rock through her body. "You'll wait for me like a good human."

Closing her eyes, she arched her back and moaned. He moved himself inside her, one slow millimeter at a time. It was delicious torture.

He stretched and filled her, never stopping his sexy rumble. It vibrated into every place their bodies met, and when he was fully inside her, his rumble hit deep and hard. She shook, on the brink of another orgasm.

"Wait!" he ordered.

"I can't," she gasped. "I…oh!"

He started moving, thrusting in and out of her at a measured pace. The strength of the vibrations would ebb and flow with his movements, never quite providing enough to push her over the edge.

"Harder," she begged. "I need you to pound into me."

Ignoring her pleading, he let go of her legs so he could support his upper body with his arms on either side of her. He lowered his head and captured her mouth in his. The kiss grounded her even as his thrusting kept taking her to the brink and back.

She wrapped her legs around his waist and tried to hold him close so she could grind into him. He started moving in small little thrusts that dragged the base of his giant cock against her clit. His rumbles become more intense.

Tension gripped her body. She was so close!

"I can feel you on the brink, my human," he whispered against her mouth. They were both panting now. "You're gripping my mating shaft as if you want to draw it further inside your body."

She couldn't talk. She could barely breathe. Whimpering, she reached up and cupped his cheeks in her hands. Bonding oil coated the sides of his face, and under her fingers, more flowed from his scent glands. She stroked her fingers over the glands, making him shudder and moan.

The scent of caramel got stronger as the oil coated and warmed her fingers. She spoke without thinking, her words barely audible over her harsh breathing.

"I want you to rub this on my pussy next time," she demanded. "It's warm, sweet, and silky. I want it to mix with my slick so you taste us both when you lick me."

He must have liked the idea because he jerked and then moaned, "Yes!"

His thrusts grew erratic, and his frantic movements pushed her over the edge. Her vision whited out as the most powerful orgasm of her life slammed into her.

"You're squeezing me tight," he cried out. "I can't control myself any longer."

No sooner had he said those words than she felt herself flooded with heat. He filled her with so much cum it squished out the sides as he thrust. The dirty sound and feel of it triggered a smaller second orgasm in her. Or maybe it was a continuation of the earlier one. It didn't matter because her heart was trying to beat out of her chest.

Letting go of his face, Kasi wrapped her arms around his neck and held tight. She clung to him with her arms and legs as they both shook and shuddered through their pleasure.

She couldn't tell how long they stayed with her limbs locked around him and him firmly locked inside her. Could they shower like this, she wondered feverishly.

"I should bathe you," he mumbled but didn't try to move.

"We've got plenty of time to get to that," she murmured. "I don't want to separate yet."

"Neither do I," he admitted.

They went silent, and Kasi's limbs started to relax as contented fatigue took over. She let go of him so her arms fell to her sides. She untwined her legs and let them relax down to the floor, thighs still widely parted around Ignatias's hips. "We might need to take a nap before bathing."

Slowly, as if not to startle her, he levered his shoulders up with his weight on his hands. "You remain relaxed. I'll bathe you."

She blinked up at him lazily. "Can we snuggle together and take a nap afterward?"

"Of course," Ignatias agreed as he gently withdrew himself from inside her and sat back, his gaze looking over her wrecked body. "Nothing would please me more."

Kasi let her eyes fall closed as Ignatias got to his feet and gathered bottles of cleansers and some cleaning cloths, then ordered the room to start up the water. She'd never felt so pampered in her entire life. Everyone should have a Talin of their own.

CHAPTER 25

Kasi

Waking up cuddled against Ignatias was the way Kasi wanted to start every morning.

Or early afternoon?

Blearily she looked at the display on the wall near the bed and tried to work out what time it was on Sorana. Someone told her that all Talin stations and ships kept the same hours as their homeworld, but for obvious reasons, colonies couldn't do that. The Ever Prosperous III had kept a constant shift schedule which meant there were no day/night cycles, only shift changes. She and Ignatias kept the same sleeping schedule she had on Sorana but that would need to change while they were on Whykeen.

Palforma told her that Sorana's days were shorter and the solar year longer than on Talarian, except they kept all the same days of observance. The first time she'd been awoken in the middle of the night by a Somber Reflection alarm, the tri-yearly celebration of the Ancestors, Kasi had learned to deactivate all the Talin-installed default alarms in her domicile.

This time an alarm hadn't woken her. It was her body's readiness to get up that pushed her from sleep. It took her three times of counting in her head, but she worked out that it was probably early evening on Sorana but late morning here on Whykeen. She was going to have some serious trouble adjusting back to Sorana time once they got home.

"Are you ready to start the day?" Ignatias asked, stroking a hand down her back. She was on her side, lying half on top of him. She'd lifted her head to look at the display but lowered back down to rest on his chest, her new collar making a slight clicking sound as it came in contact with his keratin plating. He was a hard pillow but warm.

"I think so," she answered. Then she thought of something and sat up, tapping her hands on Ignatias's chest with excitement. "Are we visiting Harquias and the green area today?"

Sounding a rumble of amusement, Ignatias captured her hands in his. "Yes but let me contact Botanical Specialist Harquias and verify the time she and Volormus arranged."

"Yeah, you should do that," she agreed, wide awake and eager to start the day now.

Tugging her hand free, she moved off the bed. Because she wasn't used to being naked, she tugged off one of the many soft blankets from the bed and wrapped it around her shoulders like a cape. Feeling better, she hunted for Ignatias's Ident. It didn't take her long, and by the time she returned, he was standing next to the bed and stretching. She took a moment to admire his powerful body before shoving the Ident at him.

"Here," she said. "Make sure she knows it's fine if she can't show us around. I don't want to mess up her schedule or anything. We could always explore the area by ourselves. I'm sure there must be a guide to all the plants on the station's Unibase or something."

"I knew you found plants interesting," he commented as he accepted the Ident and started tapping on it, "but this level of eagerness marks a high degree of fascination instead of simple curiosity."

"Remember that field you kidnapped me from?" she asked, glancing over to the main room of their cabin. She needed to go through some of the purchases from yesterday to find a clean, undamaged wrap to wear. But before she did that, she wanted to make sure Ignatias got hold of Harquias.

"How could I forget," he grumbled without looking up from the Ident.

"I know you don't approve, but you have to understand, that was my field," she said, then winced when she thought about her precious plants.

Ignatias looked up in time to see her wince. "Are you in pain?"

"I'm fine, but my poor plants are probably all suffering," she said with a sad smile and shake of her head. "I left instructions, but I doubt anyone is going to care enough to monitor the soil balances or adjust the agricultural-bots. I'm probably going to have to start from scratch when we get back."

Ignatias was silent for a moment, making it impossible for her to figure out what he was feeling. At least his body wasn't tense, so he probably wasn't upset.

"You don't have to labor," he finally said. "But you choose to anyway."

"I don't really see it as laboring," she explained. "It's fun, not work. There's nothing better than getting everything right and seeing your plants produce food, especially something that probably hasn't grown in hundreds of years!"

He sounded a rumble comprehension. "It gives you great satisfaction and a sense of purpose. I read that humans don't need those things, but I can see the literature was wrong. As it was with many facts."

Kasi snorted out a laugh. "Are you really that shocked?"

"Not any longer," he admitted with an amused rumble. His Ident pinged, and after reading something off it, he sounded one of his happy rumbles. "The agreement with

Volormus is still in effect. Harquias is eager for our visit. We need to hurry, I didn't realize how close the time was."

"Give me a few minutes, and I'll be dressed and ready," Kasi replied, sweeping the trailing end of her blanket-cape out of the way so she could march into the main area of their cabin and start looking through packages. It didn't take her long to find the large container of wraps they'd purchased and the matching slippers. She'd tried to argue about the shoes, but Ignatias insisted that she needed a variety because "having colorful choices makes humans happy."

If she was being honest with herself, she was enjoying taking a bit of time to pick out what she'd wear. As much as she wanted to get back to Sorana and her fields, she was also determined to enjoy her vacation with Ignatias.

She picked out a light blue wrap with matching slippers and then put on the belt with the bells. Before the belt, she hadn't realized how much she enjoyed the sound, but now she wanted to wear it all the time. Even when she worked in her fields!

"I should feed you first," Ignatias commented as he joined her in the main room, rubbing a hand roughly over his head. He was wearing the same pants from yesterday, his belt holding them together where he'd ripped them while taking them off.

"I'm not hungry yet, maybe later," she responded, eyeing his pants. "Did we leave all your clothes back on Sorana?"

"I have other pants on my ship, but I can't access it while it's in the repair bay," he explained. "I was so focused on getting you on board the Ever Prosperous III that I neglected to pack items for myself."

Guilt hit Kasi hard. She'd been enjoying the shopping but didn't think once about Ignatias's needs. "We can buy you stuff today. I saw some really nice looking pants and belts with matching pouches at one of the stores we passed by yesterday." Getting excited, she wiggled her hips. "Maybe we could find you a belt with bells too. We could match!"

Ignatias sounded a rumble of amusement and draped an arm over her shoulders to guide her out of the room. "Perhaps later. You wouldn't want to be late to meet Harquias, would you?"

"I'll hold you to the shopping!" Kasi laughed, knowing a distraction attempt when she heard it.

It took longer than Kasi liked to get down to the first floor. Everyone stared as they went by, but no one tried to approach. A few called out and offered candy, but she waved and called back that they were meeting someone. One male wanted to give her the candy so badly he tossed it to her with a little too much force. It would have hit her in the eye if Ignatias hadn't caught it midair.

"Be careful, humans are delicate and easily damaged," Ignatias admonished with a growl, and the offending Talin mumbled an apology as he ducked his head and hurried off.

She tried to get Ignatias to let her take one of the lift platforms alone, but he refused. It was a little disconcerting how many Talins around them stopped what they were doing to watch her and Ignatias. It was eerie.

Ignatias tried to get her to eat at one of the dining establishments, but she adamantly refused. She didn't want to waste time sitting down for a meal when there were so many interesting plants waiting for her!

They settled on a piece of flatbread covered in the vegetable smothered gravy Talins had at every meal. Kasi ate it quickly while they walked, much to Ignatias's disapproval.

"You accidentally aspirated on your food while sitting," he reminded. "I worry you'll do the same or worse while trying to eat and walk at the same time."

She rolled her eyes and swallowed another bite before answering. "That was a rare thing. I promise. Every human who grew up on Wimol learned to walk and eat at the same time. I think some of us learned to walk and sleep!" Ignatias didn't sound any amused rumbles at her joke. Hopefully someday he'd realize how funny she was.

She was about to explain her comment when Ignatias moved with lightning speed. Skittering to the side, she watched him grab the arm of a Talin, twist it behind her back, and press her hard into a nearby wall.

"What do you think you're doing?" he barked.

"I only wanted to touch her mane," the Talin said with an anxious rumble. "I've never been so close to a human before, and I wanted to know if her mane was as soft as it looked."

Kasi dumped the last of her meal into a nearby waste receptacle and rushed up to the two of them. Feeling bad for the woman, she tugged at Ignatias's arm. "You can let go; she didn't mean any harm."

"She was going to touch you," he growled. "She doesn't get to touch what is mine."

Hearing him say *mine* in such a deep, commanding tone shouldn't have made her go hot all over while they were in public. No, bad Kasi, this was no time to be thinking about sex. Forcing herself to focus on the issue, she stopped tugging at Ignatias's arm. Force wasn't going to move him. She needed to re-center him.

"Easy," she murmured, petting his bicep. "I'm right here. No one is going to take me away."

By now, several people had stopped and were asking if she was hurt or if they needed to call the station's law keepers. He wasn't responding to any of them, and Kasi was worried he might be experiencing another flashback. Then he moved.

Releasing the woman, he pivoted and grabbed Kasi up in his arms.

"Ignatias?"

"I need a moment," he confessed, his voice pitched so only she could hear him.

"Did you cause this fuss, Ormantus?" one of the bystanders asked. "You've been warned about your lack of *stellian* and impulsive behavior before."

To Kasi's relief, she and Ignatias were mostly ignored as everyone focused on Ormantus. Kasi felt bad for the woman as several Talins moved Ormantus away while loudly vocalizing their disapproval. She couldn't object because she had to deal with several other Talins who were trying to get Ignatias to take her to the healers and not listening to her at all.

Her fun day was turning into a disaster! It was a relief when she saw a familiar face appear.

"Harquias!" Kasi shouted, probably too loudly for how close her mouth was to Ignatias's earhole. He didn't flinch or sound an annoyed rattle, only turned a little.

"I heard the commotion and thought I'd check," the botanist explained. The others made way for her, probably because Kasi had called out her name.

"Ormantus was acting out again," someone said. "How does the human know you, Harquias?"

"She's going to show me all the plants!" Kasi announced.

There was a general wave of purring from the gathered Talins as voices murmured around her.

"How cute!"

"Lucky Harquias. I wish the human found inner-engine balancing systems interesting."

"I've heard humans like to cut flowers from plants and bring them inside domiciles. Such a quaint idea!"

"Don't they realize the bloom isn't the entire plant? They must be heartbroken when it dies!"

"Even if Harquias would let her cut off the flowers, the human is going to be disappointed. Nothing is blooming right now."

"But some of the plants have decorative leaves, maybe she'll be content with that?"

Harquias stepped up close, ignoring everyone's commentary. "It seems Ormantus has been dealt with. If you are well enough to continue, we can begin our tour. Unless Kasi needs to isolate or see the healer?"

Kasi wasn't going to miss a tour of the green space! "I'm great, and if I don't get to see all the plants I'll probably get really upset."

She could tell Ignatias understood her threat because he sounded an affirmative rattle. "I might have overreacted to Ormantus trying to touch my human. We had a difficult moment when we first arrived, and it colored my reaction."

"Perfectly understandable," Harquias assured him. "Caution is warranted because humans are stolen all the time. They're also so delicate they can feel physical agony from emotional pain. Any distress could cause irreparable harm, so vigilance is always the best course."

"You make valid points," Ignatias agreed. Kasi could feel some of the tension leaving his body as he talked to Harquias. He was probably relieved that no one was noting his actions as odd. "As Kasi said, she's fine, so we'll follow you to the green space."

The crowd moved out of the way as Harquias led them the short distance to the beginning of the green space that occupied most of the first floor. She heard a few people talking about reporting Ormantus to a supervisor. All of that for trying to touch her hair! It was rude but not life threatening.

Their treatment of Ormantus was another example of the strict nature of Talin society. It made the often uptight Talins on Sorana seem like wild heathens in comparison. The next time they were alone, Kasi was going to praise Ignatias for letting go of his cultural taboos to allow her in.

Soon they were surrounded by plants and Kasi was thoroughly distracted. She wiggled in Ignatias's arms until he set her down with a grumpy, annoyed rattle. She wanted her hands free to touch everything, so when Ignatias tried to hold her hand, she pulled away from him.

It was only when he froze that she realized he'd seen the move as rejection.

"I want to feel the plants," she explained quickly as Harquias had a cargo-bot crouch down next to one of the planters. Grabbing his hand, she tucked it into the back of her belt. "There, you can keep hold of me, and I can still have my hands free."

He sounded a brief, purring rumble before going silent as Harquias pointed to the crouching cargo-bot.

"You can stand on this to see better."

Kasi didn't have to be told twice. She jumped onto the cargo-bot's back, it was only knee high, and peered into the planter. Harquias launched into a description of the plants, and to Kasi's delight, she didn't dumb down her descriptions at all.

This was going to be everything she'd hoped for!

CHAPTER 26

Ignatias

"Does that mean the one with the red-tipped leaves reproduces with heterogenesis?" Kasi asked.

For the most part, Ignatias hadn't been paying attention to what the women were talking about. Botany was one of the many general education courses in cresh curriculum, but he'd never been interested. Once he passed his exams, he'd let the information be forgotten. Kasi's use of a specialized term he vaguely remembered pulled his attention into the conversation.

"That is correct," Harquias answered. "The official name for this plant is Umarg Deltorn Um, but most refer to it as Blood Dipped, for obvious reasons."

"That red is pretty bloody looking," Kasi agreed. "Is it safe for me to touch?"

"I checked on everything I'm growing and found only one plant you shouldn't get close to. We'll skip that planter so you're free to touch anything we talk about."

Kasi carefully stroked one of the small, red-tipped leaves of the Blood Dipped plant in front of her. "It's warmer than I thought it would be."

"This plant uses heat to attract prey to support the n-Um under them," Harquias explained. She pulled a few branches aside to show the sticky juvenile plants. "Those are n-Um. Blood Dipped have three alternating generations: n-Um, n1-Um, and n2-Um. Often n-Um and n1-Um will grow together, and when they die back, n2-Um will flourish. Their n-Um phase is strictly fed by insects while the rest of their phases use photosynthesis."

"That's fascinating!" Kasi said, leaning in closer to peer at the long, thin strands at the base of the plant. Ignatias had no clue what any of it meant, but he did rumble with amusement when Kasi touched one of the strands and wrinkled her nose in distaste.

"Ew, sticky! I see how they catch the insects." Harquias was ready for that reaction because she was holding out a damp cleansing cloth even before Kasi finished touching the plant. Kasi took it with a grateful smile. "Thanks!"

"Our ancient Ancestors used the sticky substance covering the n-Um to waterproof our tents and bags against rain. Every plant in here had a use in our past. That was my specialty during my studies, practical plant use of our Ancestors."

"I want to know them all," Kasi insisted and tried to hand the cloth back to Harquias.

The Talin sounded a negative rattle. "You should keep that. You'll probably soil your fingers and hands repeatedly as we explore."

Kasi shrugged and tucked it in her belt. "Do they spore or use some other method?"

The question launched Harquias into a long and technical explanation of the plant's reproductive methods and life cycle. Ignatias was lost after the second sentence, but Kasi asked a complicated question the moment Harquias paused.

When Kasi told him she liked to grow things, he dismissed her. He hadn't thought she was lying because it was obvious she enjoyed mucking around in the dirt. He had assumed her interest was superficial.

As the two women talked with a level of understanding that would've been appropriate in a high-level academic setting, Ignatias was forced to reassess his estimation of Kasi. This human wasn't simply interested in plants, she was an expert!

The two women climbed into the massive planter so Kasi could closely examine a yellowish fungus that looked like something that would grow on food left unattended for too long.

Unwilling to let go of Kasi, Ignatias climbed into the planter with them. He was forced to duck to keep from hitting his head on the low branches of the tree planted in the center.

"Give me a moment and I can show you the bioluminescent aspect of this fungus," Harquias said. "Please remain here. I'll be right back."

Harquias easily jumped down from the planter and disappeared. Kasi squatted and put her face close to where the tree's trunk disappeared into the dirt.

"Did you attend lectures on botany when you lived on Wimol?" Ignatias asked.

Kasi snorted out a laugh but didn't look away from the dirt. "There was only one educational institute for the entire hemisphere we lived on and only Ugarian's were allowed to go there. Wimol was about producing food, not scholars."

Her answer only bewildered him further. "Then how do you know so much?"

Standing up, Kasi looked up at him with raised eyebrows. "I can read, can't I? One of the good things about Wimol was they had a free Unibase. As long as I had an information square sophisticated enough to access it, I could read anything I wanted to, so I read about plants."

"There was no other entertainment available?" Ignatias asked.

Kasi shook her head. "We had a limited library of Old Earth media. There's only so many times you can watch the same vids or read the same book. Ugarian's produce some great entertainment vids, but they can be expensive to buy or rent. All of it leads to the same thing, reading during evening downtime. Besides, it was fun to learn about plants I didn't think I'd ever get to see or grow. It's probably like reading about places you want to visit but can't."

"You're a human of rare intelligence, Pretty." He expected her to react with pleasure at his compliment, but she scowled instead.

"We are not dumb!" she hissed, poking him in the chest with a single finger.

Ignatias sounded a rattle of surprise. "I said you were intelligent, not stupid! Why are you upset?"

"You said I was smart but implied all the other humans were stupid," Kasi explained. "That's not nice. I know we have a reputation among Talins as a low-intelligence species, but I expect better of you, Ignatias."

Her words were like a physical blow. Not only was she upset, but what she said was true. The short time he'd spent on Sorana revealed humans doing many difficult and highly-skilled tasks, and still he harbored the belief that Kasi was an anomaly among them.

"I'm sorry I spoke poorly of human intelligence. That was unfair of me. You are still prettier than any other human though," he said defensively. "And I will not be persuaded differently!"

To his surprise Kasi didn't get angry at his words. The corners of her mouth curved up and her eyes twinkled with happiness. "That's acceptable."

Humans could be such contrary creatures! He refrained from pointing that out, only made a note to himself that he could call her prettier than everyone else but not smarter.

Suddenly artfully hidden lights in the planter all shone far brighter, making Kasi blink then shut her eyes and sway a little. He let go of her belt to wrap his arms around her. Before he could move her out of the planter, Harquias was back, her Ident clutched in her hand.

"Is the little human well?" she asked.

"The artificial lights suddenly got brighter, and I think they hurt her eyes," Ignatias explained.

"That's my fault," Harquias said, sounding a worried rumble. "I had to disconnect this planter from the main timer circuit so it would cycle independently. I didn't think to warn you."

"I'm fine," Kasi said, slitting her eyes open. "But it's going to take me a little bit to get used to this light."

"It will dim in a few submarks," Harquias told her. "Perhaps keep your eyes closed until then."

Kasi was already shutting them again. "Sure. I noticed the fungus is imbued in the soil but only around the trunk. Does that have anything to do with its development, or is that a byproduct of living on the tree?"

"That is an excellent observation," Harquias exclaimed as the light began to dim. By the time she finished explaining the complex symbiotic relationship between the fungus and the tree, the light in the planter had gone completely dark. "There, now you can open your eyes."

Ignatias watched the fungus start to glow a soft pink. It was a familiar sight. There had been a small area of the same trees at the cresh where he was raised. Their pink light reminded him of warm summer evenings when the children were allowed to remain outside until after nightfall.

Normally he'd try to push that kind of memory away for fear of triggering a memory episode. Being with Kasi made him feel strong enough to embrace it. He let the images from his childhood float into his consciousness. He even heard Darsinum's voice telling him all about how the pink glowing trees were gateways to a land full of giants.

Nothing bad happened to him as these memories unfolded. Kasi and Harquias talked, and he let himself get lost in things he'd been afraid to remember. Tension left his neck and shoulders. Some of Darsinum's stories that he thought were long forgotten surfaced, and he decided he could tell Kasi about them later. It felt like he was getting pieces of himself back.

This was all because of his human. She was a gift that he would never stop being thankful for.

Halfway through the green space, Ignatias realized one of the items he should've bought Kasi was an information square small enough for her to carry around. She kept expressing disappointment that she couldn't take notes or capture images.

Not only should he buy her a small, easy-to-carry information square, but also a nice big one so she could watch any entertainment vid she wanted. Whykeen was a diverse enough station that they probably had a stockpile of vids from other species. They might even have some Ugarian soap operas she hadn't seen yet.

She'd probably object to any more purchases, but he was determined. Kasi deserved to have anything and everything that made her happy!

"Can I take a clipping from this one too?" Kasi asked.

Harquias's answer was predictable. "Of course! Let me clip off a few stems from the base and package them for travel."

The cargo-bot used as a stepstool earlier was now following them around, its back piled high with bags of seeds, plant growth formula samples, carefully packed clippings, and several small specialty tester units. Ignatias wasn't sure what they tested, but it had to have something to do with plants.

As he followed Kasi and Harquias from plant to plant, he worked hard on not looking up. The first balcony wasn't far above them, and they'd attracted a crowd of Talins, contentedly watching Kasi. There was a constant buzz of conversation from the crowd, and every time Kasi moved under any of them, there were loud comforting rumbles.

Among Talins, having human pets was always framed as a rewarding hobby, but it was clear humans had become far more important to Talin culture than anyone wanted to admit. These individuals were all spending valuable time doing nothing more than viewing a human at a distance. They couldn't even interact with her in a meaningful way, but still they lingered.

Something colorful caught his eyes. Looking up and to his right, he watched something small flutter down from the balcony above. Before it could hit the ground, he captured it. Opening his fist, he found a piece of insulation used for engine or weapons compartments. This type of insulation was a final, thin layer that was often painted over in more muted tones to cover the bright red of the product's default color.

There was no reason it would be out here. Even more strange was the fact that it had obviously deliberately been cut into this small shape with scalloped edges.

"What's going on?" Kasi asked, drawing his attention away from the bit of insulation in his hand. Following her gaze, he saw more of the small, carefully cut, bright red bits of insulation raining down on them in gentle fluttering waves!

"Blooms for the human!" someone shouted from the balcony. Following the voice, Ignatias saw the source of the red insulation flowers. A pair of female Talins were holding a bag between them and taking turns grabbing handfuls of "flowers" and tossing them out.

Kasi laughed in delight and started plucking them out of the air. "They're beautiful!"

The Talins throwing them sounded loud rattles of excitement while one of them shouted down, "Harquias had no flowers to give you, so we decided to fix that!"

Harquias sounded a rumble of amusement. "Thank you for adding blooms to my green space, but I expect both of you to come down here and clean up after the human leaves!"

"Can I keep some of them?" Kasi asked, her cupped hands overflowing with insulation flowers.

"You can keep as many as you like," Ignatias assured her.

"I need enough to make a bouquet!" Kasi announced and thrust her handful at him so she could gather more. "These are going to look so pretty when I secure them to bare twigs. I want to put them all over my domicile back home."

By now it had stopped raining flowers and the two Talins were leaning far over the balcony's edge to watch Kasi gather them up. Because the two women were almost directly above them, he could hear them talking to each other. They were overjoyed at Kasi's response to their gift and wondering if they should cut more insulation flowers to have on hand the next time a human visited.

No Talin would ever think it was a worthwhile use of the time to cut stylized flowers out of red insulation except in the case of amusing a human. Humans let Talins do and feel all kinds of things they weren't allowed. It was adorable!

"Here is a bag," Harquias offered, holding open an empty seed bag and pulling Ignatias out of his thoughts.

Ignatias poured the flowers in his hands into the bag and then Harquias offered it to Kasi. After emptying her handful of flowers in the bag, she took it from Harquias and started scooping them up off the ground. He and Harquias helped and soon the bag was full. Activating the seal at the top, Kasi carefully tucked the bag on the back of the cargo-bot.

Leaning over, he put his mouth to Kasi's ear. "You are the bright flower in my life."

Smiling, she turned and jumped at him, wrapping her arms around his neck and hugging him tightly. "Remember that when I do something you don't like."

Her words forced a loud amused rumble out of him as he embraced her.

CHAPTER 27

Ignatias

With yet another personal cargo-bot following them, he and Kasi made their way back to the cabin. Kasi had amassed more items in two rotations than he'd gathered in several solars. He decided it was only fitting because he'd always been able to purchase anything he wanted, and she'd rarely ever had the opportunity to buy anything.

Besides, he got a lot more joy out of getting things for Kasi than he'd ever felt selecting something for his own use. Although she seemed to enjoy shopping for him earlier.

As if reading his mind, Kasi flicked the bell on his new belt pouch while they walked down the now familiar hall to their cabin. "This has a nice sound, but I still wish you'd bought that belt that matched mine."

The idea of wearing something as attention grabbing as Kasi's belt went against his years of military training and his own minimalist sense of style. He'd given in on the decorative belt pouch because it delighted Kasi, not because he was a fan of bells.

"This is enough," he said as her bells jingled musically while they walked. He would've thought all the different bells would make a discordant sound, but Kasi walked with such grace she made them chime melodically. It still shocked him that she thought herself ugly when she was everything beautiful and elegant.

He looked forward to spending the rest of their lives convincing her of her magnificence. When they got back to the room, he should strip her down and point out everything about her that he adored. That would be every inch of her, and it could take many marks to complete the task. He couldn't think of a better way to spend the time.

"Are we in a rush?" Kasi asked.

Her question made him realize he'd started walking faster. He slowed his pace. "Sorry, I'm eager to be back in our cabin."

Kasi gave him a shy grin. "After spending so much time in the green area, we should probably use the cleansing unit again."

He sounded an excited rattle. "Yes, that's a most excellent idea!"

She chuckled and her bells started to ring more quickly as she took a few running strides before tugging at his arm. "Suddenly I'm in a rush. Hurry up!"

With a playful growl, he let go of her hand and scooped her up in his arms. There was no one in the hall to see him sprint to their cabin. The cargo-bot's metallic tip-tap sounds got faster as it worked to keep up. They were designed to carry heavy loads and avoid pedestrians, not move quickly.

He was forced to pause at the door of their cabin to let the cargo-bot catch up. Once he opened the door, it moved to stand with the other three in the room and lowered to a waiting position.

When he'd checked the rental agreement for the first three cargo-bots he'd found that they were assigned to him until he left the station with only one rotation being charged. Yet another example of the station's largess where Kasi was concerned. This bot would probably be the same. If things kept going as they were, there would be an entire parade of cargo-bots following them to his ship when it was finally repaired and they could leave.

Giving the bot a friendly pat on the small control box on the side of its body as she passed, Kasi headed to the cleansing room. He was right behind her when the cabin door chimed.

Kasi paused and looked at the door. "Do you think that's Volormus?"

Before he could answer, the door chimed repeatedly, as if someone wouldn't remove their hand from the entrance request on the door's outside display.

"Someone's impatient," Kasi commented with a laugh as she hurried over to the door. He snatched her up as she tried to pass him.

"This isn't Sorana or Wimol," he admonished, setting her down with him between her and the door. "There are dangers here that you've never faced before."

"There are only Talins on this station," she scoffed. "You guys are the most rule-following species I've ever met. There's no danger here, especially after the station director told everyone to give me space."

Ignatias sounded a negative rattle as the door chimed again. "You're naive to what lengths a Talin will go to for a human. Human thievery is one of the most common crimes right now. You are a highly valued commodity among us, Kasi."

Kasi's brows drew together. "That's so dumb. You guys all need affection lessons, that's all. When I hugged Solmance you'd have thought she'd never experienced it before. And I barely hugged Volormus and he was thrilled. You do realize you guys could," she pretended to look around as if someone might be listening to them. Then she leaned in close and whispered loudly, "Hug each other, right?"

Ignatias wanted to be amused by her antics, but the topic was too serious. "Laws and deep-seeded cultural taboos will not change on the insistence of a single human, Pretty. Even one as wonderful as you. Please trust me. Whykeen and any other places that aren't designed specifically to protect humans are dangerous for you. You shouldn't even let other Talins touch you."

The door continued to chime repeatedly, filling their cabin with insistent sounds. They both continued to ignore it.

"Fine, I'll be careful," Kasi agreed. "But you can't say no touching. I'm going to want to hug people occasionally. My family were all huggers and a lot of the people from Wimol like to hug. You need to let me hug some of the Talins we meet."

It was difficult, but Ignatias kept from sounding a rattle of annoyance. "I'll try to be patient, but there will be times I won't be able to deal with you touching others. I know it's unworthy, but I want all your affection for myself."

"You need to remember that I've picked you," she pointed out with a gentle smile. "I'm not one of those people who falls in and out of love easily."

"Are you declaring your loyalty to me?" he asked.

"Sure," she agreed with a merry laugh that matched the sound of the bells on her belt as she threw herself at him. He caught her easily and hugged her to his chest. Her arms twined around his neck, and she nuzzled her face to his. "I'm going to say *I love you* and then you say *I love you*. I don't want to hear anything about love being a human emotion, just give it a try, Nace. I love you."

Although he had doubts about Talins experiencing human love, he didn't hesitate to do as she requested. "I love you, Pretty."

"See, that wasn't so hard!" she said and pressed her lips to his right scent glands. Pleasure shot down his spine as he secreted bonding oil. He moaned as blood rushed down to his mating shaft.

"I love this smell," Kasi murmured, her voice turning husky.

Fists banging on the door started accompanying the door chime, making Kasi jerk in his arms. Setting her down, he pressed his lips to hers briefly.

"Stay here, I'll be back as soon as I've executed whoever is at the door!" he growled.

"You don't have to kill anyone," she laughed, trailing behind him. "We can tell them to go away."

"They at least deserve to be severely reprimanded," he said, then ordered the door open. A startled rattle came out of him at what was revealed.

"Nalia!" Kasi squealed and rushed past him to embrace the other human. The two females hugged, and both started talking at once.

"You don't look like you've been kidnapped!" Nalia declared.

"It's so good to see you, but what are you doing here?" Kasi asked.

They both paused, then started speaking at the same time again.

"We're here to rescue you, silly!" Nalia answered.

"I left everyone messages so they'd know I wasn't kidnapped!" Kasi exclaimed.

Both humans stopped talking for a submark, then dissolved into laughter. It was clear Kasi knew this human, but who was the Talin behind her?

Ignatias stepped close to Kasi and sounded a questioning rumble.

"I'm Committee Citizen Ignatias of the Towiv family within the Rolinan clan," he announced with the traditional fist strike to the chest.

"Captain Derani of the Jorean family within the Anize clan," Derani responded. Another Talin and human stepped into view and stood next to Derani. "This is Commandant Holian of the Suz family, within the Torm clan, and his human, Jinna."

Ignatias was stunned to be meeting the famous Commandant Holian. This Talin basically controlled an entire clan. A man with immense wealth who was also good friends with Prime Son Searin. For Ignatias, the most intimidating aspect of Holian was his highly distinguished military career. He'd been awarded honors in such abundance that no one had come even close to duplicating his achievements within living memory.

Before Ignatias could start speaking the formal words of introduction, Holian pointed to the cabin. "We should move our conversation into a more private area, Committee Citizen Ignatias. There's a great deal we need to discuss and none of it should be done in a public space. Even though it seems to be an empty hall."

He knew this time was coming, but he thought it would be further in the future. He was going to have to convince Holian to let him and Kasi stay together. Failure would be a death sentence.

Ignatias reached for Kasi. He needed her in his arms to ground himself. She didn't resist as he picked her up and cradled her against his chest. Without another word, he turned and led them into the cabin. He heard them follow and then the sound of the door closing.

"Everything is going to be fine," Kasi soothed him. "My group is made up of good people. No one is going to force us apart."

He started up a rumble of comfort and wished he had her level of confidence.

Kasi

Ignoring Ignatias's wariness, Kasi focused on her friend. "How did you find us? We didn't even know where we were going to end up!"

"I got lucky with my calculations," Nalia said with a little shrug.

Derani hugged Nalia from behind. "Nalia is being falsely modest. She has an amazingly fast mind that can work out the best course for ships."

"We broke down not long after we left Sorana, so we weren't on course for very long," Kasi pointed out. "How did you track us here? Magic? Sacrifice to the cosmic gods?"

Nalia shook her head with a chuckle. "Nothing so dramatic. The moment we got the message from Sorana about you two leaving, I figured out the most likely destination and course based on what type of ship Ignatias was flying."

"It sounds simple, but she worked for a rotation straight doing nothing but calculations," Derani interjected. "She refused to rest. She was determined to find Kasi."

"It really helped when Jinna joined us," Nalia said and nodded her head over at the other human. "She's really good at setting up auto-run programs and then organizing the data into something intelligible."

"It wasn't hard," Jinna said, speaking up for the first time. "I used to do it all the time at one of my old jobs."

That comment made it obvious Jinna was a wild-caught human, like her and Nalia. They should form a club, with matching belts!

"How did all your calculations even work?" Kasi asked with a raised eyebrow at Nalia. "We broke down and were brought here. How did you figure that out?"

"My calculations and Jinna's program got us close," Nalia explained. "Then we crossed paths with the Ever Prosperous III. When I asked for a sensor readout so I could see all the ships they'd passed by recently, they made it easy by telling me exactly where they'd dropped you off!"

"And now we're here," Jinna said with a flourish.

"Are you going to take Kasi away from me?" Ignatias asked, making Kasi gasp.

"They wouldn't," she assured him.

"We would've," Holian countered, making Jinna frown up at him.

"Holian!" she protested.

"I said *would've*, not *will*," Holian replied, wrapping his arms around Jinna. "The original plan was to separate, but it's clear they've scent-bonded. Now we have no choice but to accept him."

Jinna shook her head. "I'm not sure that sounded any better." The movement of her head made her stagger a step and clutch onto one of Holian's arms.

Holian sounded a rumble of concern. "Jinna?"

"I don't feel right," she whispered.

That's when Kasi realized she felt a little lightheaded also. "I'm feeling off too. Like there isn't enough oxygen in the room."

Nalia's knees gave out and Derani caught her before she could fall to the floor. "Same," she gasped. "What's going on?"

Holian was quick to lift Jinna into his arms and march to the door. "We should leave in case there is something wrong with the room's eco-monitors."

Derani and Ignatias moved to follow, but the door wouldn't open for Holian. With a growing sense of dread, Kasi looked up at Ignatias.

Her brain was fuzzy and she had to focus to get the words out. "I think someone's trying to kill you again."

CHAPTER 28

Ignatias

All three of the humans were struggling to breathe, and he could feel the effects of whatever was being pumped into the room himself. They needed to get out quickly before they succumbed to the scentless toxin.

He knew there was no forcing the door open or breaking through the walls with their bare fists. He glanced over to see Derani was holding Nalia with one hand and manipulating his Ident with the other.

"I can't contact anyone," he muttered.

"Dampening field," Holian declared grimly.

"Bots," Jinna whispered and lifted an arm to point.

Holian carried her to the cargo-bots without question and knelt down next to the nearest one's control box. Jinna squinted at it then started tapping the small display. She mumbled under her breath and finally relaxed back into Holian's arms.

"What did she–" Derani started to ask only to have his words cut off when the cargo-bot stood, backed up all the way across the room, then ran at the door. When it bounced off, leaving a good-sized dent, the next one did the same. All four cargo-bots took turns running into the door until they finally pushed the mangled metal out of the tracks and into the hall with a crash.

Fresh air from the hall swept into the room. Ignatias immediately felt his head starting to clear. He hadn't realized how much his thinking had started to fog until then.

"Your human is brilliant," he murmured to Holian as he followed the man out of the door. All the cargo-bots followed them, one of them limping due to a damaged leg and another one listing a little as it moved.

"Poor botty-bots," Kasi murmured, blinking up at him. "They got hurt saving us."

"I'll make sure they're all repaired and get a good meal of electrons," Ignatias assured her. Kasi giggled and patted him on the chest, then closed her eyes and dozed off. Shouldn't she be waking up and becoming more alert now that they weren't in the room anymore? "We need to take the humans to the healers."

Holian sounded a negative rattle. "I gather from Kasi's earlier statement that this is the second attempt on your life. That means there will be more. We need to leave before anyone has another chance to kill you."

"My ship isn't repaired yet," Ignatias pointed out.

"We can't trust your ship," Holian countered. "Even if the repair techs give it a complete fix, someone could sabotage it again. We're all leaving on Derani's ship. I have medical training; I can care for our humans until we get to a healer."

Ignatias didn't argue with Holian as he followed him and Derani through the network of corridors in the living quarters section of the station. It was only after they'd been walking for a while that he noticed he hadn't seen another soul. This area wasn't highly populated, but he should at least see one or two people in the halls. It made him uneasy.

"Hey, did I fall asleep?" Kasi asked, sitting up in his arms and looking around. It was a relief to see her waking, and he could hear similar comments from the other two humans as Kasi asked, "Where are we going?"

He didn't get a chance to answer. Ten Talins stepped out from an intersection of corridors, taking up the hallway and making it obvious they had no intention of letting anyone pass.

"I was afraid of this," Holian muttered, stepping back and setting Jinna down gently on the floor. "Don't move."

Ignatias cursed himself as a fool, also putting Kasi on the ground next to Jinna. "Stay here, Pretty."

Derani was quick to set Nalia next to the other two women with similar instructions. Then he joined Ignatias and Holian in facing off against the strangers.

Ignatias could only hope that because these people had tried sabotaging his ship and then poisoning the air in his room, they wouldn't be competent in a direct fight. Holian had a reputation as a skilled fighter and Ignatias kept up his training regimen. Between the two of them, they could easily take out several of the men, but could they take on ten and win?

Derani was an unknown factor in this battle. He came from a merchant family, but all Talins were expected to train for combat to some degree. He could only hope Derani followed that ideal.

"I'm Commandant Holian of the Suz family within the Torm clan. If you let us pass, none of you need to die," Holian announced, then sounded a deafening war rattle that filled the corridor, making several of their opponents flinch back with surprised rattles.

Ignatias had to admit it was a good tactic. He added his war rattle to Holian's at the same time Derani joined. Neither of them was as loud as Holian, but all together, they made an intimidating sound.

Holian raised a hand and cut off his rattle with Ignatias and Derani stopping a half submark later. "Go now and there won't be any reprisal. Stay, and we will send your souls to meet your Ancestors. Make no mistake, they will be disappointed."

For a brief moment, Ignatias thought Holian's intimidating presence and strong words were going to make the men retreat. Then one of them squared his shoulders and stepped forward.

"It's not my Ancestors who will be shamed, it's yours," he declared with an angry rattle. "You're a disgrace to all of us. Being able to kill you along with Ignatias today is a gift from the Ancestors. It shows that our mission is both sanctioned and blessed by them."

Pure confusion made Ignatias speak up. "Why me?"

Ten sets of eyes focused on him before the leader spoke. "I was supposed to get the position you have with the Committee of Pet Welfare."

A rattle of surprise came out of both Ignatias and Derani, but Holian remained silent. He was famous for his ability to hold in his rattles and rumbles, making it hard to know what he was thinking or feeling.

"Getting close to human pets was important enough to murder me for?" Ignatias asked. "Are you suffering from Fading?"

This time it was the leader of the group that sounded a shocked rattle. "What does Fading have to do with your position? You were going to be assigned to inspect Prime Son Searin's facilities after you finished on Sorana."

Ignatias was still confused, but Holian seemed to understand. "If you had the job, it would give you complete access to Prime Son Searin's home and property, a perfect time to set him up to be assassinated. With him gone, you would be assured Prime Daughter Halieni would be named as the monarch's successor."

The leader focused his face on Holian. "I see you understand."

Ignatias finally understood. "You believe Prime Daughter Halieni will support a Traditionalist agenda, even though both her brother and mother are Reformists. This is all about political maneuvering."

Derani sounded a desolate rumble. "When did we turn into a species that murdered for politics?"

"We aren't murderers," one of the other men spit out. "We are warriors fighting for the survival of the Talin Empire."

Ignatias knew the division and animosity between the Traditionalists and Reformists had become heated over the last few solars, but he never realized it had become this violent. He assumed his ship's sabotage was a case of the wrong ship being tampered with. It didn't occur to him that it was all part of a far larger plot that included plans for assassinating a member of the Prime Family!

He wished he was armed but all he had was his natural weapons: teeth, claws, and quills. Both his companions were in the same situation. Due to the strict security on the station, their opponents weren't carrying any projectile weapons, but they were all armed with something that could either stab or bludgeon.

This was going to be a difficult fight they might not win, but what made it so much worse were the three vulnerable humans behind them.

"Enough of this!" the leader said, taking a threatening step forward. "If you give up now, I'll make all your deaths painless."

Ignatias didn't have time to scoff at the male's words before Holian was in motion. The warrior launched himself at the leader, covering the distance between them before the other male could raise his dagger. Holian did a complicated move Ignatias had seen in training but never witnessed being used in actual battle.

Holian performed flawlessly, as if he was with a sparring partner. The leader of the group went down under the attack without getting the chance to even rattle out of surprise. There was a sickening cracking sound, and the leader went limp.

Straightening up with the leader's dagger in hand, Holian regarded the other men. "Which one of you would like to meet our Ancestors next?"

If it was Ignatias facing off against Holian, he'd be tempted to retreat. By the way they looked at each other, the rest of their opponents were contemplating that exact thought. Then one of them decided to take over as leader.

"This doesn't change the plan," he announced. "We still have assets in place within the Committee of Pet Welfare that will take Ignatias's spot when he's gone. The plan is still good."

"They know what we're doing. We can't let them live," another pointed out, sounding a pathetic war rattle. All three of them focused on the Talin with a sad, quiet war rattle and sounded rumbles of amusement. It wasn't planned, but their amusement pushed that individual into an unwise attack.

He rushed at them without much skill, swinging his weapon in a wide, predictable arc at Ignatias's head. Moving on instinct honed from years of practice and real-world experience, Ignatias ducked to the side and brought his clawed hand up. He tangled his fingers in the quills of his opponent and twisted, forcing the arm into an unnatural angle and causing the attacker to stumble and drop to his knees with a pained sound.

To his credit, the fighter attempted to recover. He dropped the weapon from his captured hand and tried to pick it up with his free hand, but Ignatias was already anticipating the move. He kicked the blunt weapon with his foot, sending it tumbling over to Derani.

With the weapon safely out of reach, Ignatias twisted the male's arm until it cracked. The male let out a scream and went limp. Ignatias released him, his body slumping to the floor. He wasn't dead, only passed out from pain.

"That shouldn't have been so easy," Ignatias commented, looking up to see the group now dwindled to eight. "Perhaps you should rethink your strategy."

"He was the only one among us who didn't have training," one of them mocked. "You won't find the rest of us easy targets."

"Yes, but we are armed now," Derani said, holding up the bludgeoning weapon Ignatias had kicked to him. "At least three more of you will die. Wouldn't you rather live?"

Their numerical advantage continued to give them confidence despite the truth of Derani's words. They advanced half a step, sounding war rattles and speaking words of confidence. They were working themselves into attacking, it wouldn't be long now. Normally all this noise would've gotten someone's attention and perhaps even station security, but no one came. The group must have done something to assure privacy.

Holian took a few steps back, and Ignatias and Derani mirrored him. Holian kept his eyes on the enemy even as he spoke to them in a low tone.

"We need to win or our humans' fates are in question," he murmured. "They could suffer and even perish under the control of these men."

Ignatias didn't need the reminder, but it was good to know that Holian and Derani understood the gravity of the situation. It wasn't just their lives at risk.

There was only one suitable response to Holian's words.

Ignatias repeated the same words he'd said before every battle or incursion. "Fight well and bring honor to our Ancestors."

Both Holian and Derani responded at the same time. "Honor in life and death."

"Make them come to us," Holian instructed, standing tall and proud at the center of their trio with his weapon in hand. "Don't press forward. Don't get separated. If they separate us, we're all dead."

"I won't let them flank you," Ignatias promised. Derani sounded a rattle of affirmation; then all three of them started up loud war rattles again.

"Let them beg the Ancestors for mercy," one of the men screamed out, brandishing his weapon and stepping forward. "Because we will show them none!"

Displaying an unfortunate level of good sense, the remaining eight all attacked at once. They were out of time.

CHAPTER 29

Kasi

Her head hurt, but the sound of angry voices helped Kasi focus on something outside her pain. When she got her eyes open, the first thing she saw was a lifeless Talin body on the ground. Lifting her gaze, she watched Derani, Ignatias, and Holian trying to intimidate a bunch of armed Talins into walking away.

Holian was holding a really big dagger, or was it a very small sword? Either way, he was armed, but that didn't seem like much when she surveyed nine other Talins all holding weapons.

"This is bad," Nalia muttered, stumbling to her feet.

"I feel like I was up all night drinking," Jinna commented and held out her hand. "Help me up."

Nalia pulled Jinna to her feet while Kasi worked on standing up by using the wall for support. They were all a little wobbly. Whatever gas was used, it gave all of them a bad hangover without any of the fun.

Huddling close together, the three of them watched their Talins try to talk the group out of attacking. It didn't seem to be going well, and then one of them clumsily ran at Ignatias.

Kasi gasped and almost cried out as she watched the blunt, club-like weapon descend. Then Ignatius did something fast and complicated. The weapon went flying at Derani who caught it easily, and the attacker ended up lying limp on the ground.

"He's almost as good as Holian," Jinna said with admiration. "We might survive this yet."

"Are we planning on standing back and not helping?" Kasi asked, looking behind them, even though she knew it was a dead end back there. "Our guys might be good, but I don't like the numbers here."

Jinna frowned. "Unless you have a projectile weapon hidden somewhere, there isn't much we could do in a fight. They're all much bigger and more skilled than us."

"We don't need to fight to help," Nalia countered, voicing Kasi's thoughts.

"My memory is a little fuzzy, but didn't you make the cargo-bots run through the cabin door so we could get out?" Kasi asked Jinna. "Could you make them run at the bad guys? Maybe stomp on them or pin them to a wall?"

"It's a nice idea, but impossible," Jinna explained. "There are hardwired safeties on these things that make it impossible to turn them into weapons. Manipulating their programming to not see a door is one thing, but turning them into battle-bots isn't an option. At least not without ten days and several powerful information squares."

Kasi cursed, then stifled a cry of alarm as all the men came together in a loud crash of bodies and war rattles. The melee was so chaotic she couldn't tell who was who. "We need to get help!"

"Who can we trust?" Nalia asked. "If they were able to poison the air in your cabin and keep anyone from investigating all this noise, it means they have a lot of people on this station doing their bidding. If we ask the wrong person for help, it could make all this worse!"

There was only one name that came to Kasi's mind: Harquias.

"I know who we can go to!" Kasi pointed to the smaller version of a Talin Ident that Nalia was wearing. "Can that thing connect with the station communications network?"

Nalia nodded as she unclipped it from her belt. She frowned as she tapped at it. "There's some kind of interference," she muttered.

Jinna grabbed her arm and started pulling her down to the end of the hallway. "The field can't be that large."

Kasi followed, and they were all huddled against the far wall together before Nalia made a relieved gasp. "There! I'm connected but it's weak."

She pushed the Ident to Kasi. It took a moment of fiddling with the unfamiliar tech before she found the station directory and then Harquias's Ident contact number. She requested an immediate communication using both her name and Ignatias's on the request tag.

"I don't know–" she started to say when the Ident pinged and a small holo of Harquias's face appeared.

"It's good to hear from you so soon," she said. "And I see you have friends! Do they want to—"

"We're in trouble!" Kasi said, interrupting Harquias mid-sentence. "A group of Talins tried to kill us with some kind of aerosol poison in our room and now have us trapped in the corridor outside."

"I'll call Volormus and the law keepers," Harquias answered with a concerned rumble.

"They could be a part of it!" Nalia said, pressing her face close to Kasi's. "I know we're only humans, but you have to believe us. Anyone you call could make this worse. We don't know who we can trust, except Kasi trusts you."

A loud roar and the sound of someone hitting a wall with a lot of force made all of them flinch. Kasi looked up to see that there were more bodies on the ground. The good news was that none of the bodies were their guys, but Ignatias, Holian, and Derani all looked bad. Holian was limping, Derani was favoring his right side, and Ignatias wasn't moving as fast as he had been.

Harquias didn't question Nalia's words or try to argue. Her holo image jerked around, telling Kasi the Talin was in motion. "Are the coordinates you're sending from accurate?"

Nalia looked down at the Ident then nodded. "Yes."

"Good," Harquias grunted. "Stay safe. I'll be there soon."

Then she was gone. Kasi handed Nalia the Ident back, almost dropping it when another crash made her flinch. The three of them watched as Holian took a blow to the shoulder that sent him into a wall. Ignatias was wrestling with one man while another was repeatedly hitting him in the back, and Derani was being forced back by three men with the same type of long, blunt weapon.

"This is so bad," Jinna said with a hitch in her voice. Kasi saw her own fears mirrored in the other women's faces. "I can't stand by and watch them be killed. We have to do more."

Kasi agreed, but what? She'd never felt so helpless in her entire life. Then an idea hit her. She sprinted to the cargo-bot loaded down with items. Ripping open boxes and bags, she searched until she found what she was looking for. With a sound of triumph, she held it up to show Jinna and Nalia.

"Do you really think now is the time to paint quills?" Jinna asked, eyeing the can of quill dye.

"It's an aerosol!" Kasi said with a roll of her eyes. "I got it because I thought it would look good on Ignatias, but we could use it as a weapon. Spray it in their eyes and blind them!"

Nalia looked excited but Jinna was skeptical. "You're going to have to get close."

"Can you program one of the cargo-bots to act like a shield for me?" Kasi asked.

"No, it would move out of the way of anyone trying to hit it," Jinna answered, then grinned. "But that gives me an idea!"

Kneeling on the platform of a cargo-bot wasn't the most comfortable thing Kasi had ever done, and riding it into battle was one of the scariest things she ever experienced. She had a death grip on the single handhold near the control box and the dye spray in her other hand. The bot moved slowly but steadily, and all the battling Talins completely ignored it. Who cared about a cargo-bot anyway? Bots were such a ubiquitous sight on the station, no one even noticed them anymore.

Except Kasi was on this cargo-bot, and the moment it nimbly stepped around Derani and the two Talins he was fighting, Kasi leaned over and gave one of them a face-full of dye. The Talin screamed and reared back, blindly flailing his weapon in the air. Kasi ducked and avoided the first swing. The cargo-bot rushed out of the way of the moving Talin. That kept her safe from the second and third swing.

That's when Ignatias noticed what was going on.

"No!" he cried out and tried to move toward her. He was hindered by the two men he was battling. His distraction allowed one of them to land a solid blow, driving him to his knees.

"Get me to him!" Kasi screamed at Jinna who had limited ability to control the bot using Nalia's Ident.

"I'm trying!" Jinna called back as the cargo-bot jerked under Kasi. It took one halting step toward Ignatias and then skittered to the left to avoid someone else. Jinna could only do so much when the cargo-bot's base code kept hindering the commands.

She was going to have to get off the cargo-bot and try to get to Ignatias on her own feet. Bracing herself to drop to the ground, Kasi was about to let go of the handhold when a figure burst around the corner.

It was Harquias, wearing a strange mask over her face and carrying a large canister of something over her shoulder. Uncaring of the fighting going on around her, the botanist dropped to her knees and slid into the center of the melee. At the same time, she pulled the canister off her shoulder and used her claws to puncture the top.

A thick white gas exploded out of it, rapidly filling the hallway. The cargo-bot under Kasi swung around and started trotting back to Jinna and Nalia. The gas overtook her too fast for her to realize she needed to hold her breath.

Thankfully, when she breathed it in, nothing happened. Maybe it was only meant to be a visual barrier, in which case, she needed to get back and help.

Before she could demand Jinna turn the cargo-bot around, she heard the distinct sound of bodies hitting the floor. Twisting around she saw the mist rapidly disappearing into hidden vents in the walls. All the Talins were lying on the floor except for Harquias who was still on her knees and wearing the mask.

"It must only affect Talins," Nalia said as the cargo-bot came to a stop next to her and Jinna. Her voice sounded stricken when she spoke next. "Are they dead?"

"They can't be!" Kasi cried out as she tumbled off the cargo-bot and rushed to Ignatias's side. She could hear Jinna and Nalia doing the same thing. To her immense relief, she found Ignatias breathing. Leaning over, she pressed her ear to his chest, his heart was beating steady and strong. He was knocked out, not dead.

"The gas doesn't do permanent damage," Harquias announced to the three humans, her voice muffled from the mask. She rose to her feet, discarded the canister, and stepped over to crouch next to Kasi. "Are you hurt or injured, Kasi?"

Kasi launched herself at Harquias, wrapping her arms around the woman's neck and hugging her tight. "You saved us!"

Harquias sounded a soothing rumble and hugged her back. "I will always come at your call. Always."

If Kasi didn't already love Ignatias with all her heart, she might have fallen in love with Harquias right then!

The Talin's warm, comforting bulk and faint scent of plant soil was soothing and helped Kasi deal with the anxiety attack that was trying to roar to life now that they were safe. Her body was shaking all over, and she couldn't get her breathing under control.

All she wanted to do was dissolve into a puddle of tears and eat all the sweet things she could find while being cuddled and told she was pretty.

Unfortunately, they weren't out of danger yet, something she was reminded of when both Jinna and Nalia appeared next to her and Harquias.

"Did you get hurt?" Nalia asked.

Letting go of Harquias, Kasi shook her head then wiped her eyes with shaking fingers. She tried to talk and realized she wasn't going to be able to without bursting into tears. She held up a hand to tell the other women she needed a minute as she got her emotions back under control. As she did that, Nalia and Jinna introduced themselves to Harquias and thanked her for her quick actions.

"You looked so fierce when you slid into the center of everything and clawed at the tank!" Jinna gushed.

"What was that stuff?" Nalia asked. "It was really effective and didn't do anything to Kasi."

Harquias checked a small device on her wrist before pulling off her mask and speaking. "It's a gas that can be used for crowd control. It's not deployed often, but when it's utilized, it's highly effective, especially in confined spaces like this hallway."

"Why did you have it?" Jinna asked. "Are you a law keeper or in the military?"

"I'm a botanist, not a warrior," Harquias answered. "The second most common use for it is to combat tornel weevils. I'm in charge of Whykeen's green space. There was a bad infestation of tornel weevils last year, and I requested two canisters but only needed one. I saved the second in case of reinfestation. I didn't expect to use it for its sedative qualities, but it was the first thing I thought to grab when Kasi called for help."

There was a moment of silence before Kasi guffawed at the stunned look on both Jinna and Nalia's faces.

"You all are used to hanging out with warriors," she crowed and pointed to all the unconscious Talins. "But this proves that you shouldn't fuck with farmers!"

CHAPTER 30

Ignatias

Waking up with a splitting headache distracted Ignatias for several submarks before he realized he was lying on some type of moving platform and covered by a sheet. Shifting slightly to relieve pressure on his sore ribs, he sifted through his memories. He needed to figure out what was going on. The sensation of movement stopped, and he heard the sheet rustle.

"Ignatias?" Kasi's soft voice made him open his eyes.

"Pretty," he sighed with relief and started sounding a comforting rumble.

"Hush!" she whispered urgently. "I'll explain everything later, but for now, don't move or make a sound. Please!"

"I can do that," he agreed.

She gave him a quick lip press; then her face was gone and all he could see was the dark sheet covering him. Closing his eyes, he focused on his other senses. The distinct tang of filtered air in the main area of Whykeen Station told him they were still on the station. The sounds of conversations flowing and ebbing around him confirmed that not only were they still on the station but walking through a heavily trafficked area. One of the ports?

The familiar sound of Volormus calling out caught his attention. "Where is your owner and who are these new friends?"

"Hi, Volormus!" Kasi answered cheerfully. Ignatias could hear the tension in her voice, but Volormus probably wouldn't notice. "These are my friends Nalia and Jinna. I really wanted them to meet Harquias and see the green area."

"It was great," Nalia commented. "Very, um, green."

"Green and fascinating," Jinna added.

"The three of you shouldn't be out on your own," Volormus protested. "It's not safe."

"They aren't alone," Harquias pointed out. "I'm escorting them."

"It's a kindness that you've agreed to entertain these humans," Volormus chided. "But you're a Botanical Specialist, not a warrior or trained law keeper. There isn't much you could do if someone decided to take one or more of the humans away from you."

It was faint, but Ignatias heard Kasi mutter, "You'd be surprised," before speaking up to address Volormus. "Then I guess it's a good thing we're heading to meet our owners now."

"The direction you're going is to the Section C ports. Is that why you have all these cargo-bots?" Volormus asked. "Are you leaving?"

Nalia spoke up. "She's going to come with us. My owner's name is Derani, of the Jorean family within the Anize Clan. Our ship is called the Bountiful."

Volormus sounded a rattle of agreement. "It's good that Ignatias has found alternate means of transportation. I've sent him several requests for communication but haven't gotten a response. I need to speak to him about his ship, even if he's leaving it here. It's urgent."

Ignatias guessed that Volormus wanted to talk to him about the blatant sabotage of his ship and probably wanted to initiate an investigation for attempted murder. It was good to know this male could be trusted.

"We're behind schedule and I need to get these humans to their ship. I'm afraid we spent longer exploring the green space than appropriate," Harquias said.

Jinna spoke up first. "I had a lot of questions."

"And I got distracted by the flowers," Nalia said.

"Flowers?" Volormus asked. "There's nothing blooming right now."

"Stop helping," Kasi whispered to Nalia, almost making Ignatias rumble from amusement.

"She's referring to the adora fruit," Harquias explained. "You know humans. They aren't the smartest of species."

"Her confusion is understandable. Adora fruit does look a little like a flower," Volormus blatantly lied. No one would ever say the small, berry-shaped fruit looked like a flower. But if Volormus felt the need to lie to spare Nalia's feelings, then he must believe their ridiculous story.

The idea that he, Holian, or Derani would let their humans wander the station with only Harquias to guard them was ludicrous. Not that he could pop out from under the sheet and declare his presence. He didn't even know how he ended up here. How would he explain it to Volormus?

"I need to rush these humans to their ship, or they might miss their departure window," Harquias said. "I'll inform Ignatias to contact you."

Volormus sounded the whooshing-snap of a decisive rattle. "I'll come with you. Even if you're in a rush, I can speak with Ignatias while the humans are being loaded and secured."

"We aren't cargo," Nalia muttered. "And I heard the low intelligence comment. I'm getting even with someone for that."

He heard Kasi and Jinna chuckle at Nalia's words and then he felt the bot start to move again. Volormus must be walking close because it was easy to hear him.

"These four cargo-bots look to be in disrepair," he commented. "I'm surprised the station issued them out to anyone."

Harquias made some excuse about the station being low on small-sized personal carrier cargo-bots. Kasi was quick to ask Volormus several questions that distracted him from the cargo-bots and launched him into a long explanation about the station's highly elliptical orbit. It was easy to tell when they entered the dock area. The scent of machinery filled his nose, combined with the metallic sounds of maintenance-bots and voices shouting at each other across vast distances.

The pitch of the cargo-bot changed, telling him it was walking up a loading ramp. Volormus was still insisting he talk to Ignatias, even to the point of rudeness.

"You should wait here," Nalia insisted over Volormus's objections.

Volormus gave in with a demanding rattle. "Only if you make sure Ignatias knows it's important that I speak with him."

"We will," Jinna assured him.

There was silence for a few submarks before the cargo-bot came to a halt and the humans started talking rapidly.

"How long until Derani wakes up?" Kasi asked. "We kinda need him to get the ship going!"

"I don't know," Harquias responded.

"This is bad," Nalia hissed. "I don't think Volormus is going to give up and go away."

"Don't worry about that," Kasi said, and he felt the sheet being drawn off him. Sitting up, he took in Harquias and the three humans.

Jinna's eyes went wide, and a broad smile covered her face. "You're awake!"

"Your timing is exemplary," Harquias said. There was a sound of someone groaning behind him. "It seems that everyone is waking up."

"Help me," Jinna said and rushed out of his field of vision. "Holian is going to roll right off onto the ground!"

Harquias and Nalia moved out of sight while Kasi threw herself onto his cargo-bot.

"Nace, I was so worried," Kasi said. His arms didn't respond quickly but Kasi made it on top of the cargo-bot without his help. Sitting on his lap, she grabbed his face with her little hands, a few tears streaming down her face. "I love you and I'm so happy you're alive."

"I—ufff!"

She didn't give him a chance to respond. She dragged his face close to hers and pressed her lips firmly to his. She ended the kiss much too soon and pulled away a little. "Don't ever scare me like that again!"

He sounded a soothing rumble. "I will do my very best."

"Captain Derani? Committee Citizen Ignatias?" Volormus's shouts were accompanied by the sound of feet coming up the ramp.

Letting go of his face, Kasi started to scramble off his lap. "There's too much to explain, but I need you to get yourself together and talk to Volormus."

Grabbing her before she could fall, he eased her to the ground then got to his feet. He was surprised at how steady he felt, although his limbs still seemed to be responding slowly.

"I know what to do," he assured her, then moved past where Holian and Derani were standing unsteadily, both leaning heavily on their cargo-bots.

"Don't let him board," Holian croaked.

"I won't," Ignatias answered and then he was walking through the hatch and down the ramp with Kasi on his heels.

"There you are," Volormus said, striking his chest at the same time he looked past Ignatias. "You were a good human by fetching Ignatias for me, Kasi. Now go back onto the ship. I need to talk to your master alone."

"This is so stupid," Kasi grumbled. Ignatias turned in time to see her glare at Volormus before stomping up the ramp and back into the ship. With Kasi gone, Volormus stepped up close and spoke in low tones.

"You're in grave danger," he said with a worried rumble. "I had a lengthy meeting with the repair technician put in charge of your ship. The damage done was deliberate and malicious. They meant for you to die on that ship. I believe the only reason you survived is the timer on the mechanism that caused all the damage wasn't synced correctly and went off four entire rotations later than planned."

Ignatias thought about what that would've meant for him. If it had been synced correctly, it would've stranded him far from any colonies, stations, or commonly traveled trade routes. With no help nearby, he would have died long before anyone came looking for him.

Now he knew someone with intentions to kill Prime Son Searin would have taken his place. He felt ill and only partly due to the leftover effects of the gas.

"The other thing you need to know is that whoever did this had access to your craft for at least four marks," Volormus continued. "That's the minimum amount of time it would take to do something this involved. The last port this craft was registered at was at the capital port on Talarian. Someone powerful enough to gain access there wanted you dead in a very underhanded way. There is a plot here, Ignatias, and if you're not careful, you might not survive. Even worse, it could mean Kasi's demise also."

Ignatias made a sound of agreement. "I've acquired knowledge recently that means your news doesn't surprise me."

"That would explain why Commandant Holian is here to fetch you himself," Volormus said with an approving rumble. "I saw his name on this ship's passenger list. Bountiful is registered as a merchant craft. Is that accurate or subterfuge?"

"Accurate," Ignatias responded, deciding to trust Volormus. If this male was part of the plot, he wouldn't be warning Ignatias. "The belief is that if I leave quickly and without warning, it's unlikely anyone will have time to do anything to us."

"It's not an entirely unwise plan," Volormus responded. His choice of words made it clear the male thought he could wait. He probably wanted them to travel with a full contingency of military ships instead of setting off on a ship with no weapons and little in the way of defense. "Perhaps you should leave Kasi with me until your enemies have been dealt with. I'm scheduled to return to Talarian in forty-three rotations and I could take her there with me. While living here, she could witness all types of interesting celestial events and cultural exchanges. I'm sure she'd find it entertaining."

Ignatias sounded a decisive rattle. "No, that's not possible."

Volormus sounded a rumble of amusement. "I didn't think you would agree, but it was worth voicing anyway. Contact me if I can be of any help."

Feeling relieved at Volormus's easy acceptance of Ignatias's refusal, he took another risk. "I need you to wait for at least a rotation before anyone enters the room we were staying in."

Volormus went perfectly silent for a submark before he roared out an amused rumble. "I won't ask so you don't need to lie. I'm going to guess that I'll find the evidence of another attempt on your life."

Instead of answering, Ignatias slapped his fist to his chest. "Our time together has been of great value. Thank you for gracing me with your company." He didn't stop at the end of the formal farewell but added personal words so Volormus knew he meant it. "Keep in touch with me and we'll make plans for a visit."

"It's I who must thank you for the pleasure of this conversation. I look forward to more exchanges in the future," he responded by rote, then spoke with hope in his voice. "It would be good to see you again, but would the visit be with Kasi also?"

"Yes," Ignatias agreed as Holian shouted his name from inside the ship. He started walking backward as he spoke. "Who knows, perhaps there will be other humans I can introduce to you."

The last thing he heard as the hatch shut was Volormus's loud, excited rattle.

CHAPTER 31

Kasi

Sipping a mug of sweet Delorta tea while sitting on Ignatias's lap, Kasi finally felt herself relax. It had been a rough day for all of them.

Only after Kasi, Nalia, and Jinna were thoroughly checked out in the med bay did the guys check each other over and administer a few vials of medication each. She'd watched Ignatias's shoulders drop from relief after drinking down his vials. He must have been in pain but refused to acknowledge it. It made her want to scream at him in frustration, but one look at Nalia and Jinna's resigned expressions told her he wasn't going to change.

Stubborn should be the first species descriptor under Talins in every Unibase!

Now they were sitting around a table in the galley, enjoying tea and snuggle time as they talked about everything that had happened.

"I just realized we stole four cargo-bots," Nalia commented after taking a long drink of tea. She'd spent time on a Delorta station and was fond enough of the tea to keep it in stock on Bountiful. Kasi decided she wanted to keep Delorta tea on hand as well; it was delicious.

"Don't be concerned," Derani told her. "It's not an uncommon occurrence to accidentally leave with a cargo-bot or maintenance-bot. The station will add them to Bountiful's port fee."

"Can I buy them from you?" Kasi asked.

Derani and Holian sounded rattles of surprise at her question, but Ignatias only purred and asked, "Have you named them yet?"

"Not yet, but I will," Kasi answered.

"Why would you name bots?" Derani asked while Nalia chuckled and Jinna gave her a knowing smile.

"Those aren't just any cargo-bots," Kasi answered. "They helped get us out of the poisoned room and I rode one into a battle like one of the animals people used to ride into war back on Old Earth."

"Hedgehogs?" Jinna murmured. "Hamster? Hawk? Oh, horse!"

"Yes," Kasi exclaimed, excited that Jinna remembered the name of the animal. "I think that's the right one!"

"But they aren't animals. They're bots," Derani objected. "They have alpha-numerical designations, not names. It's not as if they have personalities. They aren't sapient. They're not even sentient!"

"Shhhhh!" Kasi admonished, sliding her eyes to the open galley door. "It would hurt their feelings to hear you talking like that!"

There was a moment of silence; then all three Talins burst out in amused rumbles. Kasi ignored them and focused on Nalia and Jinna. "You guys have to help me name them. I'm going to fix them up and then teach them to carry all my plant stuff around."

"You have to name one of them Gimpy because of the damaged leg," Jinna insisted. "Even if you get it fixed."

That started off a playful conversation about names. Their Talins joined in with enthusiasm. Holian even suggested naming one of them Carrier of a Warrior Human

Female, which caused peals of laughter from her and the other women.

It was entertaining until Kasi felt her eyes starting to get heavy. She'd finished her tea, and her body was telling her it was time to rest.

"Nalia and I need to return to the control room," Derani commented as he stood up, Nalia cradled in his arms. "I need to check in on the crew and verify our flight plans."

Nalia nodded her head. "I need to make sure Yulian isn't trying to do anything fancy with the navigation."

"Does your crew know?" Ignatias asked; no one needed him to explain his question.

"They do," Derani answered. "They are all honorable Talins who are Reformists to their cores and loyal to our monarch and prime family. Both Larimus and Yulian want to retire on Sorana one day and have already gotten permission from Prime Son Searin to move there whenever they're ready."

"That's the reason I asked for Derani's help," Holian explained.

Derani made a sound of agreement. "I'll always be willing to assist. Contact me if you require anything further. The next communal meal will be in nine marks."

No sooner had Derani and Nalia left than Holian stood up, holding Jinna against his chest. They said goodbye and were gone. Kasi was yawning when Ignatias stood up and carried her to their cabin. She giggled when the door opened to show all four cargo-bots crammed into the little space.

"I'm too tired to deal with this right now," Ignatias grumbled and edged around them to get to their bed. Setting her down, he lay next to her and pulled her tightly against him.

"I don't even know what time it is," Kasi admitted. "It could be afternoon or the middle of the night. I've completely lost track. No wonder Zia had a hard time conforming to Sorana's day/night cycle. She spent years living and working on ships, and that has to mess up your body's natural rhythms."

"It doesn't matter what time it is," Ignatias answered, rubbing his cheek against the back of her head. The scent of caramel blossomed around her. "We will stay here until you are fully rested and ready to wake up. Only then will we vacate the bed and begin a new rotation."

"That sounds perfect," she answered. She was tired but not ready to sleep. "Derani said we are traveling to Talarian and then he'll take us back to Sorana. Are we going to collect your children and take them with us?"

Ignatias

Kasi's question caused him to jolt from surprise. He didn't answer right away because his first response was to remind her it was illegal for him to remove them from the cresh. But was it?

In truth, it could be done, and with his ties to Holian, it wouldn't be difficult. The moment anyone saw Sorana as the destination on the forms, the request would be fast-tracked without question.

"I could raise my children," he whispered, testing the words. Nothing bad happened. There was no crack of lightning or sudden swarm of disapproving officials barging into the room.

He said them again. "I could raise my children."

Kasi wiggled in his arms until she was facing him. "Do you want to?"

He spoke before thinking. "Not alone."

"No one wants to raise kids alone," Kasi responded with an easy smile. "That's why we set up the nursery and school on Sorana. All caregivers need breaks and help."

He thought about his brief time at the nursery. "The children all seemed engaged."

"If you mean they looked happy, then you're right," Kasi said. Bringing one of her hands up to his face, she stroked her fingers over his scent gland. Her touch was light enough to be soothing instead of erotic.

"I don't know if my children are happy," he admitted. "But I want to know. I want to interact and teach them everything I've learned in my life."

"Maybe not the combat stuff until they're adultlettes," Kasi teased. "I'll be there to help too. I always wanted kids."

"You're a generous soul, Pretty," he murmured, lowering his face to hers. Their kiss was more about comfort than passion. There was no rush, just a languid kiss, and when they separated, he knew what he needed to tell her.

"When my time in the military was done, I had no intention of going into politics. I thought I'd return to my estate on Talarian and take on a second career. I thought of studying something for the pure joy of it, perhaps history or interspecies astro-politics."

"Those don't sound like difficult goals to achieve," Kasi pointed out. "How did you end up working for the Committee of Pet Welfare and getting involved with inspecting us? Not that I'm complaining. I wish our first meeting had been better, but I'm happy with where we ended up. If you hadn't tried to rescue me, I might never have gotten to visit Whykeen or Talarian!"

Ignatias felt a small rumble of amusement burble out of him. "I agree. I wish things could've gone differently, but I'm content with our current situation."

"What made you enter into politics even though you didn't originally want to?" she pressed. "Why the Committee of Pet Welfare?"

"I didn't want to eat."

Kasi's brows knitted together in confusion. "What?"

He pulled a deep breath into his lungs and admitted everything. "The meal you fed me by hand the first night I was restrained on Sorana was the first time I'd eaten in several rotations. You made the food taste good again."

"Fading," Kasi whispered, obviously horrified. "You were dying of Fading."

He sounded a quiet, affirmative rumble. "I didn't want to die in that way."

"My friend Lasha created a clinic to help Talins who are Fading," Kasi said slowly, as she put everything together. "She said the only reason she was allowed to was because Talins think humans are the only cure for Fading. You must've believed that too."

He sounded another affirmative rumble. "There have always been rumors about humans and Fading. Then the clinic was showing amazing results. The clinic's success gave me the idea of going to work for the Committee of Pet Welfare."

"Why didn't you go to the clinic?" Kasi asked. "Lasha would never turn anyone away."

"Shame," he admitted.

"Shame," Kasi repeated the word slowly, as if confused. Then she made a sad sound. "You know, I'd like to give you a hard time, but I get it. There's always been a stigma about seeking aid for mental health issues among humans. Your species and mine aren't that different in this."

"Perhaps," Ignatias agreed. Privately he believed humans were far more forgiving of each other's weaknesses than Talins.

"You thought the fastest way to be around humans was this job?" Kasi pressed.

"Exactly," he said. "I leveraged any favors that would get me in with the Committee. I was given an inspector position ahead of many other, more qualified candidates. I should feel guilty for my actions, but it's difficult because I can still clearly remember my fear and desperation."

Kasi's eyes went a little wide. "That's why the guy in the hall back on Whykeen was saying something about you taking his place."

"He must have been one of the candidates I ousted," Ignatias said, then rushed to explain to Kasi so she wouldn't think the worst of him. "When I realized I was starting to Fade, I tried other things first. I would routinely visit the open-air market at the capital. They have a well-stocked booth that sells human items, and I would shop there every other rotation. I only ever met one human. I found out after spending many rotations there that most Talins won't bring their humans into public because they worry for their human's safety. Human theft is at an all-time high right now."

"You would know," she teased, making Ignatias sound an amused rumble. "Who did you meet? The human, I mean. I probably don't know them, but I'm still curious."

"It was a small female named Sora," he said and rumbled with amusement again when she gasped.

"You don't mean my Sora, do you?"

"I believe she's officially Searin's Sora, but yes, I'm referring to that Sora," he answered. "The same human who your colony is named after. Our meeting was brief, but she was kind and told me about the location of the small community of humans she was born into. I sought out the place, but they were all gone."

"Dead?" Kasi asked with a frown.

He gave her the honest answer. "I believe so. I asked around about their group, and I was told an infectious disease had taken most of them. The few that were left didn't live long after. I was told they died of heartbreak."

Kasi sighed. "I've heard stories like that about other human communities. It's a tough universe, especially when you don't have a homeworld or government to back you up."

"Indeed," Ignatias said, and started up a comforting rumble. "I returned from that trip with little recourse but to force my way into the Committee for Pet Welfare. That led me to Sorana, and here we are."

Kasi didn't respond right away. When she spoke, it was in a thoughtful voice, more to herself than him. "You weren't trying to rescue me. You wanted to steal me all along. Not even me, any human would've been fine. You were desperate and I was convenient."

Her words sounded despondent. She wasn't crying but her eyes looked bright, as if they might fill with water soon. He pulled her tight against him, rubbing his scent glands into her hair as he spoke.

"That's not true at all. My goal changed the moment I saw you," he argued, determined to have her believe him. "I had no intention of abducting any human. My primary desire was to simply spend time with all of you. The initial studies coming out of the Fading clinic note that even being in proximity to an interactive human pet is beneficial. I planned to stretch out my inspection for at least ten rotations. That was ten rotations I could interact with the humans and perhaps be cured."

Kasi's mouth tightened into a frown. "Lasha is doing a lot more than hanging out with Talins at the clinic. She's developed a whole program and she closely monitors everyone there. She sends vids to us all the time to share what she's doing and introduces us to the Talins staying with her and the human volunteers."

"I didn't mean to belittle Lasha's efforts," he assured her. "I used the example of her clinic to point out that even a little contact with humans can help Talins. It was that knowledge that gave me hope and pushed me to Sorana. I had no intention of forcing any human to be with me. I hoped to gain someone's favor with gifts and attention. The census data on Sorana showed a 1.5-to-1 ratio of Talin to human. That meant that some of the Sorana humans might welcome someone who would take them off Sorana and to a place where they were the only human."

"Because according to you guys, humans always need more attention," Kasi murmured, her face relaxing. "We demand almost constant hugs and cuddles. Sorry, I mean clutching and clinging."

"Exactly correct. I know better now, but you can't fault me for believing the literature from the Committee of Pet Welfare. It was all I knew before."

She tilted her head a little. "And then you saw me."

"Then I saw you," he agreed with a comforting rumble. "You looked beautiful. Your deep brown hair was gleaming in the bright light of the setting sun. Despite your disheveled appearance, you looked happy. It hurt my soul to see a creature as perfect as you laboring in a field."

"Even if that field made me happy?" she asked.

"Now that I understand what was really going on, I'd be willing to dig in the dirt with you," he rushed to assure her. "I only reacted badly because I thought you were being forced to work. I thought I might even end up settling on Sorana if a human bonded with me and didn't want to leave. I was sure Prime Son Searin would grant me land and colonial citizenship if a human's health and happiness was at stake. He and his mother, the monarch, are known for their leniency toward Talins with humans."

Kasi's eyebrows winged up. "You planned to stay?"

"It was a potential outcome I was prepared for," he answered. "You're surprised?"

Her lips curved into a small smile. "A little, I guess. I thought of you as this big, commanding Talin, going around and expecting everyone else to bend to their will."

Ignatias couldn't help the rumble of amusement that escaped him. "And yet I'm helpless to do anything but whatever you want."

Her smile faded a bit. "You feel fine now, right? Normal hunger?"

"I'm fully recovered," he assured her. "And the moment I have access to the Talarian Unibase, I'll submit my resignation from the Committee of Pet Welfare."

"But you'll submit a report on how perfect Sorana is doing everything first," she prompted. "Oh, maybe you should talk to Holian first. I know Kalor is next on the list to be inspected. If we have you working for the Committee, then we don't have to worry about hiding humans or hybrids."

"As you wish, Pretty," he agreed, closing his eyes and nuzzling his cheek against the top of her head. Bonding oil started seeping out and soaking into her luxurious mane. "I'm yours to command."

CHAPTER 32

Ignatias

It felt good to be able to hold and feed Kasi while surrounded by others and not having to worry about revealing the truth of their relationship. The two of them had woke up in time for the communal meal. He would rather stay in the room keeping Kasi to himself, but she was eager to spend time with Nalia and Jinna.

"Neither one of you celebrated the Twelve Nights of Halloheen?" Kasi asked as Ignatias held a bite of food to her mouth. Instead of accepting it, she plucked it out of his hand and set it back down on the plate without looking away from Nalia.

"I've never heard of it," Nalia said with a little shrug, then accepted a nibble of flat bread from Derani.

"I haven't either," Jinna added with a curious tilt of her head. "What part of Old Earth did your colony originally migrate from?"

"I think our Ancestors came from a couple of different places," Kasi said. "But I thought the Twelve Nights of Halloheen was a universal human holiday."

"I don't think so," Jinna said. She and Holian had started eating before everyone got there so they were already done. "But if you celebrated it, then it must've come from somewhere on Old Earth."

Ignatias didn't like that she hadn't eaten the bite. He picked it back up and pressed it to her mouth. With a small huff of annoyance, she accepted the food, ate it quickly, then started talking again.

"We were all so busy with working on the Ugarian farms that the Twelve Nights of Halloheen were our only yearly break and we made the most of them. Isla threw a great one on Sorana last year, so I hope you can come for this year's celebrations."

Nalia and Jinna looked intrigued.

"What types of things do you do?" Jinna asked.

"It all starts with Green Night," Kasi began. Ignatias waited patiently for her to take a breath so he could feed her another bite, but she turned her head at the last moment and he accidentally smashed the food against her cheek. There was a brief moment of silence before both humans and Talins expressed sounds of intense amusement.

"Nace!" Kasi exclaimed while she laughed. "What were you trying to do, feed me through osmosis?"

Feeling foolish, he tried to point out the obvious. "You moved your mouth away."

Leaning close, he licked the food off her face. She gasped, then pulled away. She looked at him with a strangely blank expression on her face before she leaned in and put her mouth to his earhole.

"I might have liked that. A lot." Her voice was a husky whisper, making desire shoot up his spine. His scent glands filled and his mating shaft swelled.

"What do you do on Green Night?" Jinna pressed, reminding both him and Kasi that they weren't alone.

"Later," she whispered to him. "We're going to revisit this licking thing later."

Clearing her throat, Kasi turned her face to the woman and started explaining what everyone did for each night. No one noticed her voice was a little unsteady and only he was close enough to smell the faint scent of desire emanating from her.

He fed himself as she told the other humans about each of the twelve nights. The traditions sounded quaint and entertaining, and he looked forward to participating next solar with Kasi. He'd make sure it was the most memorable Twelve Nights of Halloheen she'd ever experienced.

He pressed food to Kasi's lips when she stopped talking, so Nalia could describe a holiday her family celebrated. It filled him with an enormous sense of satisfaction when Kasi ate from his hand. He had no illusions that if she wasn't distracted by the conversation, she'd probably object to it. Every other meal she insisted on feeding herself and only letting him put a few bites in her mouth.

"Do you have land on Talarian, or family that can accommodate you?" Holian asked, distracting Ignatias from the humans' conversation.

"I have land," he assured Holian. "You don't need to worry about where Kasi and I will reside while we're on the homeworld."

Talarian had strict laws regarding housing. Unlike almost any other place in the universe, there was nowhere a Talin could rent a place to stay on Talarian. If you didn't have land, family, or an employer to provide lodgings, you weren't allowed to leave your ship.

It made Ignatias sad to know that there were Talins out there that lived their entire lives without ever getting to visit Talarian. There was supposed to be a program that allowed Talins a tour of their homeworld, but there were few spots and many applicants.

"We won't be staying long," Derani told him. "Five rotations at most. Will you be ready to leave by then?"

"Is it possible for me to buy space in your cargo hold?" Ignatias asked, already making plans to pack up his house and order items and supplies for his new life on Sorana.

"You can have up to a quarter of the main hold for free," Derani offered. "The Prime Family is paying for this resupply trip to Sorana, so I won't charge you for what they've already purchased."

Ignatias sounded an embarrassed rattle. "We left my ship behind on Whykeen. It was still full of the items I was asked to transport to Sorana. I need to replace them."

"I bet my new agricultural-bots were there!" Kasi wailed, breaking into their conversation. "And my agri-heaters! I forgot all about them!"

"I can purchase any items you want on Talarian," he promised quickly.

"You better!" she threatened. "Or I'll use my shiny spray paint on you when you're asleep!"

"I don't mind if you want to paint my quills," he offered.

"I'll paint rude words on your chest!" she answered, making him sound an amused rumble.

"Anything you want," he agreed.

"You make it really hard to stay mad at you," she grumbled, obviously trying hard not to smile.

His answer was succinct. "Good."

A klaxon sounded, making Kasi jump and Jinna cry out in alarm.

"Command room!" Nalia demanded even as Derani was jumping to his feet and sprinting out of the room with her in his arms.

He and Holian were quick to follow, also carrying their humans. They all made it to the command room to find everyone at their stations. The moment Derani stepped inside there was a rapid-fire explanation from Mileanem.

"Two ships are matching our speed in flanking positions. They refuse to answer any request for communications. None of our sensors are picking them up except for the live vid feeds. I can see them, but I can't tell you much about them."

Derani set Nalia down at an empty workstation where she started tapping on the display in front of her. Taking his captain's chair, he pulled his large display forward and started going over data.

Ignatias and Holian took up positions near the hatch. It allowed them to stay out of the way but still observe everything that was going on.

"They've got some kind of tech blocking our sensors," Nalia informed the room. "Every time I switch modes, I get a blip of information and then they disappear. Whatever they're using is new and adaptive. I've never seen anything like it."

Larimus sounded an anxious rattle. "It's hard to tell from the vid feeds, but I think one of them has a pulse cannon."

"Change course now!" Holian barked. No one questioned his order and within a submark the entire ship jerked. Ignatias had to scramble to stay on his feet. The moment the sharp movement was over, he rushed to a spot where he could pull a seat out of the wall. Holian took the one next to him.

"What's going on?" Kasi asked, holding tight to his neck.

Ignatias sounded a comforting rumble. "We're under attack."

Jinna voiced the biggest issue facing them. "Bountiful is a mostly unmodified merchant ship, correct? Can we outrun them, or defend ourselves?"

"No." Holian hugged her to his chest, sounding a loud comforting rumble. "They haven't fired on us yet so there's hope they want something from us. That gives us leverage."

Kasi dropped her forehead against him with a moan. "We were doing so good and now this!"

"They've matched our course and speed again," Larimus reported. "This time one is above us and one is to our port side."

"I can see a pulse cannon on the one above us," Mileanem said.

"Pilot into the one above," Holian shouted. "Bountiful will sustain damage but not as much as the other ship."

Yulian didn't move to change course. "Captain?"

"Do it," Derani commanded. "That is where our ship's hull is the thickest and there are no primary systems that could be damaged."

With Derani's permission, Yulian tapped at his display and the ship moved sharply again. A loud and jarring impact made the ship shudder around them. Ignatias was impressed when Nalia didn't even flinch. Her eyes were focused on her display, her hands moving rapidly over its surface.

"We did some damage because I can see them flickering on the sensor now," Nalia said. "Damn, they are moving in behind us."

"We need to do something more drastic," Holian shouted at Derani. "Is there anything nearby?"

"There's a small outpost but that's several marks from here," Nalia told him. Something she saw on her display made her jerk, then she twisted her head to look back at them. "Everybody ho—"

Nalia didn't get a chance to finish her warning before the entire ship shook violently.

"Did they ram us?" Kasi asked.

"Pulse cannon," Holian explained before Ignatias could. "They're targeting the engines. They want to disable the ship."

"Not that I'm complaining, but aren't they trying to kill Ignatias?" Kasi asked. "Why bother disabling the ship?"

"They might want him dead, but they want us alive," Jinna stated grimly and Holian sounded a rattle of agreement.

"Even if they don't want a human themselves, they could sell all three of you for a lot of money," Holian agreed.

"I didn't think of that," Kasi admitted. "I'm used to being seen as cheap, exploitable labor, not as a prized possession. As much as I hate it, at least it means we're all still alive."

Derani looked to Holian. "They won't get close enough to let me ram either of them."

The ship jerked violently again. Kasi let out a little whimper and buried her face against his neck. He wished he could tell her everything was going to be fine, but he didn't want to lie to her. He settled for half-truths.

"You'll survive this," he promised. "The warriors on Sorana are skilled and dedicated. They'll find all three of you. Your life might be unpleasant for a while, but all you need to do is endure. You'll be rescued, I know it."

She pulled away to meet his gaze. "I'm not doing this without you!"

He sounded a comforting rumble. "You have to."

"No!" she cried out, then looked at Holian. "All the guys back on Sorana told me what an amazing planner you are. Think of something!"

Jinna had tears in her eyes when she spoke up. "I can't lose you, Holian. I won't survive it."

"Who's this now?" Nalia muttered at her screen loudly, drawing everyone's attention.

"What?" almost everyone asked at the same time.

Nalia didn't look up. "There's a third ship, coming in fast. Fully visible to all sensors. It's a little bigger than either of the other ones and it's…" Her voice trailed off and she squinted at her screen and tapped a few things. Suddenly she pulled back, her eyes going wide. "This new ship is hot!"

"Hot?" Kasi whispered.

"I think she's referring to weapons systems," Ignatias explained, his eyes still on Nalia. "Loaded and ready to fire weapons usually show up in reds and oranges on sensor images."

"They aren't only hot, they're firing!" Nalia screamed, pushing back against her seat as if getting further away from the screen would protect her. "Incoming!"

All hope drained out of Ignatias. This third ship wasn't interested in taking the humans alive. They were all dead and it was because of him.

"I'm sorry, Kasi," he whispered, pressing her tightly against him. "You were the best thing that ever happened to me. I regret that I'm the worst thing to have befallen you."

She hugged him back. "Never say that! I made my choices. Even though we're going to die, I wouldn't change a thing."

In the background Derani, Nalia, and the rest of the crew were all shouting about trajectories, angles, and evasive maneuvers. He ignored them so he could focus his last moments of life on Kasi.

"I don't want to join my Ancestors in the Domicile of the Souls," he whispered. "I don't want to be parted from you."

"Then we'll create our own afterlife," she promised, smiling brightly with tears sparkling in her eyes. "The Village of the Loved."

"Yes," he agreed. "That sounds perfect, Pretty."

A loud boom percussed through the ship. Ignatias could feel it vibrate through his body. He'd never experienced anything like it, but he'd also never been on a ship this small when it got hit by a large caliber, ship-to-ship weapon.

He expected to see the ship start ripping apart around them. Or perhaps disintegrate into a fiery wreck, burning them alive.

Neither happened.

Strangely, everything got quiet. Ignatias looked around to find the crew staring at their displays but not interacting. Nalia looked surprised and Yulian was sounding a loud rumble of confusion.

"Why are we still alive?" Jinna asked.

"One of the other ships disappeared," Mileanem said. "I don't think it's the sensor jamming tech."

"They didn't disappear," Larimus corrected her. "Do you see all the debris? They were hit!"

"Did the third ship miss us?" Jinna asked.

"No, I don't think so," Nalia answered, a wide grin unfurling across her face. "The other smaller ship is turning away!"

"The new arrival is requesting open coms with us," Derani said, tapping on his display. "This is Captain Derani of Bountiful."

A confident voice responded to Derani. "This is Captain Sherianan of Devastation, a defender class gunship. Volormus requested I escort Bountiful back to Talarian."

Holian sucked in a breath. "Sherianan is Dalt's sister. She contracts as an independent protection ship and is in high demand. She's never failed."

"And I don't plan to start now," Sherianan said with a rumble of amusement. "Is your ship able to keep going? Do we need to plot a course to the nearest station for repairs?"

"There's only minor damage, Captains," Larimus answered. "We can wait until we get to Talarian to do the repairs."

"Good," Sherianan said. "Start your journey. We're going to do a wide turn to sweep the area and then put ourselves in your energy wake. My second-in-command is sending you detailed instructions on how to program your comms. We need encrypted closed channels from now on."

"I've received the information and I'll start modifying our comm system," Mileanem said, tapping rapidly on her display.

"Good. We can talk further after you've finished," Sherianan said. Then the comms crackled and went silent.

Kasi looked up at him as everyone started talking at once around them. "I guess we aren't dying today."

"Apparently not," Ignatias agreed.

"That's good. I wasn't ready to die yet." Kasi's smile turned to a grimace. "Looks like I could've called Volormus for help when you guys were fighting on Whykeen."

"You called the person you knew you could trust, and she got the job done," Ignatias assured her, surprised that was where her mind went. "This gave both Harquias and Volormus chances to save you. That seems fair."

Kasi giggled. "They saved all of us."

"But they were only really concerned about you," he countered. "And for good reason. You are the best human."

Her expression turned soft, and she put her face close to his. "You're the best Talin."

He could've argued with her but instead decided kissing would be a far better activity.

As usual, he was correct.

CHAPTER 33

Kasi

"What's taking so long?" Kasi asked. She couldn't sit still so she was pacing the perimeter of the room.

They'd sent a report about the attack on Bountiful the moment they were within range of a comms array powerful enough to get the message all the way to Talarian. That meant the moment they landed, they were all "invited" to sit in individual rooms within the port authority building. Because the port authorities didn't see the humans as independent entities, they weren't separated from their owners.

"Impatience won't make this process faster," Ignatias said with an annoying amount of calm. "Would you like some tea? Someone mentioned Nalia likes Delorta sweet tea, so they brought some for you as well."

Kasi stopped pacing, faced him, and put her hands on her hips. "I don't want any tea; I want to go! Your kids are waiting for us."

Ignatias didn't respond to her show of temper. He stared at her, remaining quiet and tranquil. It was infuriating!

"If we're late, they're going to be upset and think we don't care!" Kasi exclaimed, loud enough to potentially be heard in the hall. She realized she shouldn't be that noisy and lowered her volume but not the emotional intensity behind her words. "I don't want to disappoint them before I've even gotten a chance to meet them!"

"Are you worried they won't like you?" he asked with an uncomfortable level of accuracy.

"No. Yes. I don't know," she wailed, throwing up her hands.

Standing up and purring loudly, Ignatias walked to her with open arms. She collapsed against him with a dramatic sigh. "This is an usual amount of fretting for you. It can't only be about meeting my children."

"I might be scared that they're going to separate us and send me off to live with another Talin. I don't have any rights here. If they took me away from you, they probably wouldn't even let me contact Zia back on Sorana."

The moment they'd finished docking, all the mavins, the civil law keepers, had swarmed inside Bountiful. As they'd marched everyone off, she'd started getting scared. The reality of what could happen was finally hitting her.

If the Committee of Pet Welfare decided she needed to be "reallocated," she could end up with anyone! Her owner could force her to breed and have children. It was frowned upon, but not against the law. The Apogee Assembly only recently outlawed a dangerous drug that put human women into heat but also ran the risk of killing them. What other dangerous drugs were out there that were harming humans and perfectly legal?

That got her thinking about what kind of punishments owners could enact on her if she wasn't a good little pet. Could they beat her? Isolate her? Many gruesome images filled her head, like a reel of all the worst scenes from Old Earth horror movies put together.

She didn't know how Lasha could stand to live here, under the constant threat of having your bodily autonomy taken away.

Her anxiety was rising, threatening to turn into a full attack.

"Can you get the cresh to bring—" she stopped, realizing she didn't know the names of his children. "What are their names?"

"We named the boy after one of Jacilius's distinguished Ancestors, Solorium," he told her.

"Ah, I could totally call him Lor or Lori. Or maybe Sully. Those are all cute," Kasi said, some of the anxiety fading at the adorableness of that name. "If he doesn't mind, that is."

"I'm sure he'd welcome an affection name from you," he answered. "I was allowed to name the girl. I picked Darsinus."

"Darsinus is almost the same name as Darsinum," Kasi murmured. "I'm assuming that's not a coincidence."

"It isn't," he agreed. "I named her after my friend. I changed the last letter to an S so Darsinum would know I was honoring, not replacing her."

Kasi made an "aww" sound. "That's sweet. I'm glad you did it. I know in my heart Darsinum would be happy with the tribute."

"I hope so," he answered. "What were you going to ask about Solorium and Darsinus?

"Can we get the cresh to bring them here?" she asked, wrapping her arms around Ignatias and squeezing hard. "We could pretend to give them a tour of Bountiful, then shut the doors and take off!"

"That wouldn't work," Ignatias murmured. "No one is going to take you away from me. Even if they did, I would be quick to get you back, I promise. We have powerful friends now that will help keep us together."

"Except people keep trying to kill you," Kasi muttered.

"That's the exact reason we're here," Ignatias pointed out. "It's rare for a Talin ship to be attacked within Talin-controlled space. We weren't even on the edges of our empire or near a place known for piracy. It's suspicious enough that they want to investigate."

Kasi scoffed. "We were the ones attacked; why are we being treated like criminals?"

"Did they let criminals lounge in comfortable rooms and offer them food and drink of their choice on Wimol?" Ignatias asked with a rumble of amusement.

"I'm not talking about that," Kasi said. "They separated everyone into different rooms to see if our stories match up."

"They are trying to minimize trauma," Ignatias explained. "They need each of us to tell our story but if you're not used to violence, it can be difficult to recount events, especially if you have to hear others talk about it over and over again. It's standard practice for interviewing civilians."

"Why didn't you say that before?" she shrieked, hugging him tightly. The anxiety that threatened to overload her started easing. Her heartbeat slowed and the room didn't seem too small anymore with danger lurking just outside the door.

The door opened to reveal one of the mavins. "Is there a problem?"

Kasi kept her face pressed to Ignatias's chest as he answered. "My human was worried she would be taken away from me. She suffers from separation sickness and is easily upset."

The mavin started purring and stepped into the room. "I'm sorry to hear that. Can you assure her that she's safe?"

"I don't think she'll feel better until we leave here," Ignatias told him.

"I've read that some humans are more sensitive than others," the mavin said. "I can conduct your interview now, then you'll be able to leave."

Ignoring the "sensitive" comment, Kasi pulled away from Ignatias to address the mavin. "Ask us anything!"

The mavin looked down at her and kept purring. "I will, but first, would you feel better if your master sat down so you could sit in his lap and cling to him?"

Kasi stifled a sigh. "Sure, thank you."

Without warning, Ignatias picked her up and carried her a short distance to the nearest chair. After sitting, he arranged her in his lap so she was facing away from the mavin.

Probably a good idea. She wasn't good at hiding her emotions, and she didn't want to make this mavin suspicious of anything.

"You can cling to me if you feel anxious," Ignatias said as he urged her to snuggle against his chest. Playing her part, she leaned against his chest and let out a long breath. It seemed she wasn't needed for this.

On their trip here, they'd decided how much and what details to tell the authorities. Ignatias recited a story that was mostly true. Holian had insisted they needed to be honest about the three attempts on Ignatias's life. If the mavins did nothing but file reports, then they'd know who they couldn't trust.

Holian had warned them that a battle was brewing. The only question was how big it would be: an insurrection or a full out civil war.

"I've received an initial report from Whykeen security verifying what happened on the station," the mavin said after Ignatias finished. "It seems you are being systematically targeted. I'm assigning you mavins as guards while you're here on Talarian. Captain Derani informed me that you will be departing back to Sorana with his ship. I'm going to make arrangements for a military escort and at least one ship to stay in orbit around Sorana for as long as you're there."

Kasi sat up, startled. "We don't need a military escort! Sherianan, uh, I mean Captain Sherianan is going to be with us. Her ship is really…"

Kasi trailed off when she realized the mavin was staring at her and had stopped purring. Had she messed up? Did she get them in trouble? She should've read the pamphlet on Talin culture more closely…or at all.

In her defense, she'd always hated homework! Did any of them really expect her to read that dry, overly technical and badly translated tome? Honestly, it was all Ignatias's fault. He should've given her the highlights or something if he really wanted her to know anything outside of her interests.

Of course she'd read and re-read all about Talin flora! That was fascinating, especially the julun shrub. She really wanted to take a few samples home with her. Would they let her take whole plants, or was she going to have to be content with clippings?

"Kasi?" Ignatias said, nudging her a little. "The mavin asked you a question."

"Oh, sorry," she said, feeling her skin get hot with embarrassment. Leave it to her to distract herself from an anxiety attack by getting lost in thoughts about plants!

"I wanted you to know that this situation calls for more than one independent gunship, even if it's one as well run as Captain Sherianan's ship. We will contract with her to be a third ship so you can have familiar Talins protecting you, but we still insist on two military ships accompanying you. They need to be stationed at Sorana because we believe this plot is linked to the attack on Holian's colony, Kalor. If the pattern continues, Sorana will be in danger."

Kasi fought not to wince. This was going to make it hard on the Sorana humans. They were going to need to be on their "best" behavior the entire time the ships were there. Even worse, she might have to abandon her experimental field. All that work for nothing.

Maybe she could ask for a greenhouse!

"I also need to inform you that your ship is evidence for the foreseeable future," the mavin explained. "Do you want compensation for its worth or will you wait for it to be released?"

"I choose the compensation," Ignatias said.

The two men discussed details of the ship still on Whykeen, Volormus's report, and the mavins who would be guarding him. Kasi tried to pay attention, but her mind kept drifting back to greenhouses.

It was better than letting her anxiety think up worst case scenarios such as Ignatias's kids deciding she was a monster and running away from her screaming.

"I'll send you the date of our next meeting so I can apprise you of any changes to your case before you leave," the mavin said as he stood up.

Ignatias stood as well and set her on her feet next to him. "I look forward to any insights you can reveal."

They said goodbye as the mavin tried to push some candy on Kasi, and then they walked out of the building. Kasi swore the air never smelled better, even if the scent of engines and fuel tickled her nose.

Everyone was gathered in a small group just outside. There were several transports waiting, and standing next to them were armed mavins. It looked like everyone was getting a set of guards during their visit.

"Did everything go okay?" Nalia asked.

"They believed everything I said," Kasi responded with a grin, making Nalia and Jinna laugh.

"We didn't get to say a word either," Jinna commented. "At least they seem to be taking it all seriously."

"They are," Holian agreed. "Though I worry it might be too late. We ignored and dismissed the extreme Traditionalists. None of us expected them to gain traction, but they've proven popular and amassed a large number of followers."

"You really think there's going to be a civil war?" Nalia asked. Derani stepped up behind her and drew her back against him.

"I think that's the worst possible outcome of several," Holian said. "I can't give you details, but I have a plan in play that might reveal the true leadership of the Traditionalist extremists."

"If we can find the ones organizing everything, we can deliver a blow harsh enough to destroy their plans for open rebellion," Jinna said, sounding very much like a Talin.

Kasi smirked at her. "Are you going to run for a seat at the Apogee Assembly too?"

Jinna blushed and rolled her eyes, then looked at Holian. "That would get in the way of my cuddling schedule."

"Will you guys be coming back with us to Sorana?" Nalia asked. "There seemed to be some doubt about that when we were talking to the mavins." She made a face. "I mean when Derani was talking to them."

"No, we need to see about the 'plan in play' Holian mentioned earlier," Jinna explained.

"Good luck," Kasi said, glad it wasn't her going off on a secret mission. She really missed her family and friends back on Sorana. As amazing and interesting as this trip had been, she didn't want to spend another moment fearing for her life. She really wasn't designed for that kind of adventure! "Try to stay safe, okay?"

"I'll take good care of Jinna," Holian promised with a purr.

"Really good care," Jinna murmured, her eyes meeting his and a naughty grin curving her lips.

"Save it for later," Nalia said with a clap of her hands. "Our rides are waiting."

They all said their goodbyes and headed off to their different transports and mavin escorts.

CHAPTER 34

Ignatias

Ignatias would never admit it, but he was nervous to see his children. Probably even more nervous than Kasi. Having her at his side gave him something to focus on instead of his long-buried desire to spend time with his offspring.

"Which ones are they?" Kasi asked as they stepped outside to find at least thirty children engaged in various activities. He recognized most of the games from his childhood. The activities were all carefully constructed to teach important lessons in coordination and athleticism, but all he could remember was enjoying them.

At least he enjoyed them until Darsinum died. After she was gone, nothing was as joyful as it once was. He was suddenly determined his children would never know that kind of sorrow. If they wanted to tell stories or spend an entire day doing nothing productive, he would let it happen.

Kasi's plan of taking them back to Sorana no longer seemed like a good idea, it was now an imperative.

"Ignatias?" Kasi pressed.

"I don't see them," he admitted after searching the area. Had it been so long that he didn't recognize his own children?

Thankfully the caregiver escorting them pointed to a spot hidden from view by artfully planted trees. "They should be right over there. They're scheduled to practice balance during this time."

No sooner had he said that then a group of children appeared from behind the trees and made their way in a well-ordered line toward the building. There was a caregiver in front and one at the end.

The thing that made Ignatias want to sound a mournful rumble was the lack of sound coming from any of the children. They weren't talking, rattling, or rumbling. He remembered barely being able to keep his rattles quiet during lessons at that age. How were they so silent?

"They aren't rattling," he commented, looking at the caregiver.

"We are one of the creshes instituting the silence statute," he explained. "It's believed to be good for discipline and learning to teach the children to remain as silent as possible when not interacting with someone else."

Kasi huffed out a breath but didn't say anything. He already knew she didn't approve. He didn't like it either.

As the children got closer, he was able to pick out his two. They were almost at the end of the line with Darsinus walking in front of Solorium. It was shocking to see how much bigger they'd gotten. Darsinus had his mother's dark red coloring while Solarium took after his side of the family.

"Darsinus, Solorium, please come over here," the caregiver called out. The two left the rest of their classmates and made their way without comment, rattle, or rumble. It didn't take long before both children noticed Kasi. Startled and excited rattles came out of them as they rushed up to her.

"You're a human!" Darsinus declared, sounding a comforting rumble. "Are you lost? Do you need to be comforted? I heard humans need to clutch and cling to Talins to feel safe. I might be a small Talin, but I'm strong. All my caregivers say so. I'm Darsinus of the Towiv family within the Rolinan clan. This is my brother Solorium, he could comfort you too."

Kasi dropped to her knees and opened up her arms. "You do look strong, and I love clutches."

Darsinus started to hug Kasi, but stopped and pushed her brother into Kasi's embrace instead. Solorium stumbled a little and then let out a comforting rumble as Kasi folded her arms around him. His little body relaxed, and he pushed in close.

"Please don't ever let go," he whispered.

"Solorium!" the caregiver admonished, making the boy flinch and go silent. "You don't say things like that. You don't need the human; she needs you. Remember our lessons on inner strength and resilience."

When he tried to pull away from Kasi, she refused to let go. "I'm scared of you," she hissed at the caregiver. "You're loud and mean! I need to cling to Solorium to feel safe."

At her words, the little boy hugged her tighter and started up a comforting rumble.

"I'm doing my job!" the caregiver argued, sounding a loud angry rattle. At the same time, Darsinus put herself between her brother and the caregiver. She didn't make a sound, but it was obvious she was protecting Solorium.

Ignatias didn't think he could feel both pride and heartbreak at the same time.

"Your assistance is no longer needed," Ignatias informed the caregiver. Taking a step to stand next to his daughter, he faced down the caregiver. "You are free to go back to your duties. Thank you for your gift of time and skill."

The caregiver mumbled a response and left quickly. Ignatias ignored the looks he was getting from several other members of the staff and looked down at his daughter.

"I wish I'd been as brave as you when I was your age," he said.

Darsinus sounded a rattle of excitement. "Thank you, Father."

"You know who I am?" he asked with a soft, surprised rattle.

She sounded a short derisive rattle. "Of course. The last time you visited was 107 rotations ago. You brought element blocks as a gift and walked the entire perimeter with us. You gave us almost five marks of your time. It was a pleasant day."

Ignatias remembered how awkward he felt during the visit and the amount of relief he experienced the moment he left. It never occurred to him that the visit he saw as a task was a joy for his children. Guilt hit him hard.

How could he have been that selfish for so long?

He'd been so blind to all the hurt Talin culture and laws did to the most vulnerable in their society. Even after his experiences as a child, he still let himself believe this was the best option for his children. The only option.

But that wasn't true any longer for his children. And if he helped support Holian, Searin, and the other Reformists, there might be more options for other children. It was a worthy battle he was proud to play a part in.

"I'm moving to a new colony called Sorana," he told her. "I'm going to take both of you with me."

When Darsinus went perfectly still and silent, he worried he'd been too blunt and abrupt. The children had probably only been outside the cresh a few times in their entire lives; leaving it permanently might be a frightening prospect. He should've left telling them to Kasi who was far more skilled with words than him.

Before he could start really panicking, a loud, excited rattle sounded from her. With an eager hop, she turned to face her brother. Solorium was still holding Kasi and they were whispering to each other.

"Solorium!" Darsinus cried out, rushing up to him. "We're leaving with Father! We're going to a colony far away."

He didn't let go of Kasi, only turned his head to look at his sister. He sounded a desolate rumble. When he spoke, his voice was full of fear. "What will the cresh be like?"

"Wonderful," Kasi assured him. "There are only a few children and I'll be there all the time. When you're not in lessons you can come help me in my greenhouse."

"What greenhouse?" Ignatias asked. He didn't remember there being any greenhouses on Sorana.

"The one you're going to build me," Kasi said with a cheeky grin.

There was only one answer he could give while sounding an amused rumble. "Of course."

"Yes, I can do that," Solorium agreed. "I can stay close and be ready for clutching and clinging whenever you get scared."

"That's exactly what I'm going to need," Kasi agreed. Ignatias noted her eyes looked watery, but she was smiling.

Darsinus tugged at Solorium's arm. "We need to pack our things."

Letting go of Kasi, Solorium looked up at Ignatias. "Thank you, Father. I will make you very proud."

"You already have," Ignatias assured his son.

Impatient, Darsinus started dragging Solorium away. "If we pack now, we can be gone before evening meditation."

Ignatias recalled evening meditation. It was done before the daily meal, and he remembered it being one of his least favorite activities. He couldn't blame either of his children for wanting to leave before having to participate.

"Yes, you should hurry," he agreed, even though there were several rotations before Bountiful departed. He couldn't stand the thought of leaving the children at the cresh for even another submark. Without another word, both children rushed off, talking quickly about what to pack in which bag as they disappeared into a nearby building.

"It's amazing how easy it is to take the kids away when the Prime Son himself asked the government to fast track everything," Kasi said as she stood up. Taking one of his hands in hers, she smiled up at him. "You're doing the right thing."

"I have no doubts," he agreed, turning to face the human that had changed everything for him. "Thank you for opening my eyes to both my past and my future."

"It's one of the many benefits I offer," she responded. "Clutching, clinging, and life coaching. I'm a full-service human."

"You need to add savior to that list," he murmured.

Kasi beamed up at him.

Kasi

It took Solorium and Darsinus only five days to settle into a routine on Sorana. By the time fifteen days had passed, both of them acted like there had never been a life before Sorana.

They spent half the day at school where Ignatias taught the children several subjects. Then they decided what they wanted to do with the rest of their day. Solorium spent most of his time with her in the greenhouses.

At first, he probably wanted to stay close to her, but within a few days, he was showing real fascination and enthusiasm for the plants. Kasi suspected she had a budding botanist on her hands, and she couldn't be happier.

Darsinus would drop in to check on her brother but rarely spent much time with them. She wanted to go out exploring and Ignatias was quick to indulge her. The two of them would hike deep into the forests of Sorana. At every evening meal, Darsinus would regale them with new discoveries and death-defying events.

Because he spent so much time with Darsinus during the day, Ignatias was quick to ask Solorium questions about his day. Both children were flourishing and scoring far better on the standardized tests than they had been back on Talarian. Kasi couldn't ask for things to be any better.

Well, one thing could be better.

"How much longer will the ships need to be here?" Henni asked Holian.

Holian had decided to make the trip to Sorana and check in on the colony before going off on his super-secret mission. Kasi worried about Holian and Jinna, but both of them had assured her they were taking plenty of precautions.

If Kasi was honest with herself, she didn't want anyone leaving Sorana. It was a safe and happy place. She couldn't wait for the day when all the fighting between the Traditionalists and Reformists was in the past and no one needed to go on "super-secret missions" any longer.

"It could be for an entire solar," Holian answered.

"I'm tired of being on my best behavior," Isla grumbled, making several people laugh.

"This is your best behavior?" Tisuran asked.

Isla rolled her eyes. "I haven't gone wandering off into the woods by myself, have I?"

"Only because I won't let you!" Tisuran commented with a rumble of amusement. "I found you trying to climb on top of our domicile yesterday."

"That doesn't count as bad behavior," Isla argued. "The toktok bird was stuck! I was being a hero."

"The bird wasn't stuck," Tisuran argued. "It was playing. If you'd stayed on the ground, she would've flown down to you."

While Tisuran and Isla argued about the toktok bird who'd gotten fond of Isla, Kasi focused on Holian.

"Will they keep giving us warning before they come down here even after you leave?" she asked.

So far, the crews of the two ships orbiting Sorana hadn't been on the planet much, making it easier to keep up the charade of Sorana being a normal Talin colony. If that changed, Kasi worried their secrets might get out.

Even though everything ended well with her and Ignatias, that didn't mean the next Talin who witnessed a human and Talin kissing or saw one of the hybrid children wouldn't go running to their superiors.

"Ignatias will be their contact after I leave," Holian answered. "I'm afraid you're going to have to accommodate crew members visiting; they need time in the fresh air. But the captains are well aware that they have to keep their crew in order or visiting privileges will be revoked."

"I don't blame them for wanting to get off the ship, but I'm still scared something is going to happen," Kasi admitted.

Ignatias reached over and lifted her onto his lap. "I wouldn't worry. One of the ships in orbit is mostly staffed by people Holian trained, and both ships are well aware that this is Prime Son Searin's colony. They wouldn't want to do anything to upset the monarch's son and potential heir to the throne."

She was still concerned, but Ignatias's words went a long way to making her feel better. Solorium got up from his chair and hurried to her side, Darsinus right behind him.

He petted her arm as he spoke. "Don't be scared, Kasi. I'll protect you."

"And me too!" Darsinus said. "Father has been teaching me combat. I'll be able to defeat anyone who tries to steal you!"

Kasi raised an eyebrow at Ignatias. "Combat?"

"Basic skills everyone should know," Ignatias said quickly, then looked at Darsinus. "I believe we were going to keep that to ourselves."

"But Kasi needs to know I'm going to be a warrior like you," Darsinus argued.

"I'm going to be a botanist, like Kasi," Solorium announced. "We're going to develop all kinds of plants that don't exist yet. Then we'll grow plants that haven't existed in hundreds of years. Kasi knows all about how to work with the different machines to make seeds grow into different plants."

"That's fascinating, Solorium," Ignatias praised. "You couldn't have a better instructor than Kasi."

Darsinus sounded an angry rattle. "Your seeds won't be any good if I'm not there to protect you from invaders!"

Solorium stood his ground. "Invaders might not happen, but we will always need the food plants produce!"

The siblings got into an argument over which one of them was learning the more important skill. Ignatias was quick to stop the argument and assured both children they were invaluable, and Kasi got off his lap to demand hugs from each of them.

Lamarin appeared behind the siblings. "Do you guys want to play toss?"

There were excited rattles of agreement and then all three of them were running outside to play a game so complicated Kasi still couldn't understand the rules despite having multiple Talins explain it to her.

Strong hands grabbed hold of her and she was hauled back onto Ignatias's lap. "You didn't finish your meal."

She nestled against him. "I'm full. Solorium insisted on bringing me a huge snack earlier."

"He's a thoughtful child," Ignatias murmured.

"He's following the example you're setting," Kasi pointed out. "I think it's an indication you're doing a good job with those two."

He sounded an anxious rattle. "I worry because they seem to fight often."

"That's kids being kids," she assured him. "They don't hit each other, and they're quick to calm down. I know it probably goes against Talin culture, but getting into arguments with your siblings is simply a part of growing up."

"I hope you're correct."

"Trust me," she said before giving him a quick kiss. "Besides, there are plenty of parents here with older kids that can help guide us if things start getting out of hand."

"This is a generous community," Ignatias agreed.

Kasi met Ignatias's eyes. "Are you happy here?"

"The happiest," he assured her.

"Even though you're not off doing some important prestigious job?" she pressed.

"I'm doing an important prestigious job," he countered. "I'm your Talin and a father to Darsinus and Solorium. I can't think of anything more important."

Kasi's heart melted. "Good answer."

Ignatias pressed his cheek to the top of her head. The scent of caramel filled her nose. "True answer. I feel like I'm living in one of the fabulous worlds Darsinum would make up when I was child."

Closing her eyes, Kasi melted against Ignatias. "You might be. She could be out there, rumbling with happiness that you're doing well."

"You don't think she'd resent me for what happened?" he asked.

"Never. She loved you." Kasi was quick to shush the objection she knew Ignatias would have. "Yes, yes, I know you guys don't think Talins can love. Call it bonding, or friendship, or whatever, but you guys had a deep and meaningful connection. She knew you probably as well as she knew herself. She wouldn't resent you; she'd be joyful for you."

"I think about writing the stories she told," he admitted.

"Do it!" Kasi encouraged. "I can't think of a more fitting tribute. I know I'd love to read them and so would a lot of the humans here."

They both went silent as the conversation flowed around them and Kasi could've sworn she felt a warmth pass by her.

"The room's enviro controls must be off," Ignatias muttered.

"Or it was Darsinum telling you she approves," Kasi suggested. Ignatias didn't respond but kept purring and hugging her. She knew him well enough to know that was his way of agreeing with her, even though he couldn't bring himself to say the words—yet.

These Talins had so much love to give, they only needed to learn how. She felt the warmth again, and then it was gone. Darsinum agreed with her.

"Don't worry," she whispered. "This is only the beginning."

Dear Reader,

I can't tell you how much fun *Stealing Captivity* was to write. Ignatias was far more stubborn than I expected and Kasi was perfectly tenacious. I was especially surprised at Harquias coming to the rescue and showing us that you don't need to be a warrior to win a fight! I'll admit this book had me chuckling a few times as I wrote.

My wonderful editor Chrisandra (Chrisandra's Corrections) managed to make me snort tea as I was going through her edits. At the very end of chapter 15, I used the term pussy-blocked and I left a note with her asking if she thought this was okay. Not only did she like it, but she gave me a list of suggestions I have to share with you:

Box blocked
Clitorference
Beaver dammed
Carpet cutting
Cooch checked
Clam-jammed
Bushwhacked
Taco blocked
Honey-pot blocked
Muffin muzzled
Snatch snagged
Scissorsceptioned
Cunt punted

I think we all need to work hard to bring these into common parlance. From now on when the kids, pets, or life interrupts our hubba-hubba time, it's clitorference! (Yes, I'm laughing as I write this.) I hope you found this as amusing as I did.

As always, if you enjoyed *Stealing Captivity*, please leave a review on the platform or your choice. Your good reviews keep me writing. The next book is up for pre-order: *Redeeming Captivity*. This one is going to be one of the more tough story lines, but we're going to find out who's behind the scenes stirring up the Traditionalist Extremists.

As always you can visit my website for links to free novellas, my writing schedule, and links to social media:

www.RK-Munin.com

Have a Fruitful Rotation,
Rye

Other books by RK Munin

-Science Fiction-

Hissa Warrior Series
Rescuing Halin (Mian and Halin)
Buying Tiran (Mara and Tiran)
Tempting Selon (Lara and Selon)
Defying Kilan (Deena and Kilan)
Healing Mavito (Raleen and Mavito)
Claiming Yopin (Mouse and Yopin)
Teasing Woken (Safena and Woken)
Defending Revin (Kamaril and Revin)
Trusting Warik – Coming soon

Human Pets of Talin Series
Loving Captivity (Sora and Searin)
Escaping Captivity (Lakin and Dalt)
Negotiating Captivity (Nalia and Derani)
Fighting Captivity (Zia and Palforma)
Tender Captivity (Jinna and Holian - This is a novella you
can get for free by signing up for my newsletter)
Craving Captivity (Lasha and Tamerin)
The Twelve Nights of Halloheen: A holiday mashup novella
(Isla and Tisuran)
Stealing Captivity (Kasi and Ignatias)
Redeeming Captivity – Coming soon

Origins (A Human Pets of Talin Series)
Creating Captivity (Ari and Bazium)
Gossamer Chains (Rain and Hesarium)
Golden Cages – Coming soon

-Paranormal /Urban Fantasy-

Ours Evermore Series

Two Wolves for Soren (Soren, Kalli, and Quinn)
A Hacker, Vampire, and Chimera Walk into a Bar….(Tobias,
Briar, and Memphis)
When Darkness Meets Dawn (Imani, Lex, and Mac)
Tag, You're It (Novella)
Kidnapping Their Third (Cora, Pike, and Kimble) – Coming
soon

Alpha Series
Alpha Mage (Emma and Kade)
His Alpha Mage (Avery and Jason – Novella)
Alpha King (Cathleen and Lazlo)

New Clan Series
Stray Wolf (Steph and Eli)
Lost Lion (Maeve and Cyrus)
Reluctant Cervid (Tavi and Donovan)
Broken Thorn (Sabina and Theodosius)